NORTHUMBRIAN WESTERNS

These were formed out of a few crazy ideas in a pub in Northern England. Over five years they evolved through numerous drafts and short stories into a series of novels.

Blending empirically based scenarios with Spaghetti Westerns, the books link dystopia, noir-fiction and border history into a unique set of stories.

Burnt Horizon is book one. Book two is *Blighted Land* and the third is *Blasphemous Isle.*

ABOUT THE AUTHOR

Ian Chapman was born and raised in Northumberland, only leaving when he was lured to the Midlands to study Economics at the University of Wolverhampton. He was so impressed with the place he went on to gain a PGCE and MA in International Studies, staying in the Midlands to teach economics and strategy at a number of colleges and universities. When not teaching he wrote stories or rode one of his three motorbikes with the odd Glastonbury Festival thrown in.

Moving north to Lancaster he took an MA in Creative Writing at St Martin's College before completing a PhD at Lancaster University. Around this time he had a play performed and won a (small) poetry competition. He also had several short stories published.

He now lives on the edge of the Lake District, still teaching and writing but the motorbikes have been replaced by three children.

BLIGHTED LAND

Ian Chapman

Book two in the Northumbrian Western Series

First published by Lakeland Writers in 2016.

www.lakelandwriters.co.uk

ISBN: 978-1-910875-15-5

Visit www.lakelandwriters.co.uk to learn more about other books available.

To Debs and the kids. Always there for me.

CHAPTER ONE

Machine

The bike misfired but picked up speed and I rode fast across town, down to the West Bridge where the setting sun lit the wind turbines, their blades turning slowly as they picked up the breeze from the North Sea. Along the quayside cargo ships' masts and rigging appeared in the sea-fret that hung over the harbour and shouts came from the taverns rammed with drunks from Scotland and the continent. As we thundered across the bridge I could see something going on at the far end of Harbour Bridge that ran parallel. Smoke curled up and figures milled around in the mist.

I swung us down Spital Lane alongside the river and round onto Main Street. It was barricaded partway up with vehicles parked sideways to block the roadway and pavements. At the far end was whatever was causing all the noise, some great machine, an angular outline, dark coloured with protuberances, hatches and brackets. Bullets ricocheted off it as it manoeuvred around, making this clanking and grinding sound, crushing everything in its way.

Nico had his men lined up halfway up the road. They hid behind the cars and vans and fired rifles and machine guns, a pointless cacophony.

I stared at the thing as it crept forward, materialising out of the shadows. Now it was closer it was recognisable. On top of the sloping body was a separate structure fitted with several weapons. There were no wheels just metal tracks. I'd seen these on television when I was a kid, in the days when there was TV, but never in the metal, close up. It was a war machine; a tank, designed to kill. Destroy. Like the ones used in the Oil Wars but bigger, heavier built. If it hadn't been for the gun Gregg had on my back I'd be off, away from the centre of town. Out of the town, even.

Gregg had turned up at my place earlier in the evening, just as the sun was setting behind the west end of High Town lighting the rooftops dull red with its fading light. I'd been wheeling the Triumph up the back lane ready to put it away.

Gregg'd ridden across town on a bicycle so his beardy face was all sweaty as he gasped for breath, which was funny enough. When he told me Nico needed me I told him to shove it up his arse, that it was my evening off, which really wound him up. That was even funnier. The gun that he whipped out wasn't quite so funny. Especially when he started to wave it around. All jumpy like he was going to pull the trigger.

'There's an emergency. Serious stuff. Nico wants you there.' He pointed towards the town now turned to shades of grey.

Nico always wanted me somewhere for something but

he didn't usually send his pals tooled up. 'Going to tell me what this is about?'

'Yer'll see soon enough.'

I didn't like being pushed around by Gregg, or anyone really, but he was as edgy as hell so I didn't argue. I slid onto the bike, starting it up. There was a loud bang from across town. Like a firework going off, from the days when we had such things. It was followed by the rattle of machine gun fire. A flash lit the valley and the rows of houses down to the quayside. There was another thud.

'That's what it's about.' He sat behind me on the saddle, his belly pushed up against me. 'Let's go.'

'Where to?'

'Main Street. North end —'

Before he had a chance to say any more I pulled off: hard enough to jolt him but not make him too trigger happy.

I'd raced across town with him holding his pistol on me.

Now he nudged me and pointed over to a couple of Committee cars, the usual Volvos. I clunked the Scrambler into gear and rode over to them, parking behind a decrepit V40. He slid off and stared up the road at the tank as rumbled towards us, now driving over a van, one of the ancient vehicles so prized in the town. The Transit caught under the tank's track and crumpled. Folded up and popped its windows out before it was flattened. As a last gasp it spurted its fuel out that burnt in a shallow puddle.

'Shit,' he said. 'We need to stop that.' He looked over at me and slid his gun away. There was a slight shrug, almost an apology. But we both knew I'd not have come without his threat.

Now I was here but it was hard to see how I could make a difference. There was no way we'd stop something like that.

'Nico is over there,' he said. 'He'll want to have a word.'

Nico was behind a V70 estate, two men at his side armed with machine guns, firing down the road in short burst to save ammo. Nico's leather coat was pulled tight around him, over his ancient suit, sunglasses on top of his head. He had that look on his face he often had, the one he wore when he was thinking. Making a plan. He saw me and waved me over.

There was whirr from the tank as it stopped. Nico and the men ducked down. So did I. There was a roar and flash, a blast that shook the road before the side of the building opposite collapsed and we were showered in masonry, bricks bouncing onto the parked cars.

As the dust cleared I joined Nico, watching the tank through the Volvo's windows. It started to move again, now over a cart full of vegetables, the misshapen carrots falling out of the side as the cart was compressed. Gregg ran away at the far side, over to where my Scrambler was parked, well out of the way.

'Ain't this something?' Nico was calm. Almost enjoying it.

'Why have you dragged me down here?'

There was a clatter of machine gun fire that clanked and zinged on the tank.

Nico grinned. 'I've got a plan. That's why you're here, lad.' Despite being my junior I was always his lad. 'I want you to block the bridge. Stop it getting away. Grab the Northern Oil tanker from over the river. Use it to block

4

the way.'

'That won't stop it.'

One of Nico's men showed up — Jack, another member of the Round Up crew like me and Gregg and all the rest of us. All of us controlled by Nico. Jack carried a long box, best part of a metre long. It was dark coloured with blocked writing on it.

'Ah, at last,' said Nico. He pointed at the ground and Jack put the box down. Nico knelt, undid the clips and opened it up. There was a dark tube inside, dark green and twice the thickness of a drainpipe. It had a pistol grip, trigger and sight: some piece of military hardware he'd picked up, no doubt. 'Yeah, this'll do it. But we need to hem it in.' He stood and faced me.

'This is your plan. You sort it out.' Gregg didn't have his gun on me anymore. There was nothing to stop me going.

Nico thrust a set of keys at me. 'You do what you're told.'

For a second I did nothing, as the tank advanced towards us. It was tempting to walk away. Fuck off from him and all this.

Nico's free hand had shifted down his coat. To the pocket he kept his pistol in. The pistol he was happy to use.

There was a fair chance he'd punch a hole in my guts. Send someone else to drive the lorry. He'd done it plenty of times before with others who'd stepped out of line. I took the keys. 'All right.'

Nico grinned. 'Knew I could trust you.'

As he took the weapon out of its box I returned to the Scrambler. Gregg gave me some look, maybe encouragement or pity or just confusion. I started the bike up and it rattled into life. Gregg shuffled off over to Nico who was shouting instructions. Getting his men moving. They were in the cars and vans that remained intact, driving them out of the way, letting the tank through, towards me.

I pulled off and accelerated along the road, clunked up into second as the bike misfired at the top end. The tank was in my mirrors, a great dark shape behind me that vanished as I rode away. There was nothing to stop me riding off. Heading away from all this. But that would be me finished here, finished as part of the Round Up gang that Nico ran. I'd have to leave town before he got hold of me.

I hit Harbour Bridge at forty. It was a metal one with lattice structure up the sides, joined over the top. It crossed the River Farle where it flowed into the harbour. The bike's handlebars gave a shimmy on the damp surface and it lifted its front wheel as I put the power on, dropping back down as I slipped into third. This was it. If I meant to ride off it had to be now. My last opportunity to escape.

At the last second I eased the brakes on and took the road for the lorry park. Seemed I was happier to face the tank than Nico. All the town's heavy vehicles were lined up: several mobile cranes, a couple of low loaders and six articulated lorries. Three of the artics were out of operation, waiting for parts, another stripped bare. At the end were the two that worked, the Northern Oil one being the furthest.

I slid the Triumph up alongside it, killing the engine and jumping off. Maybe I'd made the right choice; maybe

I hadn't. I flicked the stand down and stood by the lorry. It was a Scania tractor with petrol tanker on the back. On the occasions when fuel came into town it was transported in this or the other working one next to it. The door to the cab was unlocked and I leapt in, fumbling with the keys, not sure what the hell I was going to do. It fired up after a couple of churns on the starter, the motor picking up, shaking the bodywork. I adjusted the mirrors, revving up, blurring the image of my bike parked beside it. The tank was now within a hundred metres of the bridge, picking up speed: a great metal block that lurched over the remaining barricades.

I shoved the lorry into gear, swinging it wide and out onto the road, facing away from the bridge. There was no way I was going to ram into the tank but if I reversed into it there was a chance I could wedge it while Nico did his work. That way I'd be as far away from it as possible.

I took the lorry out onto Bay Road and aimed up towards High Town. Then I stopped and set it up ready to back up across the bridge. Block it.

But it had been some time since I'd reversed one of these, and doing it in the dark made it much worse.

The trailer wandered off to the left, ending up jammed against the bank side, leaving room for the tank to squeeze through. I took it forwards then tried again, swinging the tractor unit from side to side to keep the trailer on track and provide a clearer a view of road behind. The tank was now on the bridge and I pushed the trailer back faster until one corner clipped the edge, crumpling against the steelwork. It pivoted on the back end so the front was wedged against the other side. That was all I had time to do. I had to go.

7

I got out and ran forward, well away from the lorry and tank; not stopping until I was at the steeper section of the road. I dropped down below the drystone wall.

There was a roar and the top of the trailer and half the cab erupted. A second later there was a flash as fuel ignited in the tanker unit. It was meant to be empty but there was always some residue. Great flames licked out of the back as the tank tried drive over it.

Then it stopped, jammed in the wreckage. As it rotated its turret Nico appeared on the bridge behind it, walking towards it. Over his shoulder was the weapon. It was aimed at the tank. 'I'm sure you know what this is!' he shouted. Gregg and the other men followed after him.

The metalwork of the bridge hemmed in the tank's barrel so it was unable to turn backwards. The turret moved from one side to the other, thudding into the structure then tracking back the other way.

The tank reversed off the wreckage and parked. The whirr of the motors slowed, stopped.

For a minute, maybe longer nothing happened. The tank was parked there and Nico faced it, the weapon rested on his shoulder, all casual, like it was an umbrella or something.

Then the turret opened. A man climbed out. Within seconds Nico's people were onto the vehicle and all over him, pulling at his arms, dragging him off the tank. The hatch clanged shut as soon as he was clear. Nico lowered the gun and waved his hand, some vague gesture that got his men to hold their prisoner to the ground. With two men pinning him down the others started kicking and punching. As this carried on I walked past the burning wreckage, over to the car park. I walked across to my bike not looking back. I'd got used to not looking in this town.

I fired the Scrambler up and rode off. I was so used to their violence it hardly even bothered me anymore.

Hardly.

CHAPTER TWO

Race Day

On Tuesday I kept out of Nico and Will's way. As usual I walked the streets, kept my eyes open for trouble. Threatened several street kids. The same pattern as the last eighteen months, even since I'd joined Round Up, come to Faeston. This place I'd drifted into after wandering the roads, facing the gangs of bikers, neo-reivers and other scavengers. Trying to make a living trading, couriering. After a year of that I'd had enough. It had been different in the past, when I'd had partners. A car. Alone on a bike in the Borders was tough. Too tough, it seemed.

It hadn't been something I'd chosen or wanted. Things should have gone better but after Setmarch, well that had been such a fuck up. Losing the car and what had happened to Jamie. And Laura. Jesus.

So I came here and joined Round Up. If I didn't think about it, it wasn't such a bad life but it got exhausting trying not to think all the time. Keeping out of the way of my employers made life better, avoiding Will's snide comments, Gregg's digs: Nico's power-games.

Nico hadn't been running the show when I arrived. He'd pushed his way up shortly afterwards. I'd had my doubts about him. Now I knew he was a rotten apple. Rotten in lots of ways. But my head was too full of the night before, The Incident, as people were calling it, to worry about Nico and his cronies.

And it really had been an incident. I'd not seen anything like that since my twenties. Military vehicles had been relatively commonplace decades ago, mostly in newspapers and on the TV but even in toy sets for kids. Models that people made. In the Oil Wars the real ones had pushed their way across the desert. Hundreds of them, on our side and the other. As the fighting advanced newer and more deadly versions of them came out. The name never seemed to do justice to their true purpose: tank. It sounded so mundane, harmless. Maybe that made it worse. An invasion of tanks. They'd all been wiped out in the wars, apart from some that came back and were used by Murgatroyd in his last gasp as Prime Minister. They'd been deployed in Birmingham and London but they'd never made it this far north, not for use, at least. Despite sticking them on the streets he'd still failed. After his downfall they'd been scrapped, dumped in remote places with all their weapons striped, neutered. That had been the only time they'd come near here: as carcasses to be abandoned in woods and on the moors, like the so-called Graveyard near the Border Forest.

Now there was one here, back from the dead.

And they had it. Round Up had a tank.

At four o'clock I sloped off, heading home. Although there were some kids making a racket on Back Road I didn't respond. They were running around in the mist. Kicking a turnip against a door. Being part of Round Up wasn't something I'd picked or enjoyed so once off duty I turned a blind eye. Anyway, compared to Nico and his pals having an armoured vehicle, a few lads mucking around didn't seem important.

I headed across town with the damp settling on my jacket as the sounds from the harbour drifted over the building: shouts from workers and the clatter of ropes and pulleys. The occasional thud as something fell. I came to Clubb Road and walked up, past the ancient Victorian houses and stumps of trees that had once lined the road. I came to the place I rented and went round the back, unlocked the wooden gate and went into the yard. As ever it was damp and the drains smelled of rotting food. Beyond the yard was the overgrown garden that belonged to the Tommy, the owner who lived downstairs. Gardening wasn't really his thing. Sounds came from his place, muted guitar playing. A gruff voice singing along. He was trying to play some old pop song. Drunk as usual.

Before I went up I checked on the bike, pulling the tarpaulin off, putting a hand to the fins on the engine, tapping the tank just below the word Triumph. There was a ding from the tank with its tiny quantity of fuel, the bootleg juice I'd scrounged. Chips marked the paintwork on this forty-year-old machine, 2013 vintage. Even the replacement forks were tarnished, one seal seeping fluid. The carbs were missing, now sitting up in the flat awaiting my attention. I'd pulled them off yesterday evening after getting back, giving me something to tinker on with. Take my mind off the events. Even though it had once been fitted with injectors and all that electronic stuff, I'd converted it last July after the cheap bio-eth got the better of the original setup. That and the loom rotting away. Now even the carbs were playing up. Age caught up with everything.

I locked the gate and made my way up the steps. The wood creaked under my weight. As I fumbled with my keys there was a noise from Tommy's flat. A dull thud. Then he swore and started singing again.

My living room smelled of petrol and damp. The carbs lay on the table, parts scattered around them. There was a service manual on the arm of my one armchair, left open partway through. A hole in the carpet marked a path from door to armchair.

I needed the bike back on the road for later. But first I needed to eat. I pulled together what almost resembled a chilli using some mince, onion and spices I'd bought at the quayside. I ate sitting with the bowl on my knee, facing the window. I read the service manual as I spooned the food into my mouth. Forkful after forkful until it was finished. Then I sat back and stared out at the mist that rolled up from the quayside and hung over the houses and disused park opposite. For a moment the fog cleared and I could see over the park and down onto Faeston: the roofs that sloped off towards the river and harbour that split the town in two. The town was built around the harbour and river that ran down to it. South Side was across the bridges, a hotchpotch of run down hotels and shops and offices that sloped upwards towards the distant moors. That was where the track was, where I went racing.

To my left were the wind turbines, just ticking over, and beyond them the sea. The freezing North Sea. Framing the harbour was High Town, the best part of

Faeston with its tidy buildings and clean streets.

The mist closed in again. All that was visible were the ghosts of the houses opposite.

I went through into the kitchen, dumped the bowl in the sink and rinsed it. Tommy's singing got louder.

There were plenty of home comforts here. After being on the road it was luxury. Occasionally there was even hot water: there were solar panels that had been fitted by Tommy's parents when he was a kid. They'd been forward-thinkers his folks, also putting in wood-burning stoves and planting the garden with saplings to provide fuel.

Some people had done that back in the twenties, as the economy unravelled, as The Collapse started to fall on the so-called civilised world. There were business failures and runs on banks, power cuts. Fuel prices that shot up. Hospitals and schools run by volunteers.

When gangs started to assert themselves there was mention of martial law but the military were bogged down in the Middle East trying to hang onto a share of dwindling oil supplies. Every army in the world was camped out there until it became clear there was no point. That the game was over.

After the coalition fell apart in 2034, that was it. Neither depleted army nor the crackpot political parties with their quick fixes were up to running the country. For a while it was chaos then it settled down. Towns like Faeston went for committees, making their own rules, establishing some semblance of order. Getting thugs like Round Up to do their dirty work.

Tommy's folks had tried to see him through all this. They'd probably thought they were setting him up all right, not guessing how far things would fall apart. That he'd lose most of the cash when his bank folded. Spend the rest on booze. That was why he needed me as a lodger, as he'd told me the day I moved in.

I finished the washing up and started work on the carbs. Bit by bit I reassembled them, setting then up according the notes I'd taken when I'd striped them. On the last few runs out the Triumph had stalled and misfired. Backfiring on the overrun. Not good. Maybe a clean was all that was needed.

At last they sat reassembled on the table.

I went to get ready for the evening. For the race.

In the bedroom I opened the wardrobe, pulling out my spare boots and trousers. At the bottom was the hatch. The hatch with all the bad stuff.

For a minute I stood there, immobile.

Maybe this time I'd let myself ignore it. Not go through the ritual.

Then I lifted the hatch, drawing out two bags. One clinked as I slid it out.

I lay them on the bed and opened the lighter one first, flattening out the paper that was inside, all those documents I'd hung onto. There were the charts and maps. The plans and cross-sections of HMS Gehenna, the last sub the UK had made. The one loaded up with weapons that still was out there now, somewhere waiting to be found.

All I had were bits of paper but they'd cost so much. A lot of people.

After staring at them for some time I opened the second bag and took out the shotgun, its sawn-off barrel rough and scratched. Without thinking I knelt on the floor, sliding it into my mouth. The end of the gun tasted of metal. The sawn-off barrels rough on my tongue, sulphurous. I closed my eyes and pulled the triggers.

The gun clicked once, then again. I held onto it, staying there for a moment.

This was something I did. Something that happened. It didn't mean anything. It was just something.

I eased the gun out of my mouth, felt its weight, swung it around. Then slid it away. I bundled the Gehenna stuff up as well and dropped both bags into the hatch.

With the ritual over I grabbed my leather jacket and helmet. Shut the wardrobe.

That was enough messing around for tonight.

As I picked up the carbs from the living room I heard a piece of furniture fall over downstairs. Shouting.

The carbs took a while to fit, as I struggled in the fading light, lining them up, getting the cable in place, slipping on the race filters. Once I'd run fuel through them I thumbed the starter. It churned over, slow then faster, a cough from the exhaust before it chimed into life, the revs rising up as smoke billowed around me, off into the low vegetation of the garden: the stumps of trees Tommy had clear-felled. I held onto the choke until it settled into a rough idle. It picked up on the throttle, dropped down again. Rose and fell in line with the twist grip.

It seemed to run all right so I picked up the helmet stashed with the bike, unlocked the gate and rode round to the front of the house. I parked it with the engine running, as it wobbled on its side-stand. I pulled on the lid then locked the gate. One of the few rules of the race was that we had to wear helmets.

The fog had drifted away and been replaced by a cold

breeze. I rode off across down, over West Bridge, the one untouched by the tank, but rather than go into town I went up Hill Road at the other side of the river, to the track. The lane where we raced. The bike's engine ran all right. There was a flat spot at low revs. Some hesitance picking up. But it revved through clean enough, pulling strongly at the top end as I made my way up the hill. Hopefully enough for tonight.

I went to the start line at the western end of the track. It shrank off into the distance, to a pine tree whitewashed to mark the finish line. Beyond it, in the distance, were the wind turbines, stilled now. Beneath them lights lit houses, row up row that led down to the quayside with the motionless ships and their forest of masts.

There were several bikes waiting: two big Japanese machines and an Italian. The thirteen-hundred Suzuki was a regular. At its prime this bike would have been unbeatable, but thirty years of poor servicing had taken its toll. It rattled and hunted, giving off a stream of smoke as it misfired. Next to it was a Kawasaki. Similar capacity, similar condition. And there was the Ducati, tidy but only an eight-hundred. There were rules on capacity but they were quite vague. The Scrambler was a shade over eight-fifty so that meant it could go in the middleweight class. If I was daft enough I could go against the bigger bikes. That was my choice. The two big machines that were here tonight were ropy but still would knock out a lot of power. I'd always avoided them in the past. There were easier ones to beat.

I waved to Starter Lad, dressed in his usual trainers and T-shirt from a long-gone football team. Against the fence was a rough blackboard. He chalked my name on the list, recognising me as a regular. I was down for race two against the Ducati.

As the two big Japs lined up I parked at the side. Several others bikes rode up, seedy lightweights too small for me to race: Honda and Daelim singles. There were a few people hanging around, spectators. There'd be more at the other end, where the bets were made.

Starter Lad went over to a funnel attached to a fencepost. It was connected to a piece of metal tubing that ran along the top of the fence to the far end. A whistle on a piece of string hung down beside it. He blew the whistle into the funnel and twisted his head round to listen. There was a muffled voice as the fella at the finish line acknowledged him.

'Hayabusa 1300 and ZZR 1400.'

There was another reply.

He straightened up and grabbed his tattered union flag and raised it.

The bikes revved, their riders' heads twisted towards Starter Lad.

He dropped the flag.

They roared off, one popping and cracking as it went. They disappeared up the track leaving the smell of cooked tyres and part-combusted fuel. Soon enough brake lights glowed at the end as they passed the tree.

I started the Triumph and rode it over. Now it was my turn. The light had faded so that the track disappeared off before me, invisible beyond the Triumph's headlight beam, past Starter Lad and the spectators. The Ducati appeared beside me and I did up my leather jacket, adjusting my open-face. My opponent hunched forward and adjusted his lid. He revved his bike as Starter Lad jumped around, his torn flag in the air. I tapped the fuel tank, like I did every race.

Starter Lad dropped the flag. Race time.

I wound the throttle and released the clutch, the Triumph lurching forward as the air-cooled twin moaned. The handlebars shimmied, clocks shaking as the needles moved round to the right. I held on as the bike rattled and roared, the road flying under its wheels. I shifted up to second, the Ducati's front wheel parallel as I held the throttle wide open and let the revs touch the red before shifting up again, a gulp coming from the two into two. The road was swallowed up by the headlight, the engine bellowing as it drew through its race filters.

Then I snicked up into third. I left the Ducati and shot past the ghostly pine. Figures appeared in the headlight. I grabbed the brake with my right hand, easing my foot down on the pedal. The bike rose up at the back, its weight shifted forward, forcing the front tyre onto the tarmac. I dropped it down through the gears, blipping the throttle and braking as it slowed and swung round, driving it back to pull up at the kerbside. The two fellas at the finish line came over. The Ducati stopped by the verge further up.

'Good run,' said one of them. 'He was close.'

I turned the engine off. He had been close. Too close. I collected the winnings, minus my stake. That was how it worked; we all betted on ourselves.

The two big Japanese bikes were at the opposite side of the road and I parked near them. They were talking about The Incident. What they'd heard about the tank going through town. I didn't join in the conversation.

I wanted to see who else came along. Whether there

was someone worth racing. Someone I could beat.

Back at the start line a couple of bikes lined up, the two lightweights that had been hanging around. They set themselves up, their engines rising and falling. Headlamps swinging around.

Then they were off. They raced up to the finish line and the Honda shot past trailing a plume of smoke. The Daelim cruised through, the rider seeming unaware that racing meant going fast.

The Ducati had moved off and turned down the road to the left, the lane that we used to get us back to the far end. I fired up the Triumph and followed him. Maybe he'd be daft enough to race me again. Lose again.

He parked near the start line and got off his bike.

I pulled up beside him, ready to ask him if he wanted a second run.

Then another bike rode up. Roared in. This was one I didn't know. It was a Yamaha, late middleweight: R6 in blue and white. Its fairing was intact and alloy polished, every bolt shining. It stopped hard in the middle of the road and then settle back onto its suspension. The rider was slim, in race leathers, leathers that were close fitting. Tight enough to suggest this wasn't one of the usual bikers. In one move the helmet came off and long hair spilled out, bright red.

The woman looked me over with her dark eyes. She killed the engine and flicked the side-stand down, walking over to me and the Ducati rider. Each step was carefully placed, one foot in front of the other.

'I want to race,' she said, giving me a look. A good eyeballing. Then a smile, a smile women had given me before. A smile that made me uneasy.

The Ducati fella seemed keen so I left him to it.

I started the Scrambler's engine, manoeuvred it round. With a last look at her I rode off.

Life was complicated enough as it was.

CHAPTER THREE

Round Up

The next day a sea-fret rolled across the town, over the buildings along the roads and into the alley. The sun was a pale circle in the sky as I did my patrol for Round Up. Wednesday was my half-day. Half an hour then I'd be finished. So far the shift had been quiet, as if sometimes was in the morning. There'd been a handful of drunks sleeping out and a couple rowing. Nothing big. Nothing until now.

I heard the voices as I joined Gladstone Street. There was a group of lads up ahead, messing around, swearing and shouting. People rode past on bicycles, on their way to the docks, or pubs. Some going the other way. No one reacted or did anything. That's how it was in Faeston. Leave it to Round Up.

I moved backwards, into an alley, away from the noise. Leaning against the damp wall I curled and uncurled my fingers, forming fists them opening them out again. If I waited there was a chance they'd go away. Or I could change my route and pretend I'd never seen them.

They'd be easy enough to sort out but I didn't have the inclination. The headspace. There seemed to be too much going on in the town. This was supposed to be one of those places where nothing much happened. Nothing changed. That had been the case for the last year and a half.

Now there'd been two new arrivals in the last day: the tank and that woman. An armoured vehicle crashing in was an oddity, really out of the ordinary. But she had unsettled me as well. People like her didn't just appear. Not in Faeston.

Maybe I was just getting jumpy.

There was more noise from the street. A crash and laughter. The troublemakers were jumpy as well. I'd have to do something. I stepped out of the alley and moved along the pavement so they could see me.

If they'd spotted me, they didn't pay much heed. There were three of them: a tall one with teeth missing, one with a shaven head and a third whose face was covered by a tattooed swastika. The tattoo shifted as he laughed and shouted, reminding me of someone else, someplace else. They all wore blue overalls, the drab attire of dockworkers. One of the them snatched a wooden chair from outside a café, swinging it up into the air. It smashed into pieces on the road. The others laughed then each grabbed a chair themselves, ready to swing it onto the road.

'I wouldn't do that,' I said.

The shaven-headed lad frowned, lowering the chair. Then he raised it again, flinging it to join the other. It clattered across the tarmac. They all laughed, coarse grunts of pleasure.

'Tut-tut,' I said, walking over to them. Seemed they weren't going to be reasonable.

The swastika-ed lad picked up a chair, laughing. 'Hey, make it three, eh?'

I snatched it, yanking the lad off balance, slipping the chair out of his grip and placing it on the ground. I was getting really pissed off with them now.

'Hey, what the fuck?'

I shook my head. 'Time to go home, boys.'

Swastika-face and tall one stared at me, hard eyes as they stepped closer. The shaven headed one stayed back.

I reached into my jacket, took out a joint of confiscated home-grown and slid it into my mouth, a casual move to distract them, not escalate things. 'Just leave it.' When they came towards me some more I stepped back. Though it was tempting to knock their heads together that would take effort. And time. 'You don't want to be rounded up.'

The shaven headed one grabbed the others' jackets, stopped them. 'Hey, wait, you know —'

'He's on his own,' said the tallest.

'He's Round Up, you know…'

I lit the joint and blew out smoke that joined the fog, now thinning in the midday sun. Maybe they were going to see sense. 'Fetch the chairs and I'll forget all about it.'

The shaven headed lad let go of the others and stepped out into the road towards the chairs. He put his hand on one but moved no further. The other two faced me, motionless. Gulls cried out up ahead and there was a rattle from a chain down at the docks, the cry of distant voices. I smoked. There was a chance the lads would just walk away, leave and not force it.

'What you gonna do?' Swastika-face squared up to me.

He was the troublemaker. With him taken down the other two wouldn't cause any bother.

'Howay!' He came right up to me, shoving me with an open hand, laughing.

It looked like he wasn't going to make it easy. I stepped back, exhaling smoke, balancing and positioning myself. I balled my hand into a fist and right-hooked him on the jaw. He staggered back eyes all over the place and hands flapping.

Tall lad glanced at his companion, his expression hardening, body straightening up. Before he had a chance to join in I punched him between the eyes. Not hard but enough to unsettle him.

Swastika face lay curled up and the tall lad rubbed his forehead, holding onto one of the chairs. The joint had fallen from my mouth so I bent and picked it up, smoking some more. There was no need to do anymore. They were just kids, not serious trouble makers but annoying.

I stared at the third lad. 'About those chairs…'

He dragged the undamaged chair and placed it with the others outside the café. Then he picked up the bits of the bust one, held them in his arms and stood by his friends.

I prodded Swastika-face with my foot. 'Next time, I round you up.' Then I walked off. I'd done my job, finished my shift, sorted out some trouble.

At the end of the road I stubbed my joint out and glanced back. The two lads standing helped the third one up. Then they stared at me, looks of fear, possibly hate.

I turned my back on them and walked into town. Past the houses and workshops open for the day's trade. As I joined High Row the sun cleared through the last of the haze and shone down on the quayside, a soft light on the ships moored there, their sails furled. Some cargo was still being loaded by men who carried barrels and bundles up the ramps, now at a steep angle due to the high tide. But most of it had already stowed with hatches battened and crews making-ready for sail. Voices drifted up from the ships, instructions and orders; I passed the shops, all busy with last minute trade where red faced men queued up with bits of bust tackle from their ships, keen to get out with the tide.

The stalls were all set up further along, stacked with chunks of meat and scabby vegetables, the staple diet of the town. No one asked where the meat came from, what animal it was. Drunks slumped outside the Globe Inn and I slid past them, up Blind Lane with its cracked paving, taking the stairs down to the office below the pub.

I held the door handle for a second, let the sounds of the port clatter around me. I had to go in and claim my money, take what I was due. But Nico, Will and Gregg had started to get difficult, as bad as the kids who wandered the street. As the heads of Round Up, they'd got to be big fish in the town. Big nasty fish.

But Monday night, The Incident, was worth something. They owed me for sorting that out.

They three of them were there when I went in, sitting at the stained table, drinking whisky and playing Black Jack, same as most days. The main headquarters, Round Up Central, was on the other side of town but they like to hang around here. Drink and play cards. The light filtering through the filthy windows caught the dust and smoke in the air.

'You finished already?' said Nico. He didn't look up from his hand. As usual he was in his dark suit, black pinstripes and flared trousers, ancient and threadbare. His shades were pushed up on his curly hair, a different pair from the other night.

Will and Gregg were in overalls, Gregg's bunched up under his beard, bulging on his belly, contrasting with Wills that hung off him.

'Sit down, lad,' said Nico.

I hated being called lad but he knew that, so I didn't take the bait. I pulled up a chair and sat at the end of the table, taking a glass, pouring some whisky. There were rattles and muted voices from the bar upstairs.

Nico topped his glass up. 'Any bother?'

'Not much.' I drank some of the whisky. It burned my throat and made my eyes water. Nasty cheap shit.

'No round ups?'

'Not today.'

He looked up, the first time he'd taken his eyes of his cards. His pupils were dilated, soft in that hard face. There was laughter from upstairs and the sound of something heavy falling over. He smiled, always a bad sign. 'We might have something extra for you to do.'

'You owe me for Monday night.'

'You'll be paid. You did well. Pity about the truck but....'

'It was your plan.'

'Everything is my plan.' This was something he said a lot.

The problem was it was true.

Though there was The Committee, who ran the business side of town: the rubbish collection, water supply and electricity. All the dull stuff like paying dockworkers and fixing roads. Although they did all the nuts and bolts of running Faeston, they relied on Round Up to enforce the rules. Keep everyone in line. And Nico had used that to lever up his power. Aside from steering every decision The Committee made, he had all sorts of rackets running on the side. Carte blanche to do what he liked.

'What's the something extra?' I fingered my glass, let it catch the light. This could be one of Nico's traps, like he'd set for Jackson back in December, the one that had sent him off the quayside with a knife in his side.

'It's to do with the other night.'

Gregg laughed. 'Isn't everything!'

'You never did say what happened to the tank or the fella in it,' I said.

'No, I never did.' Nico placed a card, a two of hearts.

Gregg groaned and picked up two cards.

'Well,' said Nico. 'We have something that needs sorting out.'

'Such as?' I took another drink of whisky, felt the burn.

'Some babysitting, that's all. No big deal.' He placed an eight of hearts after Will played a five.

'And I will get extra for that?'

'Of course.'

I knocked back the rest of my whisky and took a breath to clear the taste. 'I need paying for today.'

Nico placed his cards face down and reached into his jacket, drawing out a bag of coins. After counting some out, he slid them across the table to me, the gold glowing in that dim room. Then he put fingers on two of them, dragged them back and put them under his glass. 'Monday night's money. Well, we'll sort that after the babysitting. But I'm docking some for not rounding up. Less Rounding Up, less pay.'

'Come on Nico.'

Then he smiled, a big grin. 'Only messin'.' He offered the coins and I slid them into my jacket, a smaller pile than was due. But it added to the stash, the escape fund.

The card game restarted and gruff laughter came from upstairs. Gregg placed a three of diamonds and Will a three of spades. None of them paid any attention to me. With my hand on the pocket full of money I left.

Outside I stopped at the top of the steps and counted the coins, away from them and out of sight of the drunks from the Globe. It was well down on what it should have been, just over two-thirds of what I was due. But there was no arguing with Round Up. They set the rules. Owned the town, and me.

As I walked back along High Row I gripped the money, rattling the coins together, as the ships alongside crawled with crew. Even with the under payment I was getting a good war chest. A few more weeks of this and I'd be free to do what I liked. Add in the other night's pay, Nico's babysitting and the racing wins, then I'd be set.

But set for what?

Was it time to leave Round Up? Leave town?

Maybe it was time to move on.

Taking my hand off the money I headed to Sophie's, past crews on their way to ships and drunks staggering round, one singing some old song about whisky.

CHAPTER FOUR

Sophie

She was arranging her ornaments when I arrived, setting them out on the bookcase. There were ceramic animals, cute kids, a couple of clowns. Useless crap she'd collected from house clearances, junk shops, rubbish tips. They were all lined up, watching me as I sat on Sophie's settee, the one that pointed at her huge television set. She came over pecked me on the cheek, lipsticked lips on my stubble, her blonde curls falling onto my face. Then she sat down next to me, shimmying up close, so her thigh was pushed against me, her soft flesh.

'How are you, Trenty?' she said, putting two fingers on my chin, turning my head so she could look straight at me with her made-up face, full lips and plucked eyebrows. Smooth skin. For all her faults, she was a looker.

I hated her calling me that but it didn't stop her. 'I'm fine.'

'Work okay?'

I shrugged, let her take it as whatever she wanted.

'I'm quite all right, even though you didn't ask.'

'Sorry,' I said. 'How are you?'

She turned her head to the side, looked offended, then smiled. 'Any news?'

'Some.'

'Come on!' She wrapped her arm around mine.

'Well, there was that thing the other night, The Incident.' I wanted to see what she made of this, whether it sparked some curiosity in her. See if an armoured vehicle appearing in town unsettled her as much as me.

'Oh, I know about that.' Then she leapt up, clapping her hands. 'I've got something to show you!' At that she was off out of the room, leaving her ornaments to stare at me. I picked up the telly's remote and thumbed it, knowing that nothing would happen, that it and the TV set were bust and only there for show, not that there were any transmissions now anyway. From the other room I could hear Sophie talking to herself, chucking stuff around.

Maybe she'd missed all the fireworks the other night. Or blanked it out. That was something she did with anything too complicated or confusing. Still, she was only young, barely out of her twenties, and did have a lot of energy. That was something I liked about her, her enthusiasm. Always throwing herself into whatever the occasion was. Whatever. Maybe it was the only thing I liked about her.

I went across to the window, to the side of the room where she had a bookcase filled with cookbooks. Gulls wheeled around outside, between Sophie's flat and the warehouses opposite, stacked with clothes and provisions in from the continent. Down the lane two men argued about something and behind them was the harbour where ships moving round. Some setting sail, others coming in.

I picked up a book. Put it down: more of Sophie's junk. She did love all this old shit, and it was a little odd really all the tat she collected, but it worked between us. The thing we had was fun. Enjoying ourselves. I was old enough to be her dad but we laughed and messed around like we were teenagers. Most of the time, at least. And it had been her who'd made the initial moves: she'd picked me up. Just over a year ago when I'd been in the George and Dragon. One Saturday night.

I'd finished my shift and was having a quiet drink but a fight started at the far side of the bar.

Although I could have left it and just carried on drinking I went over. A big fella from one of the ships had hold of some skinny runt, a weaselly street lad. The punches were flying but weird thing was that the runt was winning. He had the big fella back against the wall, pummelling his face. Fists pumping, landing blow after blow. I got hold of one of the bar staff and together we dragged him off. Managed to steer him to the door. He was so intent on the big fella he barely noticed us. We threw him out of the pub, his hands still clenched and insults pouring out of him. But the barman stood at the door and kept it bolted while he left off his steam out in the cold.

I went back to my whisky and that was when the big guy found his balls. He came over to me saying he'd not needed any help and I'd made him look stupid. I'd had a rough day dealing with street kids and smart-arse deckhands. I wasn't prepared to take stick in my free time.

'Listen,' I said, 'you're right. You didn't need my help. You're quite capable of making yourself look stupid.' It was a daft thing to say but it slipped out and there were a few laughs from round the bar.

The fella puffed himself up like he was going to explode.

Then he flicked a punch out at me. It caught me on the arm and knocked me off my bar stool. I staggered for a couple of steps and he laughed, a great guffaw.

That was enough. I swung a wide hook and belted him in the jaw.

Before he regained his balance I pinned him against the wall. Piled into him. After a little knocking around he decided to go back to his boat. Maybe I'd got carried away, blamed him for all the shit in the town. Maybe he deserved it. It was hard to say.

When I returned to the bar my drink had another fresh one sitting by it. And Sophie was there. She'd taken the stool next to mine, bought me the drink.

She gave me a big smile. 'That was something.'

'Was it?' I sat down and took a drink, looked her up and down. She was all dolled up in tight dress and heels. Hair up and plenty of make-up on. Not normally what I went for but she was keen and friendly.

'Not seen you here before,' she said.

'Not been in town that long.'

'Sorted those two out easy enough.'

'Just doing what had to be done.'

'I like a man who can look after himself.' At that she slid her hand onto my knee, kept it there.

We drank more and she told me about her place in town that she ran, selling off salvaged items. I hadn't realised at the time that she meant junk.

Then we went off to a club by the quayside, drank

more and danced. Headed back to hers. Spent the night together.

We've been seeing each other since then.

Now here I was in her flat. I flicked through the cookbook with its pictures of fancy food made of unobtainable ingredients.

Sophie burst in clutching a piece of paper, thrusting it into my face. 'Here we go,' she said. 'What do you think?'

I put the book back and had a look. It was the details on a house, some small place across the other side of town, on South Side. There was a poor image of it printed on the top. At the bottom was a price. 'What's this?' I said.

'House details.'

'House details?' I turned the sheet over in case there was some clue as to why this mattered.

She took my hand, held it really tight. 'For us, Trent, when you get all your savings together. We can pool it with mine. The Committee are selling some off. We get a place. Together.' She grinned. A great smile that hit her ears.

That had been a mistake: telling her about my savings. I'd only done it because I'd been drunk. Thinking aloud. Now she was staring at me. It seemed this was the point where I was supposed to say something positive and supportive. 'Right,' I said.

'What do you think?'

'About what?'

'The house? Is this the one?'

I stared down at the sheet, as if something useful would pop out, some information that would help me ease out of this. After a few seconds I said, 'It's quite a way from town.'

She snatched the sheet from me. 'Forget it. Don't worry about all the effort I put into this.'

'Sorry, I just —'

'Don't Trent.' She crossed her arms, turned her head away from me. Then she was off out of the room, leaving me there on my own. Me and the ornaments. There was clattering from the kitchen as she shifted stuff around. It was tempting to just leave. Get the fuck out of there and go home.

Sophie had ideas in her head. About her future. About me and her — us living together. There was no way I was going to move into a place with her. No chance. She really didn't get it. This was just a fling, a passing thing that we'd both slid into. It was easy and worked for now but it was nothing more than that.

She didn't come back in so I settled onto the settee. Although hideous to look at, it was comfortable. And the room was warm, heated by her gas fire, another antique but one that worked. She often complained that the Faeston gas sooted it up but it still pumped out the heat. Sophie liked things easy, comfortable. Soft furnishings, plenty of food and warmth. Small talk. Nothing was difficult here. When I stayed over we'd often lie in until midday the next day.

Maybe it was too easy.

Muted cries came from the gulls outside mixed with the distant sound of voices at the quayside. I stretched my legs and splayed out on the settee. It was odd she hadn't asked me about the other night, The Incident, when I'd brought it up.

That was what she was poor at, serious stuff. It was impossible to talk anything through with her.

My head hurt from the things that were rattling though it. The Incident, Gehenna. The new woman turning up at the races. Ongoing problems with Round Up. Now Sophie wanting to settle down. Buy a fucking house. I shut my eyes and rubbed them.

So much to think about. Too much.

Then there was a noise from outside. A great roar like a giant wave crashing on a beach. Shouts and cries. I went to the window. A wall of water charged up the lane, swamping the people standing there, rushing into doorways before it receded back down to the quayside. The cause was in the harbour. Between the smashed hulls of boats was a giant ship, a great black shape that stood above all of them. On top of its massive hull was the dark oblong of a conning tower. It was Gehenna, HMS Gehenna that was detailed in the documents hidden in my wardrobe, the ancient submarine, last of the Extinction Class. It had surfaced here. A klaxon sounded and the sub's deck opened, slid apart with a metallic whirr. A ramp extended. Several seconds later a tank emerged, same as the one the other night, followed by others. A column of these deadly vehicles. Their turrets swivelled round and took aim as they lined up on the deck. Then the weapons fired, shaking the building, knocking me from side to side, Sophie repeating my name, over and over.

'Trent?' she said.

I was on the settee with Sophie in front of me. Behind her gulls flew by the window. There were voices outside, laughter and the burble of conversation. No screams or shouts. No submarine or tanks.

'Were you asleep?' she said.

'Resting my eyes.' I sat up, stretching.

'Are you all right?'

'Fine. I should go. I have work to do on the bike.'

'You and that bike.'

I stood up. 'It's not running right, something with the carbs.'

'Bikes and work. That's all you care about.'

'It just needs to be sorted out.'

She stood and faced me, slid her hands around me. Then down the front of my trousers. 'I can see something else that needs sorting out.' Keeping one hand there she kissed me, pulling me close with her other arm. We stayed like that for a while, as voices came from the quayside down the road.

Then she led me off to the bedroom. We made love in her room filled with teddy bears and dolls. Soft toys and kids' books racked on shelves. As she closed her eyes and lay back she whispered my name. She said how much she loved me. But it wasn't her I was in bed with, it was the woman I'd seen at the races.

CHAPTER FIVE

New Racer

After leaving Sophie's I went straight home, sitting by the window in the living room, staring out at the houses and park opposite. The mist had cleared and sunlight lit the overgrown bushes and busted brickwork. Something moved in the undergrowth, a feral cat or a couple of rats maybe. Sophie'd wanted me to stay but I couldn't face her, talk about houses and plans for the future. I'd said I had stuff to do and left.

And here I was by the window, just sitting.

I got up. There was a race later. They had races most evenings but I didn't usually go two days in a row. For some reason it seemed like a good idea: a good way to build up some more cash. Get away from town. That's what it was. No more than that.

I found myself down by the bike. For some time I stood there, staring at it. Then I rolled it out, started up and rode across town. Without aim I set off. It was as if the Scrambler took me on its own, without me controlling it. Instead of going to the race track it took me on the South

Road, past the derelict retail park, onwards to the town farms. They surrounded Faeston on each side, field upon field of pigs and chickens. Animals fed by the leftovers collected in town and brought up here. It was run by The Committee, supported by Round Up, of course. I rode past the fields of stinking animals onwards to the barricade and patrol point. Two men stood at the edge of the road each with a gun. The barricade was made of barbed wire and stakes, running off in each direction around the town. A large section was roughly patched, the result of the tank coming through. I slowed and waved to the men, Tyler and Jack from Round Up. They waved back and let me through.

As soon as I left the town's jurisdiction the landscape changed. Tended fields were replaced by rough moorland. On the edges there were marks of tracks, where the tank had veered off. I carried on for a mile stopping at the side of the road, on higher ground. Ahead of me were the parched moors that ran north to Scotland and south towards the other counties of England. To the west was more moorland, lit orange by the setting sun.

The road was empty. No sounds part from distant ones from Faeston: a heavy engine, raised voices. A bell ringing. The moors were still and silent. Being here reminded me that it wasn't all bad outside towns. Maybe this was where I was at home. Staying in Faeston had seemed like a good idea when I'd first rolled in. Somewhere to recuperate, stack up cash. Have an easy few months.

But I'd got stuck. Tied to Round Up, feeling committed: to work and to Sophie.

Off in the distance there was a line of smoke that rose

straight up. Otherwise there was no sign of life. No sign there was anyone out in the wilds.

But there'd be farmers, foresters. Couriers working the roads. Reivers and bandits.

I started the bike and turned it round, back towards town, waving to the guards at the patrol point.

I rode to the track. There were two middleweights parked by the start line, their riders chatting. One was the Ducati, the other was one I'd seen around, beaten twice: a CBR with bust fairing. There was a chance of some winnings with these two. The riders gave me a wave and I nodded back. Several other men stood around with their beer and cash gripped tightly. For some reason it all seemed a little flat. Disappointing.

Starter Lad came over. 'You racing?'

'Yeah.'

He went to the other bikers and checked they were keen to compete. They each nodded and he scribbled something down.

Another bike rode up. It was the big Suzuki from last night. Not worth a race. I'd take on the middleweights, maybe make some cash then head home. There was always the option to go and see Sophie but that didn't appeal.

The Scrambler hiccupped and coughed. I revved it up and the engine backfired. Despite all tinkering on with the carbs, the engine still wasn't right. I'd been winding Sophie up about having to work on it but it really wasn't happy. Maybe it was still the carbs, or worn bores. Possibly the valves — busted valves. I laughed at this, gave a dry grunt. Busted valves were always a sick joke, after all the headaches they'd given me in the past. Different vehicle, different place, same problems. With the bike revving at two-thousand revs, I blipped it up to four-thousand, dropping it down to idle.

I switched off the Triumph, letting it ping and tick. Once Starter Lad was in place, the Ducati and CBR prepared to race.

The flag dropped and they shot off, the Ducati pouring out smoke. Near the finish line there was a dull thud and it locked its back wheel with a screech and trail of rubber, leaving the other bike to finish.

It looked like it was me and the CBR next. I'd raced him a couple of times before and won. He was fast but the bike's power was all stacked at the top end. The Scrambler was quicker off the line. If it was running all right.

Several men helped drag the Ducati off with its bust engine. Another fella walked up and down the end section of the track, presumably looking for spilt oil. The CBR turned round and put its lamp on, moving from side to side to illuminate the track where the man inspected the road surface. There was money bet on the races so people didn't want things to go wrong: bikes crashing was bad for business. After a couple of minutes the CBR swung round and disappeared off down the lane, the one that brought bikes back to the start line.

I started the Triumph and revved it up. It sounded fine. There was movement and bright light from behind me as the CBR rode up.

He pulled up alongside me, flipping up his visor and pointed up the track. 'Duke's blown it.'

'Yeah.'

'How's yours running?'

41

'Is the track clear?'

'Yep. Bone dry.' He crept the CBR up to the start line.

I joined him and slipped the Scrambler into neutral. The sun had set and I flicked the headlamp on. For a second I put it on main beam and the white tree showed spectral in the distance, standing out from the dimming landscape. When I dipped the lamp there was just the track, empty and ready for us, lit by the two bikes' headlamps.

The flag dropped and we set off. Despite giving the Scrambler all it had, the Honda was pulled ahead.

By the time we shot past the dead pine he was half a metre in front of me. Not much but enough. I slowed, dropped down through the gears and stopped by the verge near the fellas sorting out the bets. I handed over my stake and moved off to park further up. The CBR rode over and he offered his hand. I shook it and he grinned then rode off to collect his winnings.

Another couple of bikes lined up at the far end, sounding like two small machines. There was a whistle through the funnel nailed to the fence and a fella went over and shouted into it. He listened and came back chatting to the other men. Money changed hands.

I pulled off, going along the lane back to the start line. Lights were coming on across town, row upon row down to the quayside. I wasn't sure why I was here. What I was going to do now. There was no point coming to the races if I was going to lose. The Scrambler wasn't on top form but I should have beaten the CBR. I had done in the past.

At the start line there was a Kawasaki z750. I'd not seen this one for a while but he had once been a regular. Some months ago. Maybe he'd want a race. In theory it

was a fast machine but the last time he came I'd
hammered him. Won easily.

I parked the Scrambler, ready to go over to him, ask if
he fancied a race.

As I stepped off there was the sound of a bike's engine.
Fast and smooth coming across town.

It shot up Hill Road with the revs rising and falling as it
worked its way through the gears. The headlamp
appeared at the far end of the track, bright then dim as
the bike tracked the ruts in the road. It raced towards us
then dipped its nose. It was the woman on her R6,
blipping down through the gears, before she pulled a
sharp stoppie that had the bike up on its front wheel. It
bounced back down and she balanced it, braced it with
her legs in those tight fighting leathers.

She gave me a glance then Starter Lad came over. 'Are
you here to race?'

She nodded to him. 'Yeah. I am.' Then she turned to
me. 'You fancy a race?'

I looked her machine over. All clean and tidy. Ticking
over nicely. Then I looked her over, in those tight
leathers. She faced back towards me and smiled. It was
daft going up against her. The Yamaha was in great
condition and it looked like she knew how to ride it. There
wasn't much chance I'd beat her. Despite this I got back
on the Triumph and started it up, lined up alongside her.
The Scrambler settled down into a rough idle as I moved
the handlebars around, shifting in the saddle.

She held her hand out to me. 'Good luck.'

I shook her hand, the grip firm.

Starter Lad spoke into his funnel on the fence.
Unusually there was quite a discussion. He gave them

details about the Yamaha. What kind of condition it was in. What its rider looked like.

Then he picked up his tattered flag, raised it. The R6 revved hard, the whistle of the engine becoming a bellow. It ticked over and there was clunk as she put it into gear. I adjusted my lid, giving the throttle a blip. She had her headlamp on main beam. In the distance was the finish line with the whitewashed tree.

Starter Lad dropped the flag. There was a growl from the Scrambler and a roar from the Yamaha as we shot off. The R6 fishtailed then straightened up so the Scrambler was ahead but the Yamaha's engine was on the cam and it lifted the front wheel, pulling level, dipping as it changed into second then hooking up again, disappearing off. It flew past the whitewashed tree with me in its wake. As the R6 turned and parked, I hauled on the brakes, slowed the Scrambler and eased it to a stop. It stalled and had to be restarted before I rod up and joined the woman. Her bike's engine burbled, a low throb from the exhaust. I switched off the Scrambler before it stalled again.

'Well done,' she said. The R6's fan cut in and she raised her visor, looking at me. Her eyes were fixed on me. As she slid her helmet off the bike's fan stopped and she switched off the engine, a swishing noise coming from the settling coolant. Some of her red hair had pulled out of pony tail and she straightened it up. 'Good race,' she said. 'Fast machine you've got there.'

'Not fast enough.'

She flicked the side-stand down and stepped off the bike, swinging her leg over the back of it before leaning against the saddle. 'Gave me a good run.' Even though she smiled, her arms were pulled tight in front of her and her eyes were past me, focussed on the town in the distance.

I shifted my own bike. I could have got off, stayed and chatted, enjoyed the company of an attractive woman, but things were starting to get complicated. I should never have come. One of the bookies came over and I handed him my stake. He added the money to the rest in his pocket and gave it to her.

She counted the cash, pulling out a few notes and holding them towards me. 'Share the winnings?'

'No, you're okay.'

'Sure?'

'Yeah.' I couldn't take the money. It wasn't worth setting such a precedent. And there was something else, something that didn't feel right.

She slid the money into her jacket, unzipping one of the pockets on the front, slowly zipping it up. 'How about we celebrate my win?' she said. 'There must be some decent bars in town.'

I started the engine. This was too keen, too fast. I clunked the Scrambler into gear. 'See you round,' I said before pulling off.

When I glanced in my mirror the woman was getting onto her bike, watching me go. As I left the track she set off, following me.

I rode fast across town, sticking in an extra loop round the South Road. There was no sign of her in my mirrors.

Once back at my place I took the Scrambler up the back lane, gunning it through into the yard. I flicked the engine off, furling the tarpaulin over the saddle and tank, leaving the engine clear to cool off as it ticked and pinged to itself. There was no sign of old Tommy in the flat downstairs, no sounds from the road. Maybe I'd lost her. Or she hadn't really been following me.

I gave the bike once last look. This was the worst night I'd had in two months. Only the second time the Scrambler hadn't won anything.

As I bounded up the stairs to the flat I heard an engine race up the road. When I went to the living room window I saw the blue and white R6 outside, the engine pulsing away, a whirr from the cooling fan. Her on the saddle.

I waited there for a minute, to see what she did. When she did nothing I went down to her.

She switched off when she saw me, slipping her lid onto her arm and leaning back on the saddle. 'Nice part of town.' She held her hand out again, like she had at the race. 'I'm Becky.'

I ignored the hand, looking at the bike rather than her, keeping my eyes off the jacket that was open a little at the front, enough to show some cleavage; those bike leathers, tight on her body. 'What you after?'

Becky smiled. 'Just fancied a chat.' She grinned at me, all friendly.

'I don't like being followed.'

She rocked the bike from side to side as the fuel sloshed around in the tank, her eyes off, across town away from me. 'You're quite a racer.'

'Not tonight I wasn't —'

'I've heard you're the star of the race scene.'

'Really?' I laughed at this.

'I thought you might show me the town. As a newcomer…'

'Not at the moment.'

We stood there without talking. A gurgle came from the

R6's radiator. Becky put her hands on her hips holding the bike upright with her legs, those slim legs. 'Listen, Trent, I want to be straight with you. It's about the tank, I know that you're part of the Round Up scene —'

'I think you should go.'

'I only want to talk to you about what happened.'

I tapped the fairing on the bike, this rare plastic. 'These parts must be hard to get hold of.' I pulled at the fairing and twisted, letting go with a ping. Maybe I wouldn't really break it, maybe I would. 'Be a shame if anything happened to it.'

Becky frowned. 'I'm not after trouble —'

'Then keep out of my way.' I turned and walked off. She'd slipped up mentioning Round Up. I'd have gone along with all kinds of stories from a woman with her looks but not now. Not after her admitting she was interested in my day job, especially after The Incident. She was messing me around.

Back in the room I stood at the window as she manoeuvred the bike outside. She accelerated hard up the road, the whistle of the engine drowned out by the roar from the exhaust.

I made a joint, lit it but didn't smoke it. It was only when it had burned down to the roach that I moved, throwing it out of the window and going down into the yard. The Scrambler's engine had cooled to a dull warmth. I knelt and put his hands on its tarnished alloy fins. Even without the race wins I could pull enough cash together to leave town. Things were starting to unravel. Maybe I it was best to leave before everything fell apart.

I slid the tarpaulin off the bike and sat on the saddle drumming my fingers on the fuel tank. I'd thought this was odd timing, someone new turning up. Now I knew it was dodgy. Someone fast, asking the wrong questions, following me. Not only that, but giving me those looks, like I was a piece of meat on a slab. I got a bad feeling from her.

After covering the bike I went back into the house, standing at the window until the lights went off in other houses and there was only moonlight. When the road was a black strip devoid of features. I pulled the curtains and went to my bedroom, lying on the bed. Eyes open in the darkness.

CHAPTER SIX

Rounded Up

The next day was a team day, like we always had once a fortnight. This was when several of us worked together to make a show of force, supposedly to showcase Round Up's tough-but-fair approach. It was always tough, that was for sure. I was with my usual team, Nico, Gregg and Will.

We'd gone to the far end of the South Estate, where there'd been quite a few burglaries. Fights and one rape. Story was that they were all done by one gang. All working together. For some reason the theft of a crate of whisky seemed to be the worst thing they'd done. We found several lads hanging about in a derelict shop and they became the prime suspects. After taking them outside, trying to reason with them, find out what they knew, it all started to get out of hand.

Nico held a lad against the alley wall, Gregg and Will flanking him, arms crossed on their overalls as Nico shoved his pin-striped elbow further into the lad's neck.

'Where the fuck are they?' said Nico. 'Where are the bottles?'

The lad shook his head, a tiny movement, his eyes bloodshot as they bulged.

Nico pushed harder, his red face up close. 'Where?'

The lad made a gurgling sound and Gregg laughed, his beard shaking and his belly bouncing up and down.

I was behind the three of them, a cosh in his hand, the one they given to me as we'd approached the alley. I rotated it, felt the hard rubber. This was just some street-kid, a lost nobody. Not worth anything, not this.

Nico waved his free hand at Will who joined him.

Will pulled a knife out of his overalls, wiping the blade on his filthy trouser leg. 'Time for a little whittling.' He lifted the blade up. 'Whittle, whittle.'

Gregg laughed and the lad made some sound from the back of his throat.

Will sliced his jacket open and ripped his shirt. He ran the blade over his bare chest and up to his neck.

The lad shook his head as Will cut into his skin, a tiny nick that gave out a spurt of blood. Gregg and Will laughed, Nico smiling.

That was enough. He was just a kid and they weren't after information. This was sport for these three. I'd put up with all this to begin with, believed the stories about a network of troublemakers and how they needed to interrogate all the kids they picked up, build up a picture of what was going on. But it was a pile of crap. There was no network and no picture to build up. Just a load of dysfunctional kids, fallout from the lack of schools. So many having fathers away at sea, mothers with no money.

I stepped forward. 'Looks like he doesn't know anything.'

'Ha,' said Gregg.

Will ran the blade across the lad's skin. Then he sliced into the him again making him cry and close his eyes.

'There's no point in this,' I said. 'We're wasting time on him.'

Will glanced back at me, his pale blue eyes shaded by his lank hair. 'There's plenty of point.'

'All right,' said Nico. 'Let's take him in. Trent, knock him out.'

I didn't move, the cosh limp in my hand. I knew the routine, the way Round Up worked — cosh the victim, drag him off and tie him. Torture him. Send him out onto the street cut and scarred. This wasn't about fixing stuff, making the town a better place, it was about Nico, Will and Gregg getting their kicks.

'Knock him out!' Nico turned to me. 'Hit him!'

I remained still, turning the cosh round and round, a loose grip between thumb and forefinger.

'Look,' said Nico. 'What the fuck's going on?' He kept his hand on the lad's throat but turned to me. He smelled of whisky and sweat.

'He's just young,' I said. 'He doesn't know anything.'

'Ah, just a little bairn, lost his mammy and daddy?'

'Come on, there are more serious —'

'Oh yeah?' Nico snatched the cosh off me, passing it to Gregg who laughed, swinging it around.

As Gregg raised it above him I grabbed hold of his arm, a firm grip on his overalls' sleeve. 'Leave him be.'

He shifted his arm, pulled and moved around. 'Hey.'

'Trent,' said Nico. 'Let the boys have their fun.'

They stared at me and I let go of Gregg. The lad was still pinned in place by Nico's hand. 'Cut him,' he said.

Will slashed, cutting him across his face. Gregg roared

with laughter and Nico smiled.

As Will raised his arm I barged into him, pushing him and Nico aside and knocking the blade flying. The knife landed on the ground.

I turned to the lad. 'Go.'

He frowned, dabbing at the blood on his face.

'Go!'

He ran off along the alley, past us and away.

Gregg lumbered off after him but Nico grabbed his overalls and stopped him. 'Leave him.'

Gregg sighed. 'But we were going to slice him, round him up —'

'I know.'

Will stared at me then went over to retrieve the blade.

Nico shook his head. 'You're getting soft Trent, real soft.'

'Sometimes I think you're no better than the kids on the street,' I said.

'We won't win this by being soft.'

'We already lost it.' I turned to go off but Nico took my arm.

'I'm disappointed, Trent. Very disappointed. I had plans for you. Plans. I picked up. You could have been teamed up with anyone out of Round Up but you got to go with us. The top row.' For a moment he gazed at the decrepit buildings around us. Then he grinned. 'Maybe you can redeem yourself. I still have that babysitting…'

I shook his hand off him. 'Look Nico —'

'Trent, Trent. This is much more up your street. No kids. You just need to stay alert…Keep an eye on things.' As he straightened his suit he set off down the alley, the other two following him, giving me glances, looks that showed they didn't see me as part of their gang, which suited me just fine. Nico shouted from ahead. 'Come on, Trent, follow, follow. I'll show what we're up against.' He laughed. 'This will really test your mettle.'

I hung back for a moment then joined them at the main road. I had to watch my step. Play along a little.

We piled into Nico's Mercedes, one of his personal fleet. As he drove across town they chatted about betting and women. Who they'd rounded up recently.

We went to Round Up Central, the old multi-storey car park on the South Side of town. The fella guarding the entrance waved to Nico and pulled open the heavy gate. Long before I'd arrived in Faeston Nico and the rest of them had gone to a lot of effort salvaging stuff from an abandoned prison across the border. They'd hauled doors and gates all the way here and had a gang spend weeks adapting the car park. Turning it into the town's prison.

We bounced up the potholed ramp and parked on level one, where all Nico's other vehicles were: the Jaguar and Range Rover. Spoils from his confiscations.

'Follow me,' he said. Gregg and Will wandered off upstairs, to the main offices but Nico led me downstairs, to the section I'd thought unused. We went through a dim passageway, lit by bulkhead lights, the air cold, dry. There was a heavy door at the end. He had to flick through his bunch of keys before he rattled the lock open. Partway along the passage there was another door in the wall. 'Not many people allowed through here, Trent.'

'Yeah?'

He slid his dark glasses up, fumbled with the keys to unlock the door. 'This is just for the initiated. The cognoscenti, you know? Get what I'm saying. You're a lucky man.'

'Real lucky.' I followed him as the door swung open. I didn't feel very lucky.

Nico grinned. 'Here we go.'

It was a large space, high-ceilinged, covering much of the ground floor. It was all concrete like the rest of the building, but made more stark with the spotlights set up along the sides. It was plain apart from the door we'd come through and a heavy steel shutter at the far end. Several men stood around writing on pads whilst another drew on a large sheet of paper. In the middle was the tank parked an angle on one of the town's low loaders.

Close up the vehicle was massive, a dark lump that gave off heat even though we were underground, making some low sound, not like an engine more something flowing, water under a stone bridge. It was painted a dull green marked with scorch marks. There were no wheels just two sets of caterpillar tracks. On the top of it there was a squat turret supporting a gun barrel of a calibre you could fit a small child in.

Nico walked around it and I followed. 'It's something else, eh?'

'I saw it the other night.'

'But close up, close up it's really something!'

'I suppose.' Nico kicked the low loader. 'Nearly bust this. Some weight. And the cranes struggled.'

'Yeah?' There were markings on the vehicle, letters and numbers. And symbols I'd not seen before, or not since before The Collapse, yellow squares with shapes in them.

'Thing is, we can't get into it. There's no key. No lock that we can see but we can't open the hatch' He turned to me. 'Imagine if we had one of these, if we could work out

54

how to make others.' He grinned. 'We'd be unstoppable.'

'Yeah,' I said, tapping the thick steel. 'Unstoppable.'

'Problem is, we can't make one, no one can now. Someone else made this, sometime else.' He pointed at the walls and ceiling. 'But there could be hundreds of them out there, thousands, left over.'

'There are loads of them up at Otterburn.' All the border couriers knew of wrecks abandoned in the old military base.

'Not that junk. Working stuff. Like this...'

'So why am I here?'

'Because you're one of us, Trent! A trusted member of the gang, a reliable foot soldier and good team player. You belong and you're going to help us out.' We carried on walking around, circling the great dark shape. At the back of the vehicle he grabbed my sleeve. 'He's the only one who knows about it, how to get in and work it. Where it came from and whether there are more. He knows all about it. We need to know.'

'He?'

'The driver, the guy who came out of it.'

I put my hand on the steel panel at the back, above thick vents and code numbers etched into the metal. It was warm to the touch, as if the vehicle had been out in the sun. There was a gentle throb through the metal, like the thing had a pulse, a heart beating somewhere inside. I took my hand off it. 'How do I fit in?'

'Well, that's where your babysitting comes in. Unlike some of the others in Round Up, you're a slow fuse, you know? You take your time with stuff. That's sometimes a useful thing, you get what I'm saying?'

'Not really.' What I got was a bad feeling.

'We've had him under lock and key ever since he came out, since he gave himself up, but we've not got much out of him. He's not said more than a word. We tried various, ah, methods, but he's resisting.' He smiled and came up close. 'So you're going to take over, spend some time with him.' He banged on the vehicle. 'You're going squeeze the details out of him.'

CHAPTER SEVEN
Becky

That evening I went up to the track again. I parked my bike and stood on the verge. The sun was low across the town, catching the windows in the taller buildings and the sea in the distance.

Starter Lad came over. 'Seen a lot of you this week.'

'I'm in the mood for racing.'

He put me on the list and went over to the others parked opposite, an assortment from the usual suspects: the Suzuki Hayabusa, CBR and z750. Maybe I'd go against the zed. Or try my luck against the CBR again. Not the big Suki.

But there was another reason I'd come here. Now I'd half agreed to interrogate the stranger — not that it seemed I had much choice — I was tied up in the stuff going on. The tank arriving. Becky turning up. She was part of it and I wanted to talk to her. Pick her brains and see where she fitted in.

That was real reason I was here. To see her.

Starter Lad leant against the fence drinking beer from a

bottle. The riders of the three bikes chatted about oil and engines and stuff. They didn't seem keen to race yet. There was an engine sound for Hill Road — low and staccato, not like Becky's machine — and an old BWM appeared. It was an eleven-hundred, an infrequent visitor to the track, and he rolled up alongside the other bikes. The Suzuki's rider slid on his lid and started his bike. He and the BMW lined up at the start line. As the they prepared I crossed over the track, standing a couple of yards down from Starter Lad. He raised his flag and the bikes shot off. They raced to the end with a trail of fumes, the Suzuki metres ahead.

As they sorted out the winnings I looked across town. Round Up's HQ stood out at the far side of the river, lit by its office lights. The tank was in there. And the fella I had to interview.

I'd asked to see him earlier, find out who I was dealing with but Nico had been coy, evasive about where he was and what was happening. He'd promised money and promotion to Round Up's top rank. His reward.

None of it bothered me apart from the money.

An engine sounded behind me, powering along the lane. I turned to see a bright light charging towards me.

It was the R6. Her bike.

It eased to a stop a metre short of me.

She was wearing those leathers again, her lid on her arm and bright hair loose on her shoulders. She glanced over as Starter Lad approached her. They chatted for a moment then looked over at me. I shook my head. There was no point putting the scrambler against her machine. No contest.

She shifted on machine, rocking it between her legs.

'It's taken some time for me to get this machine of mine right.'

'No kidding.'

'Those forks and wheels take some looking after —'

'Look,' I said. 'Can we stop playing games?'

'I just thought —'

'We need to talk.'

She smiled at this. 'Okay.'

'Just so you know, I don't like being followed. Don't like being messed about.'

'Sorry.'

The CBR and z750 had started up and approached the start line.

'So what's going on?' I said. This was her chance to convince me she was worth taking seriously.

She put her hand on my arm and glanced around as she spoke. 'I hadn't meant to come straight out with all the stuff the other day. It just slipped out.'

'Right.'

'Can we talk somewhere else, somewhere private?'

Starter lad stood by the fence with the flag raised as the CBR and Zed both revved like mad. The flag dropped and the bikes were off, popping and cracking up the track. For a few seconds we just stared at each other. As the bikes raced.

'Here's fine,' I said.

She sighed. 'I need some information, just to know something.'

'Information?' This really was dodgy.

The bikes finished and parked at the other end. There were no other bikes ready to race. Just me and Becky parked there.

She messed with the fuel cap on her bike's tank. With those slim fingers. 'I need some help.'

'Help…'

'And I think you're the person who can give it.'

'Right.' I wasn't going to give her anything. Not a hint that I was willing to help a stranger. Especially if it was to do with Round Up. There was a chance that this was a set by Nico, one of his loyalty tests. Like the one that had seen off Jackson. Probably loads of fellas before I'd come to town.

She put her hands to her head, closed her eyes for a second. 'They have my brother.' Then she turned slightly away, looking out across town, towards the sea. 'They're keeping him. I just want to know he's all right.'

'Your brother?'

'They have him, somewhere. He was passing through. It all just went wrong.'

'Right.' Though it was tempting to fill in the gaps I wanted her to do the talking. Tell me what going on.

'He didn't mean to go through town. That was a mistake. Now they've got him. And his vehicle.'

'Vehicle?'

'You know, do I have to say it?'

'Yes, you do.'

She closed her eyes for a second then opened them and stared at me. 'He was in the tank.'

'Right.' So that was it. That was why she was here. Talking to me.

'I just want to know he's all right. That's all.'

'Why me?'

'I heard you were in Round Up, the people who run this place, and you seemed approachable…'

Starter Lad came over and stood before us. 'You two racing?'

'I'm not sure,' said Becky.

'No,' I said.

He pulled a face and walked towards the fence, his flag trailing on the ground.

Only when he was well away did I speak. 'So, tell me more.'

'Like what?'

'Why did he come through town? Shoot the place up?'

'That wasn't the plan, like I said. He was meant to go round. He must have panicked. Lost control or something…'

'Or something?'

'Anyway, Round Up has him and I wondered if you could see him. Talk to him. See he is okay.'

'I'll see what I can do.'

Becky smiled. 'Thanks —'

'But I can't promise much.'

'Okay.'

I started the Scrambler. The whole story made me uncomfortable but it was hard to work out how much of it was true. What it was she was really after.

She raised her voice over the clatter of the engine. 'Let me know how he is. I'm in The Bay Hotel, High Town. You'll find me in the bar most nights.'

'Right.' I clunked the Triumph into gear.

She smiled at me, leant back against her bike, stretched her leathers tight on her body.

I steered round her and rode off. She was lying to me about something. Maybe everything. I should have said no to her request.

I should have.

CHAPTER EIGHT

Two Women

There wasn't much rounding-up to be done the next morning: a few kids hanging around the harbour, kicking stones back and forth in the mist but I soon scared them off. There weren't many others which was just as well as my head was too full to concentrate. Full of stuff about the tank and Nico and the tank's driver. And Becky. She was on my mind a lot. I wandered around in the damp air as the waves thudded on the harbour wall. Tried to make sense of it all.

At lunchtime I met Sophie, like I had done every Friday for the last few months. I wasn't in the mood but she'd kick up a stink if I didn't show up. It was the usual venue, the Cafe Italia, a fake continental place that was as shit as all the other cafés but more expensive. She was waiting when I arrived, sitting in the corner where she always sat wearing a pink jumper, holding a menu, not that she needed it.

She stood up when I arrived, kissed me on the cheek and pointed out that I was late, as usual.

She thrust a menu at me, this stained piece of card with uneven writing on it. I didn't even bother to read it seeing as I knew it all. Knew what I'd have.

'How are you?' I said.

'Fine, as if you care.'

'Work all right?'

She shrugged then threw down the menu. 'What's going on Trenty?'

'What do you mean?' I wondered if she'd seen Becky parked round at my place, seen us chatting.

'Your head's not here! You're off with the fairies.'

'Right.'

The waiter came over, the usual lad, shaven headed, stained apron. 'What you havin?' he said.

'Stew,' I said. He wrote it down, didn't reply.

Sophie tilted her head back, like she always did before saying something ridiculous. 'Well, I'd like the spaghetti carbonara.'

'Out of bacon,' said the lad.

She grunted. 'Give me the fucking bolognese.'

The lad left.

'So,' she said, leaning towards me. 'What's going on?'

'Going on?'

'Oh, Trent. Tell me about work. What you've been up to?'

'We're busy. Got a lot of sorting out to do.'

'Oh?'

'I've been asked to lead some of it. To do with The Incident.'

'Oh?' She sat up at this. 'That's good. If you're doing that, something so important, they must think that you have prospects. That you're going somewhere. That is good.' She grinned at this, gave me a big smile. 'Oh, Trenty, I didn't know you'd taken on extra responsibilities.' Her hand gripped mine, held it far too tightly.

'It's not something I asked for...' She'd not been interested the other day. I hadn't expected her to make such a fuss.

She clapped her hands, a high clap up in the air. 'This will make such a difference. We'll be able to plan ahead, think about where we are going —'

'Hang on —'

'I knew it would all come together. I knew...' And so she went on, about us and how things were going to be great. The two of us together. Forever.

Our food arrived, the two plates slapped in front of us. Mine the usual grey slop that they called stew. Sophie's reddish-brown with lumps in it. Nothing like what she'd ordered. Usually she complained and pointed out what the food was meant to look like, quoting her beloved cook books. This time she just tucked in, ate and talked. Said more about her plans for us in the future.

I picked on with mine and said a few words, but that was it.

By the time we came to the end of the meal she'd sorted out the rest of our lives and I'd hardly said anything.

'I have to go,' I said standing up, throwing some cash on the table.

'Oh, is it time to get back?'

I shrugged. Unlike most places Faeston had clocks that worked so being five or ten minutes late did matter. But this was more about getting away from Sophie with her mindless crap.

She leapt up and grabbed hold of me, wrapping me in a tight embrace, kissing me and muttering on.

I slid free and was off and out, her still at my side, following me along Back Lane. The mist had cleared. Men hung round the workshops that made tackle and ropes, mingling with shoppers who came from the stalls along the North Quay carrying lumps of meat and filthy vegetables. Amongst them drunks spilled out of the George and Dragon, getting air or looking for a fight.

Sophie yanked at my arm when we came to her shop.

'This is all so good,' she said.

'Yeah?' We stood in front of the shop window. It was filled with old toys and books on stands. Busted ornaments and bits of machinery. Crap, really, that no one wanted. The place had been a phone shop or something in the past, the name still visible under Sophie's sign. She called it *Faeston Phantasmagoria*, whatever that meant. 'Look, I have to go.'

She kissed me again and went into the shop, dusting broken computer equipment on a stand.

For the rest of the afternoon I skulked around town. Three drunks decided to take turns pissing down from the bridge on Bay Road. We had a little chat that ended with one having a bust lip and getting rounded up. I marched him to Round Up Central, dropping him off. Aside from that there was just a couple of fights by the Skinners Arms. Sailors letting off steam. Even when I had one fella pinned against the wall I was thinking about Sophie and her plans. Nico and his. Whatever Becky was up to.

Everyone had plans apart from me.

At the end of the day I reported to Round Up's town office underneath the Globe. Nico was at his usual spot, that dirt-encrusted table, a whisky bottle before him. He was playing cards with Tyler and Noah. They nodded but Nico didn't look up. For a while they carried on playing.

'Good day?' said Nico. His shades were down so it was hard to tell if he was talking to me.

'Not bad.'

There was a roar of laughter from the bar upstairs.

He sipped whisky. 'Round ups?'

'Just the one.'

'Oh.' He smiled at this. 'One is one. Anyhow, that's you done. See you tomorrow.'

The three of them played cards, as if I'd gone.

'I have a question,' I said.

'A question?' Nico held the card he was about to place, looked at me over his sunglasses with a raised eyebrow. 'What kind of question?'

'About what we were talking about. That babysitting job.'

He took a breath, placed the card. 'That kind of question.' He looked at Noah and Tyler, then dropped his cards face down, shoving his chair back and walking to the back door, the one to the yard. He stood there until I joined him then we went out. It was a long thin yard with brick walls on each side, all topped with broken glass. The concrete paving was cracked and flaked with a drain set to the right surrounded by dried scum. At the far end was a door to the lane, bolted in several places.

Nico shut the door behind us as the seagulls soared above us. 'What do you want to know?'

'You want me to do some babysitting. For the fella from the tank.'

'And?'

'Just want to know a little more. About him.'

'What's to know?'

'Who is he? What condition he's in, you know…'

'Really? You want to do this?' He sighed, messed with the buttons on his suit. When I didn't reply he carried on. 'His name is Casper. We worked that out from a letter he had on him. He's got a few bruises but otherwise, fine. All right?' He grabbed hold of the door. 'Happy?'

'What was the letter?'

'The letter? Nothing. Just a thank you note or some shit. All right?'

'Yeah.'

Back inside he slumped back in his seat and picked up his cards, throwing one down. Noah and Tyler gave me a nod as I left but Nico didn't react.

I stopped halfway along High Row, alongside the ships. There were only a few crew members on them, the odd man doing maintenance. It was low tide and the gang planks sloped down to the decks. Some would set sail late tonight but most would wait until the morning.

I headed home, avoiding Sophie's shop and flat, passing men full of beer.

Then I stopped and turned right, heading the other way. I crossed Harbour Bridge, still marked from The Incident: sections bent and scorched. Bay Road had been cleared of the lorry's wreckage but the tarmac was gouged and melted. As the road twisted off to the left I took Hillside Walk towards High Town, the best part of Faeston. Where Becky was. The path took me up the cliffside in a long sweep. Partway up I stopped and looked back at the town. The late afternoon sun caught the water in the harbour; reflected off windows and metalwork on the ships. It lit the wind turbines as they slowly turned. The turbines that kept the water pumping and docks working, the railway running: where whisky, raw materials and fuel came down from Scotland. Food and luxuries from abroad travelling back up. From here it looked like a place that had all the answers, somewhere facing forwards not back. Then I saw the great block that was Round Up HQ. Where the tank and Casper were held.

I carried on up the hill to the Bay Hotel.

It was a big old building on the edge of High Town. It had rows of tall windows and blocks of chimneys topped by rows of black pots. They'd kept it in good nick, even giving it a lick of paint every year.

The bar was half empty when I went in. There were a few lone drinkers and a big group all dolled up in old-world clothes, probably from on one of the passenger ships that came in once a week. Down from Aberdeen or Edinburgh. Places that hadn't completely fallen apart. A couple of waiters drifted around. They picked up glasses, refilled drinks. This was a different world from the pubs at the quayside with their drunks and fights and tarts after business. I went up to one of the waiters and ordered a whisky then took a seat at a table away from the door, well away from the group.

My drink came and I sipped it. Looked out of the window across the town. At the sea that went on forever, empty apart from a couple of boats, probably trawlers trying to haul a few decent fish from the dead water. It was like the town was on the edge of the world. The rows of houses were now in darkness and the ships down in the harbour invisible. Only Round Up HQ stood out. I watched as it slipped into darkness.

The chair next to me shifted and Becky slid onto it, leaning on the table. She tapped my glass, the bracelet on her wrist jangling.

'Mind if I join you?' she said.

I shrugged. 'My pleasure.'

She wasn't in her usual leathers but a thin jacket. It was undone and she wore a light top underneath: purple, patterned, reminding me of someone from my past. Someone gone. Her bright lipstick made her look like she was on a date. Waving her hand at waiter she ordered a gin with tonic. I asked for another whisky, a double. I knocked back the first.

'You planning on getting drunk?' she said.

'Maybe.'

Music started to play, ancient pre-recorded stuff that wheezed through speakers around the room. It was some classic rock song, fast guitars, loud drums.

'This is some town,' she said. 'Lights and music. Fuel you can afford.'

'Yeah. It has its benefits.'

The whisky and gin arrived. She told the barman she was in room twelve, then examined the glass, sipping it, closing her eyes, savouring it.

'Good?' I said.

She nodded, taking the slice of lemon out of the gin, turning it round, staring at it. 'You know, I've been looking for you for some time.'

I laughed. 'Me or the lemon?'

'Both.'

I played with my glass, kept my eyes on it, not on her. I'd let her talk, see what she gave away.

'It's just…I don't know.' She waved a hand around, putting the lemon into her mouth, chewing it, dropping it back into the glass. 'Most places are so crazy. People wrapped up in stuff.' Giving a shrug she took a drink, raising her eyebrow. It was hard not to compare her to Sophie, measure them against each other. One mysterious, dangerous. The other settled, sensible, in a quirky sort of way.

Becky held her glass on the table, both hands on it. 'I know I said too much the other night, about Round Up, the tank, but I wanted to be straight with you…set things out before you got the wrong idea.'

'And what idea would that be?'

She faced me, smiled. 'That I was just coming on to you. Another woman after you. I'm sure there've been a few.'

I said nothing, let silence say whatever she wanted it to say.

'So, Trent, you know what I want. The question is, will you help me?'

The music went off and there was the burble of conversation. The bar had filled up in the last few minutes, mostly couples, all dressed up, pretending this really was somewhere fancy.

'Depends on what you want,' I said.

'Not a lot. See how he is. Talk to him.'

The music started up again, this time a pop song, a female artist from the twenties. Becky was being careful. Maybe she was wise not to trust me. Not to give away too much. Still, I needed to know she wasn't playing games. That this wasn't a test from Nico.

'How will I know it's him?' I said.

'What do you mean?'

'We have a load of people in custody. How will I know it's your brother?'

She laughed. 'You can ask him. That would do it.'

I had a slug of whisky, swilled it around to let it burn a little. 'Tell me about him.'

She waved at the waiter, called him over, stretching up so her jacket was tight on her body. 'Want another drink?'

'Go on.' Maybe her plan was to get me drunk. Or maybe she just liked to drink.

She ordered the whisky and gin then stood up. 'Let's head outside.' She walked off towards the door. I followed her.

Outside the air was cooler, fresh. Tables and chairs were set out on a flagged patio overlooking Faeston. The sun had set and lit the clouds a dull orange. The town was in shade, dotted by what few lights there were. Voices came from the harbour, distant shouts and whistles. Machinery droned at the docks, all backed by the constant growl of the wind turbines, their blades dark shadows. The spotlights on cargo ships and warehouses made them seem to float above the rest of the town. The sea stretched off into the black, featureless.

She sat at a table. 'There aren't many towns where you can do this,' she said. 'I'd forgotten how amazing the sea could look.'

'You can't see the filth at night.'

'All that water. Makes me want to strip off and go for a swim.' She smiled at me. 'You a swimmer?'

'Not really.' I didn't let myself think about her in the water, naked.

The waiter came over and gave us our drinks. Becky

thanked him. After a sip she spoke again. 'This is so good.'

'You were going to tell me about your brother.'

'Casper? What did you want to know?'

She'd passed the first test, knowing his name. 'Isn't it obvious?'

'You mean the tank?'

She took another drink, her eyes on the shadowed town. For a few seconds she stared and said nothing. Then she faced me. 'Eblis. That's what it's called. The tank. Coming through town was a mistake. He hadn't planned that.'

'What had he planned?'

She shrugged. 'Casper will tell you more.'

'And what was he doing in a tank?'

'He'll tell you.'

'Is that all I get?'

'For now.'

'Come on.'

'Our plan was, is, to go to Scotland. Somewhere better. Safe. He was in the tank I was on the bike.'

A couple came out, both in their fifties, drunk. They staggered around laughing then went back in.

'I've said too much already,' said Becky.

I took a drink and waited to see if she'd add anything.

'Once you've spoken to him, seen he's okay, we can talk some more?'

'I guess so.'

She gazed off at the sea. 'It just goes on forever doesn't it.' She laughed. 'Casper can't —' She stopped herself. 'We'll chat after you've seen him.'

I finished my whisky and stood up. I had all I needed. 'I think it's time for me to go.'

Becky took my sleeve, a strong grip. 'Hey, it's your round next. And the night's only young. There's lots to do.' She smiled and leant forward. 'I have a room here you know.'

I slid out of her grip. 'Thanks for the drinks.'

She stood and joined me. 'Listen, thanks for doing this. Watching out for Casper.'

'Let's see what happens.' I walked back to the building. She walked along side me. I stopped at the doorway. 'I'll come find you. Once I've talked to him.'

'Thanks.'

As I pulled the door open I motioned for her to go first. She stepped through but stopped and turned, so that I walked into her. Our bodies were pushed together, face to face, my chest shoved up against hers. She gripped me and held me there.

'If you want to make sure it's him,' she said, 'ask him about this.' She pulled her top down a little to show a mole on her left breast. 'Think you'll remember?' her voice was low, her breath on my face, warm, gin and lemon scented. She stepped away, smiled. 'See you soon.'

'Yeah.' I made my way across the bar and carried on out, away from the hotel. I walked back fast, thinking about Round Up and things I needed to do to the bike.

Thinking about anything but Becky.

CHAPTER NINE

Casper

The next morning I took a walk on the beach. It was one of the things that had first attracted me to the town, reminding me of long gone holidays. Jamie, my old partner — he'd had a thing for beaches. That was the last thing we'd done together, sit on a beach further down the Northumbrian coast, me and him chatting. Shortly before I dissolved our partnership.

Not that the beach at Faeston was much to look at. It was gouged and holed where sand has been removed for building work, conditioning soil, anything. Rubbish lay strewn about: busted devices with no use — computers, phones and TV sets. Relics from a different time. And of course there was the sewerage. Turds washed up that hadn't caught the tide.

Despite all the crap and junk, it felt good to walk along it, below the cliffs that protected High Town, the entrance to the bay just ahead. The stonework appeared out of the late summer fret as the sun burnt down through it. I was thinking, weighing up where this was all going. Whether I was right to tag along with Becky. Get involved with her brother.

It wasn't like I wanted to stick with Round Up. I wasn't even keen on the town anymore. This was where I'd ended up not somewhere I'd chosen. It had been easy to pick up work but I'd never planned to stay forever. I'd been drawn into the place; found a decent flat. Fixed the Triumph up and gone to the races. Sophie had latched onto me and made us into a couple. I'd got used to living in Faeston.

If living was the word.

I stopped by a rock pool and sat on a busted TV set. It was a really old one, a great box of cracked plastic. The tube had gone but the rest of it lay cock-eyed in the sand. I picked up a handful of stones and threw them into the water. Something brown floated around in the pool.

I was bored. Sick of the routine of Round Up. It was all about controlling and playing power games. There was no one with any sense of the outside. Their world was the town. They didn't want to know about other places or how people did things elsewhere.

Becky wasn't like that. She was a real outsider. Full of ideas and energy. She wasn't someone to hang around in one place. Make a home and pretend the old-world still existed. She was more interested in being on the move and free to go where there were opportunities.

More like me.

But she was an odd one. There was lots she wasn't telling me. Too much. And her brother was an unknown.

Jamie used to always go on about having a plan. And Gary. Now it was time for me to have one.

I'd got stuck in Faeston. Stuck in a rut. It had been fine

for a while but it was time to go.

I walked off the beach and into town.

When I got to Round Up Central Nico wasn't there. But Will was, sitting up in the control room that had once been the security office. He grunted at me when I told him about the interrogation, that I'd been picked to do it. Before he led me off I grabbed a pencil and piece of paper.

Our footsteps echoed off the walls as we walked along the corridor. The only breaks in the grey concrete were the low, barred windows and bare light bulbs every two metres. Round Up were allowed a much electricity as needed and Nico made sure they got it.

I'd not really thought about what I was going to ask Casper. Anyway, I'd work it out as it went along. As usual.

We turned a corner and Will stopped at a steel door. There was a narrow slit two-thirds up sealed by a metal flap: it was one of the secure rooms, where we stuck troublemakers when they were brought in.

'This is it.' Will took out a key and put it in the lock. The mechanism turned with a dull clank. 'There are two of our men inside with him. I'll wait outside.'

'I don't need the men.'

'Well you've got them.'

The door swung open. There was no light. The only illumination was from the small window high up on the far wall. Three people stood in the cell: two Round Up men, who I didn't recognise, and the prisoner, Casper. He had blond hair, cut short, almost shaved. He was in his thirties, a similar age to Becky. His face was bruised and he had a black eye. He looked as if he was having difficulty staying upright. Before the three of them was a table with a seat at either side.

'This is the interrogator,' said the Will.

I went in and he left, shutting the door behind him.

One of the guards watched Casper but the other one just stared ahead. At the locked door.

I approached Casper, trying to ignore them.

Normally we did Round Up interviews two on one. Prisoner versus good cop and bad cop. Sometimes bad cop, bad cop. I didn't like having the two guards in the cell.

'I'm Trent,' I said.

Casper didn't react. I thought about repeating it, but then he looked at me, one eyebrow raising.

'I just want to chat. Ask a few questions.'

He nodded but lowered his head again.

'Can he sit?' I said to one of the men, the fella staring into space.

The other one answered for him. 'We were told to keep him standing.'

'He needs to sit. So I can quiz him.'

He glanced at his companion. For a second they seemed to communicate with minor facial expressions. 'I suppose so,' he said.

They nudged Casper forward and he stumbled into the chair, resting his elbows on the table, sighing. I sat opposite, leaning back in my seat. The two men were rigid behind him, as if something was going to happen.

'You two can go. I'm fine here.'

The same guard replied as before. 'We were told to stay.'

'At least go over to the wall. Give us some space.'

Again they looked at one another, did that mind-reading thing. After a moment they moved towards the door and stood each side of it.

'Well, Casper,' I said in a loud voice. 'I guess you know what this is about.'

His head was in his hands and he leant forward.

'I'm just here to chat. Ask questions.'

He looked up. 'Is that so?' His voice was sharp, gruff.

'Yes, questions.' I leant forward and wrote BECKY on the piece of paper.

This got him. He straightened up, grinned at this, a mean smile, as he eyed me. Under Becky's name I wrote SHE'S IN TOWN. SAFE.

I raised my voice. 'I need to know where you came from; why are you here; who you work for?'

'Oh yeah?'

There was one last test for him. And her. I wrote: MOLE.

He smiled and tapped his chest, beside his left nipple. Then he sat back, arms crossed. Smug.

'So,' I said, louder. 'What brought you here?'

'Just passing through.'

'Passing through to where?' I had to get something from him. Something to give Nico. Keep him off my back.

'Somewhere else.'

'We need to know where you were going; where you came from?'

'Oh?' He sighed and fidgeted but said no more.

'What about your vehicle? The tank?'

'Tank?' Then nothing.

'Tell me how you got it; how it works?'

'Seriously?'

I put my elbows on the table. So did he. Now we were

face to face, up close. 'If you don't tell me something,' I said, 'then they'll send in someone else. They'll beat it out of you.'

We eyeballed each other for a moment.

'Why did you come through town. Shoot the place up.'

'Didn't mean to.'

'Go on.'

He sighed. 'I was meant to go round but took the wrong road. Then people started shooting so I shot back...'

'And where were you going?'

He sat back again, his lips tight and brow furrowed. The arms were crossed on his chest and he took a deep breath. For a minute we sat and looked at each other, him silent but lips moving as he ground he teeth.

'Look,' I said. 'You're stuck here. Either you talk to me or Nico will start hurting you.'

He tilted his head to one side but said nothing.

'We know a little about the tank.'

He put his hands on the table, licked his lips. 'The Eblis...'

Then there was a sound from the door. It unlocked and opened.

Will came in. 'We're needed on a job. Urgent.'

I crossed out everything I'd written on the piece of paper then added EBLIS -THE TANK and YORKSHIRE: something I'd guessed by the route he had come into town.

Casper looked up at me, shrugged, raised both eyebrows. I turned and followed Will out. As the door was shutting Casper watched me, the two guards now back at his side.

Maybe he was Becky's brother. A lot of her story fitted. He wasn't someone I'd warmed to. Not a man I'd trust.

Will shuffled off ahead of me. 'This is a big one,' he said. 'We've got ring leaders. We've got the main troublemakers in the town.'

CHAPTER TEN

Harsh lesson

It was short walk from Central to where Nico had the lads. They were at the Seaview Hotel, once grand but now a mess like most of the South Side. Will took me straight in, through the bust doors and up onto the first floor. The carpets were stained and ripped, much of the wooden panelling ripped off the wall. He led me on towards a room at the end where the door was open. It was a double bedroom with only a settee and bed, filthy bedding knotted up on it. The bay window looked across the town, though the glass was so dirty it was hard to see much. It smelled of sweat and piss. Nico paced up and down in front of three teenage boys sitting on the settee. They were scruffy. Thin. Gregg stood behind them and Will joined him, leaning against a busted table. I stood away from them.

'See, the thing is,' said Nico. 'You crossed the line.'

The lads looked at each other and frowned. The one in the middle sat upright. 'It was a misunderstanding,' he said. His voice wavered as he spoke.

Nico smiled and walked back and forward, playing with his shades. 'Oh, it was that, it really was —'

'We won't do it again.'

Nico laughed, a short bark that made them on their seats. He slid his shades on and pointed at each of them in turn. 'This has gone too far, too fucking far.' He nodded to Will who came round and joined him. Will felt around in his dungarees. He fumbled in his pocket for what felt like an age before he pulled out a length of cord. He wrapped it around one hand and pulled on it with the other.

Nico shook his head. 'We need to teach you a lesson. Set an example.'

The lads didn't move. They were all transfixed by the cord in Will's hands.

'Nico,' I said.

Nico stopped pacing. He turned towards me and raised his right hand. His lips were tight and eyes fixed on me. That was a look that told me to back off. Leave it. Will and Gregg stared at me as well. Gregg tapped a pocket on his dungarees. There was a bulge in it the size of a pistol, one he'd love to pull out and jam in my face. Take me out and remove a competitor from the Round Up hierarchy.

I stepped backwards, away from them all. I wasn't needed here and didn't want to be part of it. I'd ease myself into the passageway and get the fuck away.

Nico started to pace again. He nodded to Will who swung the cord from one hand, left and right. The lads watched but didn't move. Will moved up to the settee and they shrunk back. The cord jumped around in his hand above them. Then he flicked it towards Gregg behind the settee. Gregg grabbed it, wrapped it around one hand then the other. He dropped it onto the lad in front of him, over his head. His neck.

Gregg pulled hard on it. Strangled him.

I stepped forward but Will was in front of me. He had his knife out and blocked my way.

The cord bit into the lad's neck, lifting him up as he grasped hold of it, tugged at it. The other two stared at him, shuffled in their seats but didn't help. Their faces were white. Eyes wide. Gregg leant back, forearms straining as he hauled the lad up. His body lifted from the seat, his face contorted as the cord cut into his neck. He clawed at his throat and kicked his feet.

'You've made your point,' I said.

Nico laughed. 'Finish him.'

Will had half turned to watch the strangulation. He grinned as the lad's eyes swelled up.

I took my chance and punched Will, a crack to the jaw that set him off balance, out of my way. I sprung past him and went over to Gregg, pulling at his arm. As I struggled with Gregg Nico came over. I had hold of Gregg's hand and undid his fingers but he kept the pressure on. Nico went for me but I elbowed him, knocked some of the wind out of him and I grabbed at Gregg again. I hauled the cord, yanked hard slid one end out of his grip. Released the lad. Gregg staggered back as it came free.

Will stood in front of the settee. 'Looks like you were too late.'

The lad was slumped on the seat, his head to one side and his tongue protruding. Eyes shut.

Gregg laughed and slid the rope into his dungarees.

Nico was round the front again. He pointed at the other two. 'This is what happens. This is a lesson. A harsh lesson in reality.'

They didn't move. Didn't look at the body slumped beside them. The dead body of their friend.

'If you cross the line, this is the result.'

Will went over and opened the door. Nico went out followed by Gregg, like they'd rehearsed this.

'Come on,' Will said to me.

I didn't move. The two surviving lads stared at the floor. The body lay slumped beside them.

Will came over jabbed towards me with his knife. 'Get out.'

'What about him?'

'Leave him.'

I moved towards the dead body but Will thrust out at me and I had to step aside to miss being hit.

'I'm not kidding,' he said. 'Leave him. Or join him.'

I looked into Will's eyes. He meant it. Him and Gregg would be happy to get rid of me. Nico might have plans for me but they weren't interested.

So I went out into the corridor. Will shut the door and with a nod from Nico stood close to me. Gregg went to the other side. They hemmed me in as Nico came up, jabbed me in the chest. 'Very disappointing. Very fucking disappointing, Trent.'

'There was no need.'.

'Things are tough. Out there in the world.' He waved his hand around, sweeping it in a great arc. 'The other night showed us that. We need to protect ourselves. Sort things out here then expand. Build our defences.'

'How will this help?' I tapped the door. Pointed back towards the dead lad.

'See, Trent, you don't understand. You don't see the

big picture. There's no time for sentimentality. Bad people have to be wiped out.'

From the room I could hear sobbing.

Nico adjusted his shirt. He took a breath then punched me in the stomach. It took all of the air out of me. Folded me up.

Then he grabbed my collar. 'Things are changin' Trent. We've been slack. We need to step things up. Step, step, step!' He took another breath and exhaled slowly. 'But, you have a role. You're no good at this. The tough stuff. It's the other bits you're useful for. Like our man in the cell...' He eased his grip on me. 'Any luck, Trent? Any information? Anything you can tell us, hmm?'

Will had his knife out again. This was going the wrong way. I was going to end up like that lad in there.

'Yeah,' I said. 'He said where he'd come from...'

Nico smiled. 'Really? He talked?'

'Yeah.'

'This for real?'

'Yes.'

'And?'

I pulled out the piece of paper.

Nico read it. 'Yorkshire? Where in Yorkshire?'

'Just south of York.' It was the first place that sprung into my mind.

He jabbed the paper 'And this Eblis? What's that?'

'The tank's name. The model.'

Nico stepped back and patted me on the cheek. 'Well, that's something. That is something.' He nodded to Will and Gregg moved away from me as well. 'Don't think you're off the hook, Trent. But this is something. A *reprieve*.' He brandished the piece of paper and led them off.

As they disappeared I thought about going back into the room, saying something, helping with the body. Instead I hung around in the hallway for several minutes. Then I left the hotel and went straight across town.

I stopped at Harbour Bridge and held onto the metalwork where the steel had been twisted by the tank. For some time I stared down into the River Farle, as the filthy water rolled past. Maybe I should have done more. Tried harder to save the lad. Stayed and helped the other two. Not lied about what Casper had said.

Maybe. Maybe not.

I carried on across the bridge and up the pathway. Made my way to High Town. I didn't trust Becky but at the moment she seemed to be the only person I wanted to talk to.

The bar of the Bay Hotel was quiet with a couple of fellas in their sixties drinking beer and some drunk woman half slumped over a table. There was no sign of Becky.

I took the same seat and ordered a whisky. Stared out at the town and the sea. From here it looked so peaceful. But I really needed to get away. The tank arriving had changed Round Up, made it worse. They'd gone from bullies to killers.

For some time I sat there and sipped the whisky, as piano music played on the sound system and the waiters flitted around. I thought about Casper, that nasty look on his face. The way he sneered at me. I finished the drink and had another, looking out across Faeston in the midday sun.

I moved to a table by the window and ordered a beer, just to pace myself.

It was sometime later that Becky came in. By then there were a few more drinkers. Men in worn suits. Women in shabby blouses. Becky looked good again. She was in a long dress, purple with tie-dye patterns. Slim fitting. Even though I was wary of her I couldn't ignore how great she looked. I watched how she moved, how her clothes fitted her body and how her hair fell onto her shoulders.

This was the time to play it cool, see what she had to offer, find out what her and Casper were really about. She was an enemy of Round Up but that didn't make her my friend.

She took the seat opposite, pulled it up close. 'Did you see him?' No small talk. No asking how I was or what was going on.

'Yeah, I saw him.'

'Is he okay?'

'Oh, he's fine. Fellas like him are always fine.'

She waved to the waiter. He came over and she ordered a gin. Even though she spoke to him she eyed me the whole time. Once he'd gone she moved closer. 'He's all right? Casper?'

'Like I said, he's fine.'

She smiled at this but her eyes were hard, serious. The waiter brought her drink over and asked if I wanted anything else. I said I was fine and he left.

Becky took a drink and stared out of the window. She pointed towards the door that led out to the garden. 'Let's sit outside, again. It's a nice afternoon.'

'Let's not.' I wasn't in the mood to play along.

'Did he say much?'

'Bits.'

She took a drink, looked away from me. 'But he is

okay?'

'We've covered that.'

'What'll they do to him?'

This was it, crunch time. I could soften it for her. But it was best she knew how it really was. 'They'll work him over. Find out everything he knows. They won't stop until they got his full history. Where he's from; going to. How to get into the tank…'

She took another drink, finished it off. For a few seconds she sat there with the empty glass in her hand turning it around, staring into it.

'Sorry,' I said. 'That's how they work.'

She leant one hand on the table. The other she slid underneath, onto my knee. Rested it there. 'You've got to help, Trent, get him out of there.'

'Get him out?' This was new. But I should have spotted it.

'You've got to help.'

'I can't. Sorry.'

'It's not just about Casper. If they get the Eblis, you know what they'll do.'

'I know.'

'We need to get Casper free. And take the Eblis.'

'I understand. But I can't help.' I stood up, ready to go. This was too much. It was all risk for me and no reward.

Becky took my hand. 'Wait —'

'I'm sorry.'

'It's fine. I understand.' She stood and joined me. 'I want to thank you for your help. I know you've taken a risk doing this.' She pulled out a wad of cash. 'Let me treat you.'

'I don't want your money.'

'Let's take a walk. Go to some bars. Have fun.'

I was about to argue, point out I had stuff to do. Instead I nodded. Said nothing. A few drinks with an attractive woman wasn't such a bad thing to do. I'd helped her out and she owed me. The alternative was an evening alone in my flat. Or with Sophie.

We went through the hotel, onto St Cuthbert's Terrace.

'So,' she said. 'Where do you suggest?'

'I know a few places.' I led her down the High Town Walkway, a paved road the Committee had just put in when I'd arrived eighteen months ago, something they were really proud of. It was old bricks set in a zig-zag pattern with a couple of mosaics. We passed one of a sea monster.

Even though it was only early evening candles were lit at some of the bars. Becky strode alongside me slowly, her head tilted back, dress tight on her body. She moved well and was in good shape. I didn't have to trust her to find her sexy.

Music came up the road and I let it draw me towards The Web Club, one of my favourites when I first arrived in town. A couple at the doorway were locked in an embrace, hands all over each other as they stood below the metal spider's web on the wall. The music from inside was loud, energetic: trumpets and saxophones. Drums.

'Fancy this?' I said.

'Sounds good.'

I let Becky go ahead and followed her into the passageway and onto the narrow staircase, her legs just in front of me. As we twisted our way up I could see the muscles in her thighs working under her dress. She gave off the smell of some flower, something delicate.

At the top of the stairs we came to the main bar. It was a long room with tables set out in the middle and alcoves along one side. The walls were bare brick covered with posters of musicians. At the far end a band played an old jazz song. I led her to one of the alcoves.

As we slid in a waiter came over and took our orders. I asked for a large whisky and she had a small beer.

She leant over to me. 'This is quite some place.'

'Found it shortly after I arrived in town.'

'One of your haunts?'

'Not so much now.' Largely because Sophie didn't like the music or the decor. Or the drinks or High Town.

The band finished. Becky applauded, staring at me, a look that was hard to work out.

The waiter brought our drinks. Becky drank and so did I. As the band started to play again, she leant over, her breath warm on my neck. 'I'm not going to mess with you, Trent. I think I can trust you. We have to get Casper out. Get the Eblis. We're on our way somewhere…' She sat back and gave me that look again, tilting her head a little, reading my reaction.

'Go on.'

Leaning in again, she put her mouth even closer to my ear. 'I'd like you in with us, Trent, you could add something to what we're doing.'

And she needed me to get Casper out.

'We're going somewhere amazing. Really special.' Then she sat back and drank, giving some kind of a smile, a faint one, but her eyes soft. The band stopped and the audience clapped. One of the musicians said something about an intermission. There was more applause. The sound of people talking.

Becky shuffled round so she was close to me, her thigh pressed against mine. 'You're not like the others here, Trent. Round Up and their like. You don't belong here.'

'You don't know me.'

'But you know what I mean.'

I knew all right. But I was still wary. She was feeding me what I wanted to hear. Buttering me up. 'So what are you suggesting.'

'Help get Casper out. And the Eblis. Come with us.'

We sat there for a good minute, as she played with her glass, let me think through her offer. It was tempting. Leave Faeston and Round Up for somewhere else. With her and her brother. He was the worst thing about the deal. Him and the hassle getting him out, of course.

'We'd never get him out,' I said.

'I can help with that.'

'It's not like we can just walk out with him.'

'With you help we'll be fine.'

'And what is this place you're going to?'

'A town. In Scotland. Somewhere where they are doing it all right. Working together not against each other.'

It was interesting but I didn't need her and Casper. I had money and the Scrambler. There was nothing stopping me leaving town. Getting on the road again. Finding this place.

Becky stared into her glass and turned it slowly. 'Think about it, Trent.'

'Listen.' I wanted to slow this down, go off and think about it. Then the band started to play again. As they came on Becky gave me funny looks. This was the jumpiest I'd seen her.

Finishing my whisky I put the glass down. A waiter

passed by I waved him over and asked for the same again, ordering Becky another beer. Maybe what she offered was what I needed. Something different, some purpose. No more wandering alone or working for people like Nico.

'I'll think about it,' I said.

'You sure?'

'Yeah.'

We were very close. She leant forward as if to whisper in my ear but kissed me on the cheek. I looked at her and she kissed me on the lips, putting her hands on mine.

When the waiter arrived with our drinks we separated.

The trumpeter played a solo and people cheered. I closed my eyes and put a hand against my temple. I saw the three lads on the settee. Two white faced, terrified. The third dead.

'Trent?'

I opened my eyes. 'What's your plan?'

'What?'

'Your plan? To get Casper out.'

She waved her hand, dismissive as it if was obvious. 'I have stuff we can use. You know the layout...'

The band stopped. I knocked back my whisky then stood up. 'I need to go.'

'Really?'

'I've had enough.'

She joined me as I settled our bill. Left the club. I'd really had enough to drink. And my head was spinning from everything else. We stood outside. The sun had set and there were more candles lit outside the bars and cafes. The lights around the harbour shone up from Low Town. The rest of it was invisible.

'What do you think?' she said.

'It sounds like something.'

She was watching me again. 'What now?'

'Time to go.'

We moved onto the Walkway, by a mosaic of Poseidon. She shuffled around and didn't make eye contact. 'Are you going to help?' she said.

'I'll see.'

She smiled and moved over to me, putting her arms around me, kissing me again. This time full on the lips with more passion. When she moved back her eyes were red rimmed, as if she was going to cry. 'We need to do it soon.'

'Right.'

As she moved off she leant back to me, her mouth by my ear again. 'Thanks for all your help.' Then she kissed me on the cheek and walked off.

CHAPTER ELEVEN

Torture

I didn't sleep well that night. I was woken by nightmares then lay in my room as the sounds of Faeston drifted in: trains on their way down from Scotland. Ships making ready to sail. Everyone in the town seemed to be moving around.

I went to Round Up Central first thing. I wanted to meet Casper again. Gregg was in the office with Tyler and some lad I didn't know. They told me that Nico was across town at the Globe.

Gregg grinned at me. He seemed to have forgotten our altercation from the day before. 'Spent a bit of time with your mate last night.'

'My mate?'

'The prisoner. Got him singing.'

This wasn't something I wanted. 'Oh yeah?'

'Propped him up. Didn't let him sleep, eat, drink.'

'He say much?' If Casper had mentioned our chat, about Becky, that was it. Nico would be on to me.

'Nah. Whining on about bein' tired. Something about

wanting to go home. Think he's near breaking though.' Gregg thought this was great, grinning away. Tyler and the other man laughed, seeing it as a big joke.

'I'll go see him now. Try to get something out of him.'

Gregg thrust a pencil and pad of paper at me, said no more. He led me out and along the corridor, swinging his keys, whistling a tune. At the door he grunted. 'As soon as he starts talking I'm to be called.' He unlocked the door. 'Nico's orders.'

Nico's orders. They were keeping an eye on me.

As before there were two guards in the cell. One I recognised from the previous day, the one who'd spoken, but the other I'd not seen before. Casper was sitting at the table, his head slumped on his hands.

'He's meant to stand up!' said Gregg.

'Leave him,' I said. 'I want to talk to him.'

'Nico said —'

'Leave him, please.'

I sat opposite Casper, the pad in front of me. 'How are you?'

He glanced up, one eyebrow raised, then lay back down on his hands moving his head from side to side. 'Uh, Christ,' he said.

'Time for another chat.'

He sat up and yawned. His tongue was coated white, eyes bloodshot. He dropped his head forward onto his arms taking deep breaths.

He'd been kept awake for days now. It wouldn't be long before he really broke. Told them how to get into the Eblis and all about Becky. All about me.

I glanced back up at the guards. They seemed to be staring into space. Not watching me and Casper. They were probably tired as well. Bored shitless. I spoke in a loud voice. 'I need to know what's going on.'

He shook his head. Maybe he'd heard me and was responding or maybe it was just a comfort thing.

'Casper, this is important.'

When he raised his head one eye was half shut.

Then he slumped down, flat out on the table.

I asked stuff about the tank and where he'd come from, leaning forward nodding, writing notes, even though Casper was breathing deeply, probably asleep. Which was good. If he rested he'd be able to hold himself together for another day.

After forty minutes, when he sounded like he was snoring I nudged him. 'This better all be true,' I said.

He started and sat up. 'What?'

'You heard me.'

Blinking like mad he nodded and lay back down.

I gripped the pad and stood up. The guards looked at me and I eyeballed each in turn. Then I went to the door and knocked until Gregg came.

He opened it a couple of centimetres, no more. 'Is he talking?'

'Yeah.'

I grabbed hold of the door and yanked it wide then walked out, pushing him aside. 'I've taken notes.'

'You were to call me when he talked!'

'There wasn't time.'

'Nico will hear —'

'I've got notes. For Nico. I'll pass them on to him.'

Before he could ask anymore I was off. I was in no mood for Gregg to have a go. Bollock me for not letting him into the cell.

Outside I screwed up the crap I'd written and threw it into the gutter. A cart rattled past full of mangy looking turnips. Casper wasn't going to last much longer. I'd given him a break but he'd gone for days without sleep. Soon Nico would get details out of him. Details about my involvement.

I had to do something.

We'd have to break him free. Getting him out would be a miracle. Without thinking about it I'd got caught up in this.

Last night I'd dreamt about Becky. Me and her in bed together. Partway through the sub had appeared again. Not like the dream I'd had in Sophie's, more bizarre, with me floating in the water, alongside it. As it dived I was swept underwater with it, swirling and turning. Maybe it meant something.

More likely it was from all the booze I'd had.

Several boys grabbed turnips off the cart, running away with them.

So Becky had arrived and wanted me to go with her on this mission of hers. We'd break Casper out and run off into the wilds.

Just like that.

As the farmer spotted the lads he stopped the cart and jumped off, running after them. But they were too fast.

I started to walk home. Maybe Becky had just been messing me around. Playing games to get me to help her. She was interesting and attractive. Good to spend time with. But not worth getting killed for. Not many women were, if any.

But I was ready to go. Ready to leave the town and happy to give Round Up a bloody nose on the way. If she had some kind of a serious plan, some ideas about getting the tank and going then it was worth hearing.

If she didn't, that was that. I'd take my chances on Casper not talking. Leave when I was ready.

I turned round and headed across town. Towards High Town.

When I got to the Bay Hotel I went straight in. I remembered her room number from when she'd mentioned it in the bar.

Room twelve was on the first floor at the far end, by a cracked window that looked out across the town. I thumped on the door, rattling it in the frame. It was patched with an uneven piece of wood at the bottom, the number written in neat paint. From other rooms I could hear voices, someone singing way off, a slow tune. Maybe Becky was still asleep: it was only midmorning. Or maybe wasn't here, hadn't ever been. It might have all been a trick by Round Up, a test. One I'd failed.

Maybe I should just turn and go.

The door opened. Becky stood there with a towel wrapped around her, a crease of cleavage showing, her hair wet and eyelashes matted. She smelled of soap. 'Trent?' She glanced past me, up and down the passageway then waved her hand at me. 'Come in.'

I followed through into the main room. There was a window that looked out to sea where a couple of ships made their way in towards the harbour. The bed was strewn with maps and plans of buildings. Old magazines. There were pieces of paper on the coffee table with motorcycle components on them. Two panniers and a rucksack were packed beside it. Black bra and knickers lay upon folded clothes on a pillow.

'You planning to leave?' I said.

'Just been waiting for you.'

'I didn't even know I was coming.'

She smiled. 'I just need to finish washing…' She adjusted the towel, tucking it into her cleavage. Then she went into the bathroom.

I rested back in the seat and closed my eyes. Around me were the sounds of the building, footsteps and chairs scraping. Shouts and slamming doors. If I was going to go along with this I needed a lot more information. Where, why and how. If she gave the wrong answers that would be it. I'd ride off alone.

I jerked up when she came back in, still in the towel but now with her hair wrapped up as well.

'Should we thrash out the details?' she said.

'I have a few questions.'

She sat down, unfolding a map and setting it out on the floor. 'Go on.'

'Say we get Casper out —'

'Which we will.'

'Where are we going?'

She went across to the bed, picked up a magazine and handed it to me. It was a holiday brochure, decades old.

'Page forty-two,' she said.

I turned to the page she'd said. It had pictures of a castle surrounded by trees. A loch and small village. Smiling men with bagpipes. A plate full of seafood. A red deer with massive antlers. 'What the fuck is this?'

'There's a community there. A group of forward-thinkers. They have forests for fuel. Water they can fish. Farm with healthy animals. Good housing. It's all run through an elected council. And they welcome decent people. It's not like here with Round Up.'

'Sounds too good to be true.'

'The problem is its location. On the west coast of Scotland. You have to pass round Glasgow or Edinburgh and across country. A couple of other dangerous places. That's why we need the Eblis.'

'And you've been there? Seen it?'

'I know reliable people who have.'

I flicked through the photos of the place in this holiday brochure. It was possible that it did exist. That there were people trying to move things forward. Shangri-La had elements of it, Gary's oasis in the far north of Northumberland. But it was too wrapped up in hippy stuff for me. 'Is this a religious cult?'

She frowned and shook her head. 'Not at all.' She sat down on the bed and faced me. 'We've had enough of all this.' She waved her hand towards Low Town. 'Places run by thugs. So-called committees that are just gangs in disguise. Neo-reivers.' She shrugged.

Maybe that was all genuine. I still had one more question.

'Why me?'

Reaching over to one of the panniers she opened it and pulled out a handgun: a semi-automatic pistol. Her towel slid up on her legs the showing the top of her thighs. She checked the gun over, dropped the magazine out, popped it back in. 'You know your way around stuff, seem reliable...'

I shook my head. 'Come on. You zoomed in on me at the bike races. Just by chance I was the guy ready to interrogate Casper.'

'Maybe I did some sniffing around. Found out who ran

the town. How things worked. I did figure out you were in Round Up, but I didn't know you'd be doing the questioning.'

'And what about me coming with you?'

'That wasn't the initial plan.' She put the pistol away and started clearing stuff off the bed, putting it all on the floor. 'I was after someone in Round Up who could give me inside details. Information. You just happened to have more about you. A good feeling, shall we say.'

'A good feeling?'

'I knew you'd help us. Get Casper out.'

'I haven't said I'll help.'

She smiled. 'You're here, aren't you?' She reached down to a bag on the floor and pulled out another gun. Then a grenade. 'I have the kit and a plan. Bring your bike over and we'll talk it through.'

'Look, trying to get Casper out is possible but we'll never get the tank. No way —'

'We'll talk about it when you come back.'

'I'm not sure.'

She refastened the bag. As she leant forward the top of her towel came undone, slipping down a little, showing her body underneath, still damp from the bath. She took hold of the towel again but instead of doing it up just pulled it off. She stood in front of me naked. She looked fantastic, her skin smooth and soft and with a hint of tan, natural colour. She had curves but there was a firmness to her body, strength. She took my hand and I resisted. Pulled free. She was sexy but this was taking me all in the wrong direction.

'You don't find me attractive?'

'It's not that —'

'Come on, Trent...'

'I don't want to complicate things.'

She lay down on the bed on her side with a leg crooked up, one arm across her nipples and the other on her crotch, hiding the thin strip of hair. 'You sure?'

'I need to go,' I backed off towards the door, my eyes fixed on her body, part of me wanting to stay there with her. Spend the rest of the morning in bed. But I knew that would really cloud my thoughts and I needed a clear head.

Becky got up and slid the towel on following me to the door. 'Listen, Trent, I didn't mean to give you the wrong idea, I —'

'It's fine.' I opened the door and stepped out into the hallway.

She stopped in the doorway. 'Think it through. I'll wait for you. Here.' She smiled. Some kind of smile I couldn't figure out.

'All right.' But I was already on my way towards the stairs.

As I crossed town I thought it all through. Becky and Casper and their plans. Round Up and Sophie and Faeston. There was too much going on. Too much I didn't like. Round Up had stepped up a gear. And Sophie was getting all settled, with me woven into her nest. In some ways Becky's plan had come at just the right time. Appealing as it was to go off with her there were too many loose ends. Too many unknowns. Getting Casper out was going to be hard. And he was some fella. Some piece. But once we were out we'd be in the Eblis. We'd be able to go anywhere. I'd be much safer than on the bike.

But I had to go where they wanted, at their pace. I

wasn't one for taking orders and fitting in. That was why I hated Round Up.

Maybe I was best going off on my own, same as I always had. I wasn't quite ready to go but I'd soon have enough cash together to see me safe. Maybe do some final patch-ups on the Scrambler.

I came to my flat. Tommy was singing to himself downstairs. His version of a hymn.

I opened the door and went into the living room. Gregg and Will sat in the two chairs at the table.

Gregg had his hand on a pistol that lay on his lap aimed at me. 'Wondered when you'd arrive,' he said.

Will laughed as Gregg cocked the gun.

CHAPTER TWELVE

Decider

Gregg frowned. 'You're in luck. Nico wants you alive.'

'Yep,' said Will.

They both looked dreadfully disappointed.

'What's this all about?' I said.

Gregg grunted. 'You know what it's about. All your games with him in the cell. Do you think we're stupid?'

I did think they were stupid but obviously they weren't quite as bad as I'd assumed.

'Got you now!' added Will.

'Aye,' said Gregg. 'We know you've been working against us.'

'So now what?' I said. The pistol was aimed at me. Still tight in Gregg's hand.

He waved it around, onto my feet and torso and head. It was an old revolver, chipped and marked but good enough this range. His lips were tight and brow furrowed like he was thinking something through. Like he was ready to pop a shot into me. He could tell Nico it had been an accident. The gun went off in a scuffle, or something.

'We're going to work you over. Make you squeal. Slowly. Until, well…'

'Until you're dead,' said Will.

Gregg stood up. 'Come on, out.' The gun was waved again but this time to make me move.

'Right.' I went towards the door and took the handle. Tried to work out some way to get out of this. If they had something on me from Casper, I really was in the shit. Maybe he'd let on that I'd mentioned Becky. Told them that I knew his sister and had helped him. Now Round Up were going to knock me around. Finish me off.

'Wait.' Will shoved past me and took the handle himself. 'Don't want you running off.'

As he went out Gregg pushed up close behind me. He jammed the gun in my back and made me walk out. 'No funny business, you hear?'

'I hear,' I said.

Will was ahead of us on the stairs. He walked down backwards watching me as he went. Gregg came out of my door leaving it open.

'Are you going to shut that?'

'What the fuck for?' he said.

'Nico might want to go through my stuff. He won't want it stolen.'

Gregg grunted at this. Mentioning Nico always pressed his buttons. He kept his eyes on me but reached back with his left hand to grab the door handle and pull it shut. He couldn't reach it so he glanced round.

As he did I grabbed his wrist, the one holding the gun. With his free hand he punched me in the ribs but he was too close to get any force behind it. Before he got the idea to push me down the stairs I braced myself against the railing. He still wouldn't release the gun so I got both hands on it, aimed it down the stairs and got the end of my thumb on the trigger. Fired a shot.

It cracked off over Will's head. 'Get him, Gregg,' he shouted.

'I'm trying!'

As Gregg tried to pull the gun free, I launched myself at him, using the rail to shove against. I sent him off balance and he raised up his hands but I got hold of the pistol, twisted it hard and he had to release it to stop his finger being broken. He cried out and I pulled the pistol free, elbowing him in the face while I had the chance.

With the gun in my hand I stepped back and aimed it at him.

'You nearly broke my finger!' he said.

'You'll have worse in a minute.'

'Nico will hear about this! He'll have your skin!'

'Wasn't the plan anyway?'

'Now you've really —'

'Save it.' I shifted back towards the door. Will had advanced up the stairs so I aimed at him. 'Back off.' He kept coming so I fired a shot into the stairs, just in front of him. It blasted a chunk of wood off the edge and he backed down and stood in the yard. I waved for Gregg to follow him. He didn't move for a second then trudged down. As he went ahead I popped out the chamber to see how many rounds there were left: only two. He'd know that so I'd have to be careful.

Once he was beside Will I set myself on the second step. Now I had to work out what to do with them. Shooting them wasn't an option. Nasty pieces that they were I wasn't one for executions. I'd have to work out where to put them.

'Empty your pockets,' I said.

'Nico will hear about this,' said Gregg.

'So you said. Go on.'

They felt around in their overalls. Both had cash. Will had a knife and Gregg car keys. I made Will throw the knife across the yard.

'Take me to the car,' I said. I only had the two shots so I didn't have much freedom now. But they were cowards. That was helpful.

They led me across the road to the disused park. There was a track that ran through it and the Volvo was parked part way along, just under the bushes so it was hard to spot. I popped the boot and checked for guns. There wasn't anything dangerous in there, just tools and spares.

As I shut the boot Will leapt forward so I flicked out the gun. Cracked him across the face and makes his lips bleed. He staggered back with his hand to his mouth. Gregg just stared at me. If they'd both rushed me I'd have struggled to keep them off.

I waved the gun around. Made myself look braver than I was. These two weren't the brightest of sparks but they were quite capable of killing. In fact, it was what they liked doing.

Next I checked the inside of the car, going round to the passenger side while they stayed at the other. There was a crowbar and some sandbags but not much else. Under one of the bags there was a good length of rope.

'Get in,' I said.

Neither moved so I took the crowbar. I went round to the them and raised it up

'I said, get in.' To make the point I hit Will on the back,

a satisfying thud.

Once they were in the front seats I held the gun to Will's head and made him tie Gregg's hands to the steering wheel. Then I tied Will to it myself. He'd not done much of a job securing Gregg so I added a few of knots of my own. Once they were good and tight I popped the bonnet, ripped the leads off the starter solenoid and chucked them into a bush. Then I double locked the car and took the keys.

They'd get out in a while but it gave me a little time. Time to pull myself together and head off. Go and see Becky. Her deal was starting to sound better now. If I went off on the bike Nico would soon catch me up in one of his cars. Blow me off the road. Even if I hid out in a nearby town he'd use his contacts to track me down. I needed to get away as far and fast as I could in something with equal firepower to the weapons he had hidden in Round Up Central. Something like a tank.

I went back to the flat and loaded up my panniers with spare spark plugs and a roll of tools. The crowbar and pistol from Will and Gregg. I slid them into the bottom of the bag and shoved a blanket on top.

I went into the wardrobe and pulled out Gehenna and the bag with the shotgun. Took the wad of money. Counted through it and rammed it and my clothes into a rucksack. There wasn't much I wanted to take but I put it all together.

Outside I manoeuvred the bike around, started it up and rode out of the yard, facing towards High Town. The Volvo was still parked in the bushes with Gregg and Will in it. They'd expect me to ride off out of town now. They'd never guess I was going to Round Up Central to take their precious tank. With any luck it would be a complete surprise.

I shot across Faeston and was soon at High Town.

I parked at the front of Bay Hotel and went straight up to Becky's room.

She opened the door. 'All set?' If she'd wondered about me coming back she didn't let on.

'Yeah, I'm all set.' I dumped my bags on the bed and sat next to them. It was tempting to tell about all the weird shit that had gone on since I'd left. Instead I said, 'So, what's the plan?'

She picked up a map and ran her finger across it. Then she put it down and leant towards me. 'Tell me the layout of their place.'

I went through the setup at Round Up Central. The different floors: where they had Casper. She nodded, raised an eyebrow when I told her about the doors from the prison. She asked about the ways and way out. Where they kept their weapons.

'Is that where the Eblis is?' she said. 'Next to the armoury?'

'Yeah. But forget about that. We'll never get it out.'

She put her fingers to her lips, said nothing for a moment. 'If we can get the key for Casper's cell we're fine,'

'If.' If Nico was around he'd never hand the key over. Never.

'After that we can haul Casper out and he can drive the Eblis. Get us out of there.'

'Just like that?'

'The Eblis can blast its way out,' she said. 'Once we're into it —'

'Once we're into it.' It'd be a lot easier if we didn't need to get him. Especially as he was such a miserable piece. And it sounded like he'd let on to Nico. 'Can you drive it?'

'The Eblis? Well, I can get us into it but he is the expert —'

'So we need him?'

'Yes.'

I left it at that but if things got tough I'd lead her down to the tank. Leave Casper.

She grabbed her bags up. 'Ready to go?'

I didn't really feel it. Then I thought of Gregg and Will in the car. Getting free and warning Nico. 'Yeah. I'm ready.'

She led out, down the back staircase with its threadbare carpets and busted banister. Then we went through an internal door into the hotel's old garage. The R6 was parked in the centre on a paddock stand, looking as immaculate as ever. There were a few cars at the other end. A security guard sat in a hut at the far side. Becky waved to him and he nodded back.

As she loaded up I walked out round a barrier to the Scrambler parked outside. I slid onto it and started it up.

A moment later she came out as the guard opened the barrier. She stopped beside me and the two bikes ticked over, the smooth four of hers and the lumpy twin of mine: one immaculate and cared for the other worn out.

Without a word she pulled off and I followed her, heading along Bay Road. She opened the R6 up and popped a wheelie, the back wheel skidding along the road once the front end dropped down. I worked the Scrambler to keep up. It really was a good bike, and she knew how to ride it.

We raced across town towards Round Up Central, ready to spring Casper. Take the tank. End my time at Faeston.

CHAPTER THIRTEEN

Rescue

Casper was in the far end of Round Up Central, the part that joined the old shopping mall to the multi-storey. We parked across the road in an overgrown car park, behind the derelict Citizen's Advice Bureau and next to a busted ticket machine, out of view.

'Just go through the layout again,' she said.

I explained what was on the main levels. Where the office was and Casper's cell. The basement with weapon's-store and Eblis. She reached into her rucksack and took out several grenades and a semi-automatic pistol.

As she slipped several clips of bullets into her trousers, I opened my bag taking out the shotgun, sliding in the one cartridge I had. There was also the crowbar and pistol with two rounds I'd got from Gregg. Becky reached into her bag again and pulled out a whole box of cartridges, passing them over. I loaded one and put the rest in my jacket.

'Where did all this come from?' I said.

'Where does anything come from?'

I looked over at the building. The place where I'd worked for the last eighteen months.

'What's the best way in?' she said.

I pointed towards the far end. 'The fire exit. It'll bypass some of the security doors. We'll raise the alarm going in. Once we trigger it we need to get a move on.'

'We go straight for Casper?'

'Yeah.' But if we couldn't get him out I'd be off to the tank. I'd need Becky to get into it. Or find out how it was locked, at least.

We headed along the road next to the decaying BT building then up the side of the multi-storey car-park. We went to the fire exit, locked with three heavy hasps and padlocks. I raised the pistol ready to shoot them off but Becky smiled and pulled out a cloth bag, picking out a lump of soft material, playing with it in her hand. She took off three pieces, rolled them and shoved them into each padlock. Once they were in place she felt around in the bag again, this time bringing out small fuses with a detonator attached. One of each went onto the padlocks as well.

'Plastic explosive?' I said.

She nodded and lit each fuse with a lighter. 'Stand back.' As she moved over to the side I joined her. A few seconds later there were two loud cracks and the tinkle of metal falling to the ground. The third didn't fire. I was about to go over to it when it blew.

'Not the same without electric detonators,' she said.

I pulled the remains of the padlocks off, opening the door.

We went inside and shut the door behind us. There was no sound of alarms. No one running down towards us.

The staircase smelled of smoke from the explosive.

'Follow me,' I said, leading her up.

We stopped on level two. Footsteps came down towards us, fast, two people. I grabbed Becky and pulled her under the stairs. Two Round Up men went off at the floor above us. They looked like a couple of the new fellas: young, keen to see some action. Once they'd gone we carried on to level three and stopped at the door. This led to the corridor where Casper was. The door was one of the reinforced ex-prison ones. It was locked.

'Make a hell of a noise getting in here,' I said.

'Don't you have access to the keys?'

'No chance.' Not now. Not with Nico after me.

She examined the lock and door. 'We could wait for someone to come out.'

'There's not time.' There was a fair chance they'd already noticed our entrance.

She took out a piece of dynamite and wedged it under the handle, taping it by the lock.

'That won't do it,' I said. At best it was going to damage the mechanism and weaken it. Most of the blast was going to bounce back, destroying the stairwell. It would certainly alert Round Up. We'd have them all on us.

'It'll do it, don't worry.'

'We'd be better off using the plastic explosive —'

'No, this I'll do it.'

I grabbed her wrist, stopping her. This was a stupid idea.

She swung towards me with her gun in her other hand. The pistol was aimed at me. 'Back off, Trent!'

We stood like that for a moment then I released her, let

her carry on taping the explosive in place. The gun was still aimed at me as she worked. Once she'd finished she lowered the weapon. 'Look, Trent...' she said. Then made some sound from the back of her throat. A grunt. She lit the fuse and went down the stairs.

I joined her as we huddled on the second level, neither of us saying anything.

There was a noise from the passageway and the door to level two opened, the one right beside us. Two men came through, Tyler and someone I didn't know. For a second they stared at me. At Becky.

Then she raised her pistol. 'Don't move.'

I pulled out mine as well.

A moment later the explosive went off. It roared down the stairs over us and the two men. Chunks of masonry flew off, bounced around the stairwell and one hit Tyler on the head. He fell to the ground and lay there without moving.

The other man stared at his body.

I went over to Tyler and shifted the chunk of concrete that now lay on his neck, felt for a pulse. There was nothing.

'Trent,' said Becky.

'He's dead.' I stood and waved my pistol at the other man. 'Are you armed?'

He shook his head and pulled out his pockets but his eyes were still on Tyler.

'Stay here. Don't move.'

I went over to Becky. Joined her and went up the stairs. She kept her gun trained on the fella the whole time but he didn't move. Didn't shift from the side of Tyler's body.

The door to level three was still intact, the handle

blown off, metal scorched but lock holding.

'Shit,' she said.

'I said it wouldn't blow —'

'I know. I know.'

As she paced in front of the door, there were voices and shouts from below. I was ready to forget about Casper. Go straight for the Eblis. Get the hell out of there.

Then the door opened. It swung out and a Round Up fella peered out: Luke one of the regulars. Someone I recognised but didn't know well. He went to say something and Becky swung the gun towards him.

'Easy does it,' she said.

He raised his hands and moved back through the doorway and into the passageway. When he looked at me I thrust my pistol towards him.

We followed him through the door, pulled it shut and locked it.

There were voices up ahead, several men. Becky shoved her pistol into Luke's neck and pinned him against the wall. I slid past her and carried on.

When I came to the office I stopped at the doorway and looked round. There was Aaron and another man. Aaron had started in the last year. He was in his thirties. Keen but not too daft. I didn't know the other fella. He was younger and look less sensible. There was no sign of Gregg or Will.

Aaron was doing all the talking. He said they had to stay there and guard the prisoner. The other man suggested they should investigate the noises. They argued and did nothing. Didn't even notice me peering in.

Finally, Aaron sent the man off and he came towards us. I slid back towards Becky and held up one finger, then

117

made a walking motion with the other hand.

When the man came round the corner he saw me. Before he had time to say anything I hit him in the neck, a sharp blow that made him gasp and grab at his throat. His eyes bulged and he staggered backwards towards Becky who smacked him round the back of his head with her pistol. He dropped like a sack of potatoes and sprawled out on the floor.

'There's one more,' I said. I'd expected Aaron to come round and see what the noise was about. Find Becky waving a gun around.

When I went round the corner I saw why he hadn't. He was on the phone, the one recently fitted by Nico as part of his plan to use old-world technology to increase Round-Up's efficiency. Aaron bellowed into the device. He repeated the word bomb over and over. He had his back to us, making it easy to get up close. Ram my pistol against his spine, cocking it with a loud click.

'Hello Aaron,' I said.

He swung round, puzzled, especially when he saw Becky.

'Trent?' he said. But his eyes were off all over Becky and our two guns. 'What are you up to?'

'We want the prisoner,' said Becky.

His grin vanished. 'No way.'

Becky came up close and tapped him on the nose with her pistol. 'I won't ask again.'

'No way.'

We stayed like that for a few seconds but it felt longer. Much longer.

At last he gave a nod. I took the phone off him and hung it up. He stood slowly, leading us on. He wasn't especially brave or stupid but he knew his allegiance. He'd try something against us if he thought he could get away with it.

In the passageway we passed his unconscious companion.

'He's not dead,' I said.

We carried on to the door of Casper's cell. 'This is it.'

'Open it,' said Becky.

'Well,' said Aaron. 'I'm not sure if I've the right —'

'Open it!'

Aaron eyeballed her, stuck his hands in his pockets.

She lowered her gun and cocked it. Fired. The shot boomed through the passageway. Aaron hopped back with one foot in the air. She'd clipped the edge of his boot and just missed his foot. It was hard to say if this was planned or if she'd meant to cripple him. For a moment he leant against the wall. Then he took the keys out and unlocked the door.

Becky pushed it open.

Casper sat at the table, his hands over his face. He peered through his fingers and smiled. 'Thank Christ,' he said.

CHAPTER FOURTEEN
Eblis

We dragged the unconscious fella and put in the office with Aaron. Then we locked them both in.

Casper laughed, a nasty chuckle. He bruised face creased up as he smiled. 'Knew you'd get me out, Becks.' There was no mention of my part in this. No thanks or sign of relief, just a smug nastiness.

But it was too late to back out now. We'd locked up two Round Up fellas. Killed Tyler. So I led us to the end of the corridor and unlocked the door. There was no one directly outside but voices came up the stairwell. I went ahead onto the landing and peered down. Tyler's body still lay there but the other fella had gone, no doubt to raise the alarm, if they'd not heard the racket we'd made. The door on the floor below us opened and someone came through so I ducked back. There sounded to be three, maybe four people down there. One of them was Nico, another Gregg. Will would be there as well but I couldn't hear him. They'd be tooled up and ready for us. We'd certainly struggle to get past them even with the weapons we had.

Becky came and joined me. 'Well?'

'Got company down below.'

'Where's the Eblis?'

'Bottom floor. Down the stairs.'

'Is there another way to it?'

'It's the only staircase.' Which was true, but there was a disused lift. I pointed back the way we'd come. 'There's a bust lift. At the other end.' It had never worked and hadn't ever been something of any importance. Up until now.

We locked the door behind us and passed the office with Aaron and the other fella still locked in. At the far end we came to the metal doors of the lift, partially open into a dark shaft. I took out the crowbar levering it wider. There were four cables hanging, filthy, all taut, attached to the lift car at the bottom.

'Don't fancy that,' said Casper.

'There's no other way,' I said.

'You'll have to help me down.'

'Will we?' I gave him a good eyeballing.

He returned the stare then looked away, down the filthy shaft.

Becky slid her gun away, tightened her bag on her back and stepping forward. 'We need to get going.' She leapt out and grabbed hold of the cables in one move, wrapping her arms around the wires and slowly moved downwards.

'I can't do this,' said Casper.

'You'll be fine.' I stood alongside him. We were both on the edge of the shaft as Becky moved down. A shadow in the faint light.

'I just can't.'

'Look, you either come with us or stay.'

'I won't. I can't do it.'

'All right. Stay. See what Round Up does to you.'

This got him going. He reached out and grabbed hold, half fell but maintained his grip. His body swung, pivoted on his hands. Then he wrapped arms and legs around the cable. Crept down.

Once he'd descend a metre or so I slid through and held onto the lift doors, pushed them together. As there wasn't much of a ledge inside the shaft I couldn't shut them completely but I narrowed the gap, hanging onto the door. There was no sign of anyone in the passageway but they'd soon try to get through. With one hand on a door I twisted round and reached to grab hold of the cable. There was only little light, just a thin beam. I was at full stretch with the shaft below me. I released the door and got both hands onto the cable. I took a deep breath and pushed off with my feet.

The cable thudded into my stomach and my bag bounced around. One hand slipped and I slid down. Though I was tempted to drop down on top of Casper and Becky I swung my arm round the cable and hauled myself to a stop.

I started to descend.

It went fine until Becky stepped off. She shouted that she was on top of the lift. That she was standing on the hatch ready to go. For some reason that freaked Casper and he stopped moving, just below me. First I knew was when my foot stood on his head.

'I'm stuck,' he said.

'No, you're not. Keep going.' I twisted my head to see what he was up to.

'No, I'm stuck. Can't move.'

Becky shouted up. 'What's going on?'

When Casper didn't say anything I replied. 'He's stuck.'

'Stuck?'

'Can't move. Won't move.'

'Casper,' she said. 'You're nearly down. Come on.'

He still didn't move, his body now wrapped tight around the wire.

'Casper,' I said. 'You need to move.'

'Can't do it.'

'Move or I'll move you.'

'I can't.'

So I kicked him in the head. He cried out so I did it again. I was in no mood for him panicking. Getting us stuck. 'Get down that fucking cable now.' I heard movement.

Millimetre by millimetre he made his way down with my feet catching his head every now and then. Becky stood to the side with her lighter lit, its flickering flame on the three of us.

'What happened there?' she said.

'Nothing,' said Casper. He glared at me, like it was my fault.

She waved the lighter around, pointing at the hatch. 'Let's go.'

The hatch was held by two clips which I kicked off before I raised it a couple of centimetres. It was pitch black in the lift car. At least there was no one waiting for us.

I dropped down. It bounced when I landed and rubble slid off across the floor. I groped my way to the door and felt around. When I found the gap between the two halves

I shoved the crowbar into it. Levered it open a little. There were a couple of Round Up men at the end of the corridor. They talked and shook their heads. They weren't really keyed up but one had a shotgun. Maybe the other was armed as well.

Casper came down and fell back as he hit the floor. I gave Becky a hand as she dropped through.

'We've got company,' I said.

She pressed her face against the lift doors. Her lips moved as she twisted her head. Then she raised up her pistol and shoved it through the gap. 'Open the doors once I've fired.'

I was about to say that seemed a risky plan. That there was a chance she'd just draw all the other fellas down. But before I had time to say anything the gun fired. Then twice again.

I levered the two halves doors apart and we pushed through into the corridor. It was silent. At the far end was the door out to the stairs. It was being pulled closed and it clanged shut as the two men disappeared out through it. They peered through at us and Becky aimed her gun at them. They vanished away from the window.

The door to the Eblis was off to the right.

Becky tapped it. 'Is this it?'

'Yeah,' I said.

'Do you know how to get us in?'

'Nico will have the key, more than likely.' The door was as heavy as all the other ex-prison ones. We'd struggle to blow it or break our way in.

There were footsteps on the stairs, voices. I drew out the shotgun as Becky ferreted around in her bag and pulled out the plastic explosive and detonators.

'That won't do it.'

'So what do you suggest, Trent?'

When I said nothing she started wedging it onto the door handle. I examined the wall between us and the tank. There was a pipe that went through it. Some old water feed. Alongside it were power cables and a drainpipe, all through the same section.

Becky had backed away from the door. She hadn't lit the charge and fumbled around with her lighter. Before she set it off I grabbed the explosive and pulled it off.

'Hey, Trent —'

'Wait.' I jammed it behind the pipe and snatched her lighter. Lit the detonator. Then I dragged her off into the lift. Casper was still in there and we pressed ourselves against the sides.

'I hope you know what you're doing,' she said.

Before I could reply, say that I wasn't sure, and it was a gamble, there was a great blast. Debris sprayed through the gap in the lift's doors, rattling off the metal sides. Echoing around it.

Becky went straight out into the passageway and I followed. The air was filled with dust and smoke. Masonry and busted metal lay on the ground. And there was a hole in the wall. Where the pipe had been there was now a great breach that led into the room holding the Eblis.

Becky was already on her way through and I ducked through with Casper.

Into the room with the Eblis.

CHAPTER FIFTEEN

Out of town

The tank was all hard edges, bigger than I remembered. There was rubble around the tracks and parts of bricks lay across its front end and the low loader it was on. Becky was on the hull and Casper clambered up, round the gun-barrel that faced off towards the shuttered door. He placed his hands on a couple of panels. There were several clicks and the hatch popped open and he slid in. I climbed up, across the warm metal. Smooth to the touch. It still made a hum, like blood rushing round my head. Shots cracked in the passageway. Becky was halfway into the turret.

'What are you planning?' I said.

'Blast our way out.' She dropped into the Eblis.

'Of course.' I stayed at the edge of the hatch. That narrow entrance. Getting into it was probably the sensible thing to do. It was much safer than staying out here with Round Up. But it didn't feel right.

Becky popped her head back up. 'You coming?'

'I'll follow you out. Grab my bike.'

She looked as if she was going to argue then sighed. 'Whatever. See you out there.' She vanished into the turret and pulled the hatch shut.

A face peered through the hole in the wall, one of the fellas we'd scared off. When I waved the shotgun at him he ducked back. He'd soon be back. Maybe I should have got into the tank after all.

There was a whirring from the Eblis. I expected the cough of a started motor then the sound of a heavy diesel engine but instead there were whines and clicks. A dull drone. The turret swung round a few degrees until it was centred on the shutter. As the gun barrel rose up I ducked and covered my ears.

There was a thunderous roar and crash. It was like the whole room had been blown apart. The air was filled with dust and the smell of cordite. Bits of metal clattered onto the ground and the sound of the gun echoed round the building. Round my head.

The tank settled back onto its suspension. The heavy shutter had been blown apart and daylight shone through the smoke.

With a low rumble the Eblis moved forwards. I walked alongside it, sheltered from anyone coming through the breech in the wall. The vehicle barely shifted on its suspension as it crushed the end of the low loader and pushed through the smashed doorway. It moved with some speed, clanks and squeaks coming from the tracks. I ran alongside as it went onto the road then stopped.

There was a clatter as a machine gun fired from Round Up Central. It pinged off the tank's hull and thudded into the road. The Eblis's turret swivelled round towards the building and the barrel rose up.

I didn't hang around but ran across the road to the derelict car park where the Scrambler was parked. I ducked behind the bike and peered over.

The tank's gun roared and the vehicle rocked back on its suspension as smoke engulfed the building and masonry erupted from it. Bricks flew into the air and some clattered onto the ground. A dust cloud billowed out, the building now a shapeless husk in the background. Flames licked from the ground floor where the shell had impacted.

For a moment there was just the sound of burning building then the tanks hatch popped open and Becky stuck her head out.

'Are you getting in?' she said.

'I'll follow you out of town.'

'Really?'

'Really.'

'Fine. Can you pass my bags?'

They were still on her bike. I went over and grabbed them, looking the R6 over, all polished and smart. I took the bags over to the tank. 'What about the bike?'

'The Yamaha? It's not coming. This was its last run.'

I thought about saying I'd take it. It was a much better machine than mine. But the Scrambler meant something to me. It was a good bike but it was also part of my history.

She stashed the bags and gave me that look again, like she wanted to say more. 'We'll stop once we're through the check point. Out of town.' She dropped down into the Eblis, flicking the turret shut.

There were whirrs and whines from the tank as it moved forward then swung round. The tracks clattered as it took a great arc, the gun's barrel staying aimed at the wrecked building.

As I got onto the Triumph I looked over at what was left of Round Up Central. There was no movement, no sign that anyone had survived. I started the bike and clunked into gear. There was a clatter from the second floor, where the office was. Had been. A bullet ricocheted off the ground a couple of metres away.

I gunned the Scrambler and raced after the tank as shots came from behind me.

I rode off from Round Up Central for the last time.

We cut across town on New Road, avoiding the Harbour Bridge that had caught Casper out when he first arrived. For a big machine it was fast, clocking forty. They didn't slow even when carts blocked the way, crushing a barrow, driving over a barricade of planks and barrels that Round Up had set up. It was positioned halfway across the road by West Bridge, narrowing it so that only pedestrians could get through, forcing the Eblis to climb over. It rose up on its tracks, dropping down with a thud as its weight compressed them.

There was room for me to squeeze through and we carried on through North Side, the tank charging up the hill. At High Row people came out of the shops and houses and stared at us. Amongst them was Sophie. She stood on the pavement with her mouth open, watching the tank with her hands clutched against her chest, then lowering them when she saw me. I could have waved, saluted, given some sign of recognition but instead did nothing. I looked away and rode on.

We continued up the hill, past the town farms and to the barricade. If there were men at the north check point they didn't hang around. The tank rattled through without any resistance, chewing up the barbed wire.

A mile onto the moors we stopped. Casper appeared out of the hatch. He jumped down, joined by Becky.

'That was easy enough,' he said.

'They'll soon be after us,' she said.

'She's right,' I said.

Becky came over and put her hand on the Triumph's headlamp. 'We can strap this on. Then you can get in.'

'I'm fine riding it.'

'You sure?'

'Yeah.'

Casper said nothing. He went back to the tank and slid into it. Being stuck in a steel box with him didn't appeal. Even if she was there as well.

Maybe she got this. Maybe not. Either way she'd didn't argue. 'Fine.' She joined Casper and the hatch thudded shut.

I turned towards town. Smoke rose up from the far side, where Round Up Central was. There were bells ringing and the sound of distant engines.

So that was it. I'd left Round Up and the town. Sophie as well. I'd really ensured I'd never be able to return. Getting Casper and the tank had been messy: Tyler getting killed and God knows who else in Round Up Central when Casper fired at it.

But I was only tagging along. It wasn't like we had to be best buddies or whatever.

Once we were well clear of the place I'd go. It was handy to have the Eblis for the next day or so. While Nico, Gregg and Will were on our tail. We'd be safe enough with all this armour.

But once we were out of Round Up's range I'd be all right to ride on.

There were all kinds of whirrs from the Eblis then it clattered forward and accelerated along the road.

The great mass picked up speed and set off away from town.

CHAPTER SIXTEEN
On the Road

We travelled on for another couple of hours, the tank rattling ahead of me. The town and coast disappeared behind us as we passed empty moorland and the occasional farm building. Most were derelict but the odd one had a sign warning of dangerous dogs or owners having guns, or both. It was a hard life out here, risking the neo-reivers and other scavengers. But good food always sold for top money so there was a living to be made.

Up ahead a vehicle appeared, a dot on the horizon. It came towards the Eblis, initially fast then slowing down before turning off into a side road. By the size and speed it moved it was a car, traders more than likely. The side roads round here didn't go anywhere so it probably ducked off to avoid us. Not a bad move considering what the tank was armed with. And the size of it. It was quite a sight on the open road.

We cracked along at a fair pace, hitting forty on the straights. The bike thudded up through the gears with a nice loud blast from the exhaust. From the tank there was the rumble of its tracks with the occasional squeak from a dry link. Not much of an engine sound. My guess was it had a fuel cell. Either that or some kind of noise suppression system. Something they'd tried on the last few models they'd made. The old-world's last gasp.

The big questions were when, and where, I headed off.

Once we stopped I'd quiz them about their intended location. This amazing place they were aiming for. I wasn't interested in going there, just the route. Once I had the details I could work out where I when I was planning to take my leave. With the cash I had there'd be opportunities in the right town. I had plenty of options.

As we came to a crossroad the tank swung sharp to the left, onto a B road. Smaller and slower than the one we'd been on. Was this some plan or were they lost? Either way I followed them. The Eblis rocked back and forth on the potholed surface. I steered round the chewed up tarmac and chunks of road.

We bounced along for miles with nothing else on the road. We were onto the low moors, dotted with the odd birch and blackened sections of heather. Where the dried out vegetation had caught light in the summer. We were heading west now rather than north; if this was their route to Scotland it would take forever. Maybe they really were lost. After all, Casper had blundered through town when he'd meant to go round it. But Becky was with him now and she knew what she was doing. Appeared to, at least.

We passed a lorry stripped down in a field. There was only the chassis and a few panels left to rot. A chewed up tyre and some busted glass. The sun was low under the clouds and lit the scrap vehicle a dull gold.

Whatever I thought of Casper and Becky, we had made it. We were away from Faeston and Round Up. Away from Sophie. I didn't want to think about Sophie.

We carried on along the track for some time, alongside the parched moors with its stunted trees. As the sun dipped ahead of us onto thick woodland in the distance.

Then the Eblis turned right onto another road, a rough track of gravel and dried earth. We twisted past low hummocks and came upon dense woodland, the eastern edge of the Border Forest.

This was the right way but it was too small a road to make any headway. Were they planning to stop off? I was keen to push on. Put some miles between us and Nico's gang. Then again, the light was fading. And we'd be well hidden here.

As the sun disappeared behind the trees we pitched across the rough ground, snaking our way between the rows of conifers, their sparsely leafed branches casting deep shadows. After some minutes the tank slowed and pulled into a large clearing. The ground was covered with dead branches and many of the trees were brown and leafless. Some had fallen or leant uprooted. There was a dark pool over to the far side.

The Eblis stopped and I pulled the Scrambler up at its side, killing the engine. There was a pop as it backfired. Then silence. Maybe a trickle from a stream way off. Casper clanged the hatch open and climbed out. As he stood on the bulkhead Becky joined him.

I stayed on the bike as they surveyed where we were. On every side there was thick woodland. The track we'd come down disappeared off at an angle so we couldn't be seen from the road. A crow cawed from the undergrowth then flapped off.

I got off the Scrambler and checked it over. There was a slight oil leak from the crankcase. I dipped my finger in the amber drops. Felt the heat. Then I tapped the fuel tank, heard the low ping. I'd need to think about refuelling somewhere. There was a reasonable amount of Faeston bio-eth in there but only enough to get me up to Edinburgh. Nowhere near the Highlands.

The Eblis would need some more juice as well, whatever it ran on. Fuel-cells needed fuel.

Becky came over. 'We made it.'

'Yep, so far.'

'We're well hidden here, if anyone's following us.'

'If anyone survived.'

'You bothered?'

'Not at all. Just keen to get away. Anyway, what's your plan?'

'Overnight here. Head off first thing. That work for you?'

'Fine.'

She moved closer to me. 'Listen, Trent —'

'Yeah?'

'I just...I don't know...'

We stood there without speaking. As a breeze rattled the branches.

'I need to go take a leak,' I said.

'Oh, okay.'

I left her standing by my bike and went over into the trees. The twigs crunched under my feet and light filtered down through the branches. Becky was still by the bike but she went back to the tank after a minute. There was no sign of Casper. I guessed he was sniffing around somewhere.

Afterwards I went over to the pond, cupping my hands in it, rubbing them together. The water was cool and peaty.

'I wouldn't drink that,' said Becky.

'I didn't plan to.'

She had a bag with her and slid out a pan, putting it to one side. 'Trent, I appreciate what you did back then, back at Round Up's building —'

'It's fine. I'm pleased to be away.'

'Well, thanks.' She gave me a smile then put her hand on my arm. Just held it there. After a moment she moved away and started to gather wood, putting a fire together. Casper was over by the far side of the pond, wandering around, staring at the ground, like he'd lost something.

I waited to see if she said anything else. When she didn't I shouldered my bag and wandered off, round the pond, following the stream that fed it. It led me into the trees, over ground thick with leaf litter. I walked for some time, through tightly packed birch and pines, until I came to a small waterfall that ran into a deep pool. The ground was flat at the sides with sparse tree cover, letting in the evening light. I went over to the water's edge and sat on a log, peeling bark off until I found some grubs. I picked two of them up and laid them on my leg, feeling around in my bag. I found a hook and line, something I always had with me when I was on the road, and threaded the biggest grub onto it. It squirmed and jerked as I lowered it into the water, easing the line out.

I sat there as the woods grew darker and the line hung limp in the water. Birds shifted in the undergrowth and something ran up a tree behind me. The pond was dark, black, rippling with the flow from the waterfall. I could see myself staring out of it, twisted out of shape.

I reached into the bag and brought out the Gehenna stuff laying it out beside me. I opened it and tilted it to catch what light there was, going over the line drawing of the submarine, all its decks and sections, tracking it with my finger again and again.

I put it back into the bag and watched myself from the water. Becky and Casper were some pair. There was something strange about them but it was hard to pin down. He was cold. Unfriendly. But I'd met plenty of fellas like him. And she ran hot and cold. Chatty then distant. I'd have to keep an eye on them. Still, compared to Nico, Gregg and Will they were lovely.

The woods darkened around me.

The line twitched. It pulled again. I lifted it up and there was a small trout on it. The fish flicked its tail and I threw it onto the ground. It gasped and stared up at me as I watched it die. It was tempting to grab it and throw it back into the water, show some mercy. But we needed to eat and this was the main course.

I carried it back, limp on the hook. The woods were dark and I picked my way over tree trunks, branches and loose stones, heading towards the tank.

When I lost the stream I stopped. It'd be easy to wander off here, carry on into the woods and end up on the wrong side. Alone in the dark. To walk on and on, away from the Eblis, Becky and Casper.

I flicked my lighter on and the trees and ground appeared around me, all looking the same. There was no sign of the stream or anything else that would help. I walked straight ahead for several yards then stopped and turned back. There were trunks that vanished off into the distance, pine needles everywhere.

Then there was a laugh from my right, a low chuckle way off. It had to be Casper. I headed towards the sound as he laughed again.

I emerged close to where I'd come into the trees. Becky and Casper sat by a fire eating. When I joined them she thrust a plate at me with beans and sausages on it.

'Where did this come from?' I said.

'We stashed it some time ago. Ready for this,' said Casper. Empty tins lay at his feet.

I sat down and dug into the food, setting the fish beside me. The beans tasted good. I'd not eaten for hours and hadn't even realised I was hungry. I shovelled it in.

Once I'd finished I gutted the fish and hung it above the flames. Becky heated water in the pan making dandelion tea. Casper just gazed into the fire, his bruised face a flickering pattern from the flames.

'Tell me about the place you're heading to,' I said.

For a moment Becky and Casper just looked at each other.

Then she spoke. 'It's called Arcadia.'

'Arcadia?'

Casper grunted. 'That's its name. Place we're going to.' He reached into the bag at Becky's side and pulled out the maps. He jabbed at a patch of blue on the edge of one. 'Here.'

Becky moved round to let me nearer. It was hard to see much in the firelight.

'Up on the coast,' she said. 'On the edges of Loch Fyne.' As she said it she glanced across at Casper. Something passed between them but it was hard to work out what it was.

'Right,' I said.

'It's only a couple of hundred miles, maybe a little more. It should take another couple of days depending on what route we take.'

'Probably go up through the Lowlands,' said Casper. 'Head west. Not sure exactly.' He flapped his hand around the map but didn't really point to a specific road.

I didn't like his answer but didn't want to push it. Not yet.

'We'll go on back roads,' she said. 'We can't outrun your...we can't outrun the people from Round Up. I know they have cars, fast ones, but they can't go cross country. We've enough armour to survive anything reivers throw at us but I'd guess Round Up have some serious kit.'

Casper grunted at this. That was true. Nico had put some time into building up his arsenal. He'd soon pulled out that rocket-launcher the other day. God knows what else he had. If he was still around.

'And what happens when we get there?' I said.

Casper looked at Becky then she spoke, her face a pattern of rippling shadows from the fire. 'We make contact, show we're decent people...' She went into her bag and pulled out a glass bottle. Easing the stopper out she drank from it before wiping her mouth on her sleeve. 'Then we'll neutralise Eblis, dump it somewhere out of the way.'

'I see.'

She offered me the bottle. It was vodka of some type. Rough and strong. After a drink I made a joint from some grass I'd brought in my bag. The woods were quiet and the fire had died down to several logs. I lit the spliff, drew on it then passed it on to them. We smoked in silence for a few minutes.

I felt ready to probe them a little more. 'Where did you get the tank from?'

They looked at one another, said nothing for a moment. There was a scuffling noise from a tree behind us, then silence.

'It was in storage,' said Becky. Casper nodded and she continued. 'An old army base near Birmingham. Hidden in a bunker behind a warehouse. We noticed a ventilation shaft to it. Took some getting out. At least the manuals were hidden nearby otherwise we'd never have got in.'

Casper picked a twig up and threw it into the fire. It landed on the bright embers and flared up. Burnt away to nothing. Becky didn't seem keen to say any more.

For a moment we sat without speaking.

Then I stood up. 'I'll get some more wood.'

'Thanks,' said Becky.

I stepped away from the fire and wandered off into the shadows. Gathering up branches I moved further away, watching them. They were leant forward, heads close together. All that stuff about Arcadia sounded half-baked. I couldn't believe they hadn't worked a route out. They were up to something but it was hard to say what. I'd play along for the ride but keep my wits about me. Watch my back.

I picked up sticks and returned to the fire.

When I got back they were rolling their bedding out.

'Early start,' said Becky.

'Yeah,' I said, chucking the logs onto the fire. They hissed as the damp steamed out. Casper straightened his sleeping bag, sat on it and stared at the burning wood.

I set out mine, thinking of the times I'd done this before. Travelling with others: Jamie and Lawson. People I'd trusted.

Becky said good night and Casper muttered something, both of them slipping into their bedding, turned away from me. I sat by the fire, as it spluttered and flared up.

Then I lay down, stared into the clear sky at the stars. As shadows flickered across the clearing I drifted off to sleep.

CHAPTER SEVENTEEN

Pleasure Town

When I awoke Becky was next to my bag. She saw me and moved over to the fire and stacked it up with logs. There was a pan of water at her side. 'Sleep well?' she said.

'Fine,' I said, though I'd slept shallow for most of it, dreaming of movement in the woods as the fire cracked and popped into the early hours.

I slid out of my sleeping bag and stretched. There was thin cloud and the trees cast soft shadows across the clearing. 'Where's Casper?' His sleeping bag was folded but there was no sign of him.

'He's gone off to get some drier wood.' She arranged twigs in the white-edged embers. 'Look, Trent, he's not at his best...He's had a rough few weeks with the journey here and Round Up.'

'I know.' I knew he'd been kicked around. I knew that I didn't trust him.

The twigs caught fire and flared up so she added several larger sticks which she snapped first. I knelt beside her and helped. She smelled of wood smoke and dandelion tea. We added sticks for some time, breaking and dropping them onto the growing pile.

She stopped and put her hand on mine. 'Trent...'

'Yes?'

She turned towards me, her eyes soft. Then she kissed me, straight on the lips but with her mouth tight, eyes open.

Pulling away she gripped my hand. 'Casper can get very protective, so…'

'So?'

She slid her hand free, stood and snapped a branch over her knee, keeping me in her gaze. I helped her set up the fire but didn't say anything else.

Casper joined us carrying a pile of dry wood. We made small talk about the weather and how we'd slept. Nothing about Round-Up or leaving town. We stacked the fire before warming tinned sausage and boiling water for tea. As we ate and drank Becky checked the map and Casper stared off into the woods. He'd not said more than a dozen words since we'd left town. Part of it must have been what had happened to him. Being locked in that room alone for days wouldn't have been much fun with Nico dropping in to administer punishment now and then. Gregg keeping him awake all night. Me quizzing him.

When Becky went off to the Eblis, Casper started packing his bag. I approached him. 'How are you doing?'

'Doing?'

'Are you all right?'

'I'm fine.' He carried on stuffing his ripped sleeping bags into the rucksack.

'I know what Nico and Gregg can be like.'

Looking up at me he exhaled slowly. For a moment he didn't move. We were eye to eye. Then he inhaled and carried on packing the bag. 'Yeah, well, I'm out of there.'

When he didn't say any more I stashed my own gear.

Becky came back and packed her stuff, saying how it looked like a nice day and we'd picked a good spot to stop. Chit-chat that I gave short answers to. And Casper ignored. Once everything was away they laid out the map. Becky suggested routes, all back roads, adding to the distance and limiting the speed we could go, but she had a point. If anyone from Round Up had survived they would be in the town's fastest machines: the Jag and Audi A6. Nico's Range Rover. They'd have commandeered every drop of bio-eth available and be out racing after us. The Eblis was better armed but they could dig up a few nasty weapons. There was a chance that Casper had blown some of them to pieces but the weapons were stored at the far end of Round Up Central, where the walls were thickest.

The planned route looked easy enough. There was no easy way through the Lowlands so Becky suggested we skirt Edinburgh. Seemed as good a choice as any. Maybe I'd jump off after that. See what the southern end of the Highlands had to offer. I'd not been up there for since The Collapse.

'Should we head off?' said Becky.

'Suits me,' I said.

Casper just grabbed up his bag and went to the tank.

I wheeled the bike alongside. We'd not talked about fuel stops. Casper and Becky slid their bags into the tank.

'Where are we going to get juice?' I said.

'Juice?' said Casper.

144

'Fuel.'

He laughed but Becky gave me a serious look. 'We don't need to refuel,' she said. 'Didn't Round Up tell you?'

'Seems not.'

She patted the vehicle on the back, near the air vents. 'This was a prototype, the last gasp of the old world.'

'It'll never need refuelling,' said Casper. 'You're standing next one of the few nuclear powered tanks.'

'Right.' I nodded and smiled at this. Tried to seem impressed. For me nuclear meant weapons, or the sludge that lay across the west coast. It wasn't something to trust or feel safe with. Becky and Casper loaded up and chatted about some setting they had to adjust. Something technical.

I stared at the back end of the Eblis, where the reactor had to be. It had lasted for decades. Survived all kinds of military tests, as well as what it went through in Faeston, so it was unlikely to just blow. That was what I told myself. But still there was some doubt about it.

Becky gave me a wave and shut the hatch.

I started the Scrambler. The valves chattered in the cold engine and I revved it up. As the Eblis whirred off I followed after it. Along the rough track through the trees.

When we joined the road, the Eblis shot off but it was too twisty a route for it to pick up much pace. We joined the B road and swung off to the right.

I kept an eye on my mirrors for Nico and co. Watched every movement, waiting to see when they appeared.

We bounced around for a couple of hours, the road hemmed in by thick woods, a light mist hanging over the trees. Midmorning we passed a carved stone at the roadside. *Welcome to Scotland* it said but it was adorned with animal skulls and bones. Spattered with dried mud and pitched at an angle where someone had tried to tip it over. We were in the northern reaches of the Border Forest now, the old plantations merged and spread out. Birch and pine trees had taken over, the ones that were fine with the unreliable weather. It all looked pretty on a sunny day but there were some nasty places round here. Rough villages where the locals had gone feral and killed their neighbour. Stuck them in a stew. I'd seen some of them first hand and didn't want to again. So normally this was somewhere I'd avoid but normally I wasn't travelling with an armoured vehicle.

There was no sign of anyone behind, in front of or to the side of us as we made our way along the track, the Scrambler's motor blatting out. It was actually good to be on the road. It felt natural after all those years I'd spent in the wilds.

The Eblis swung off to the east. We cleared the trees in a few miles and came out onto moorland dotted with saplings and smaller patches of woods.

As we dipped into a valley we past a sign for a town. The original name had been crossed out, scraped off the metal and Pleasure Town painted in uneven lettering. I knew of the place but had steered clear in the past: it was too near the Border Forest. It had a reputation for being lively. Living up to its name.

As we came round a bend several high-pitched thuds came from undergrowth and pinged off the front of Eblis.

Gun fire. Someone was firing at us.

The tank stopped and I hauled the Scrambler up at the far side of it, sheltered from any further shooting. There were no more shots so I stuck my head up over the bulkhead. At the far side of the road there was a patch of stunted sycamores. Several of the branches moved and there were voices. A glimpse of an arm holding a rifle that lined up on the tank.

I ducked back down and there were several more shots. Silence. When I looked up this time something flew into the air, hard surfaced with a flame licking out of it. It sailed over towards us and thudded against the tank with a smash of glass and the smell of methylated spirt. The liquid caught light with a woof and flames rolled across the flank of the vehicle. The meths dripped into the vents at the rear end.

Then there was a rattle from the turret, several shots followed by a few more. They rippled through the undergrowth and one man staggered out and fell forward. Another cried out.

The gun stopped and there was no sound. Just the hiss of the burning meths.

Suddenly a figure burst from the trees. He had another Molotov Cocktail in his hand but before he could throw it the tank's machine gun clattered again. He jerked up and flopped forward. Landed flat on the road where the bottle smashed and its contents flowed out.

He lay still in the pool of fire.

The tank's turret popped open and Casper looked out. 'You hit?'

'No. I'm fine.'

He twisted round to look at the fellas he'd shot. 'Morons, eh?'

'Think we should move him?' I pointed to the man in the road. The flames had now worked their way onto his coat which crackled as it burned. The road off to his right was ablaze as well.

'You kidding?' He looked round at the rear end of the tank. The fire had died down and left sooty marks across metal. He watched them the last few flames fade then he grunted and slid back in.

Clicks and whirrs came from the Eblis. A few seconds later it moved off. The tracks clattered as it picked up speed down the road. I was about to start the Scrambler but instead stepped off and went over to the burning body. I grabbed the arm that wasn't alight then flipped him over and stamped out the flames on the road.

He lay smoking on the singed tarmac, a smallish fella in scruffy coat and threadbare trousers. I grasped his boots and hauled him over to the verge. He slid on his chest and face, arms stretched out and I pulled him in as far as he would go then got hold of his shoulders and rolled him into the bushes. The other two lay splayed further into the undergrowth. There was a pile of weapons beside them: assault rifles, shotguns and more Molotov Cocktails. They were probably the lookouts for the town. They townsfolk would eventually figure out they'd lost some people and get all jumpy. If we were stopping off we'd have to make it a short one.

A few branches were snapped from the tank's shooting so I threw them over the bodies. Roughly covered them up.

With a last look at the dead men I went over to the Scrambler and started off.

There was no sign of the Eblis as I rode down the road. They'd had time to get well ahead. For a few seconds I pushed the bike on hard before easing off. If they'd gone they'd gone. I'd make my own plans.

But then I spotted the tank at the roadside.

Casper was out at the back. Flames licked up the rear of the vehicle. Black smoke billowed out. Becky was beside him holding something. She sprayed clouds of white gas onto the flames, smothering them. It was a fire extinguisher she held: it had been such a long time since I'd seen one I'd not recognised it.

The flames were gone but smoke still poured out.

I pulled up a few metres back and walked over.

She opened up a hatch on the tank's flank and sprayed the extinguisher into the engine compartment. The smoke thinned and stopped.

'What's going on?' I said.

'What's it look like?' said Casper.

Becky leant into the hatch, poking around shaking her head. 'Halon suppression system's not working. Should have put this out…' She muttered on like that for minutes as Casper hopped around.

I waited for the tank to blow itself apart. Or for someone to appear from the trees that edged the road, hawthorns that were split and lopsided, disappearing off around us. Perfect place for another attack.

Becky straightened up and held a cluster of melted wires. 'Cooling fan circuit.'

'Is it fixable?' I said.

Casper grunted and Becky shrugged. There was a noise from the trees, a tapping.

'We need to get moving. They were probably the town's lookouts.'

'Can't go far,' she said. 'And dead slow.'

They climbed back into Eblis. Before Casper had even

shut the hatch they moved off. I remounted the bike and followed as they crept along the road. Into Pleasure Town. The whole way I had my eyes on the roadside ready for another ambush. Some more fellas with guns and homemade weapons.

There was no one, just signs advertising the town's attractions: the drinking horse, the burry king and hag racing. There were a few people on pavements but they staggered around, waved bottles. Looked drunk. Tarnished ribbons hung from broken lampposts and dying trees. The tank swung left onto a side road lined with semi-detached houses. They all had driveways and front gardens but most were windowless, door-less and the gardens were overgrown, littered with debris from the stripped houses.

I stopped at the end. Maybe this was where I disappeared off. Left them to sort out their own problems. I tapped the tank on the bike. Sloshed the fuel around. It was getting low. Really low. There'd be juice here. I rode the bike up and joined the Eblis as it slid onto the drive of one of the derelict houses. It went up the side, through the empty shell of a garage, a skeleton of rusted spars that clattered down around it. It stopped on the lawn with the tracks rested on a rockery. I pulled across to the far side, behind a lopsided shed and gigantic buddleia.

I turned off the bike as Casper and Becky slid out.

The blank windows of the house looked down on us. There were sounds from way off, shouts and music. The place smelled of rotting vegetation. Blocked drains.

'It needs to cool down,' said Becky.

There was a crash from several streets away, cheers. Casper went to the fence and peered over.

'So, can you fix it?' I said.

She shook her head. 'Not without parts. Wire to fix up the cooling circuit.' The tank made whirring noises. A couple of clicks. 'We might be able to get something in town. Might as well have a stop off. While it cools down.'

'We shouldn't hang around. Not after shooting the lookouts.'

Casper kicked the tank's tracks. 'How would they know it was us?'

That was true. Without the tank we didn't look dangerous. Pleasure Town was known for its transient population. Lots of people passed through. 'I'll leave the bike here as well.' It wasn't always wise to ride around towns like this. People took a liking to your bike and wanted it. I'd walk around, find the fuel station if there was one. Ride straight in later on. Leave.

I popped the bike's battery out and grabbed my bag. The battery wedged in with my spare clothes and the shotgun and Gehenna stuff. My little secret.

There was a distant cheer.

'Sounds fun,' said Casper.

'Remember you shot a couple of the locals,' I said.

'Come on,' said Becky. 'Let's get going.'

We left the vehicles and walked into Pleasure Town.

CHAPTER EIGHTEEN

Stop Off

There were drunks everywhere on the way into town: men and women in the road, couples lying on the overgrown verges, having sex, sleeping, fighting.

The town hadn't been somewhere I'd come to when I was couriering, so all I knew about it were the stories. Leery tales of drink and fights, the kind of gossip other drivers rolled out, too exaggerated to take seriously. Or maybe it was all true.

'Pleasure Town tries to live up to its name,' said Becky.

'You know the place?' I said.

'A little.'

We passed a young woman, all smart, in a tight dress that showed plenty of flesh. She looked up at me as we walked by. Her hair was blond with a little curl. Her face soft skinned. It was like seeing Sophie again. She smiled at me and I turned away, carried on walking alongside Becky, Casper marching off ahead.

We came to a row of smart houses, ancient Victorian places with front yards and big windows. Tidy looking. At the end was a workshop, the door open and men repairing a cart. One held it steady on jacks while two others hammered a wheel on.

Becky went up to the fella doing the steadying, asking him something. He shook his head and pointed down the road. Casper watched the party people as they staggered around. Drank and laughed. Even he had a smile on his face.

She returned and we walked on. 'He says there a workshop just off the marketplace. Reckons they might have some wires.'

'Maybe we can get a drink?' Casper turned to me. 'You fancy a beer?'

'Yeah.' I did but not with him. I'd rather he shoved off to find the parts so I could spend some time on my own. Or with Becky.

'Feel like celebrating a little. We've outrun those morons from Faeston.'

'Have you forgotten that the tank needs fixing?' said Becky.

'You'll sort that, Becks. No worries.'

'Well, we'll see. I hope so.'

We came to the town centre with a marketplace surrounded by old buildings. They all seemed to be pubs. There were tables set on the pavements and drinkers sat at them or stood around. In the middle there was some kind of a fight going on. Men rolled around the ground clawing at an object the size of a football but misshapen and ripped. There were a few thugs at the far end with pick axe handles. One rifle between them: Pleasure Town's equivalent to Round Up, no doubt. But they didn't seem bothered by it all. Spectators laughed and drank from earthenware cups.

'It's the town ball,' said Becky. 'They fight over it.'

'Town ball?' I said.

'A football that once belonged to someone famous, I think. Whoever gets to hold it at sunset wins, or something...' Tapping Casper on the shoulder she pointed towards the left-hand side of the marketplace. 'I need to find the workshop. Meet you back here. You two enjoy the game.' With that she walked off.

Me and Casper stood there as the men fought over the ball. People watching laughed as a lad got kicked in the head and went reeling off.

Some town. Still there were plenty of bars all stocked with booze by the look of things.

'Ready for that drink?' I said. Maybe a couple of drinks was what Casper needed. Loosen him up a bit.

'I reckon.'

We shoved our way past the drunks and made our way into the nearest pub. A rough sign said Biffa's Bar.

The interior was decorated with old CDs. Cracked and scratched ones stuck on the wall with nails. The plastic surfaces caught the light and bounced it round the room, onto the bare floorboards and the faces of the men who stood there drinking. There were a few women but they huddled together over at the far side. The place smelled of sweat and stale booze. I ordered a whisky and Casper nodded when I looked over at him so I made it two.

After we'd been served we stood and drank. We were given ceramic tumblers, not glasses. We didn't talk. Outside there were shouts and cheers. No one took any notice of us.

We finished our whiskies. 'Another?' I said. Casper

nodded and called the barman over, ordering two more.

There was a cheer from the marketplace.

The drinks arrived. Casper held his tumbler, stared into it.

At the other side of the room there was movement as two men manhandled a wooden cupboard out of a side room. They shifted it against the far wall and opened the doors. It was an old TV set and DVD player. Wires ran down to a couple of car batteries which themselves were connected to a lead that ran out of the room. Flickering on the screen was a football stadium. We watched as the game started and the players ran around, the image locking up then breaking before resuming. The men clustered round the TV and cheered at the ancient game.

'I don't get football,' said Casper.

'Yeah?' I wasn't a fan myself. But I didn't want some big discussion on it. Not with him.

Heads turned away from the TV set for a moment. A woman had come into the room. She was in her thirties with a good body, wearing a light dress. Her hair was long, blond. It was the woman I'd seen earlier on the way into town. She smiled at Casper. At me, as she approached the bar. She stood at the far end away from the TV set.

'She's a looker,' said Casper.

'She's not bad.'

She moved with a confidence in how she looked, the dress short enough to show smooth, tanned legs; low enough to show plenty of cleavage. She wasn't at all like Sophie and was out of place with the other women in here: big-handed country types.

The barman went over to her, smiled asked her how

she was. She flashed a grin at him then jerked her thumb towards us. He shook his head and went off to get her a drink. Then she came over to me and Casper, one foot in front of the other, a wiggle in her stride to make her body move in the right way.

'Mind if I join you?' she said.

'Fine by me,' said Casper.

I said nothing but looker her up and down. From her blond hair to tanned ankles, taking in everything in-between.

She smiled. 'I'm Maddy.'

'I'm Casper,' said Casper. He pointed at me. 'This is Trent.'

She glanced over at Casper, at the bruises on his face, then back at me. 'You not from town?'

'No,' I said. 'We're on a trip.'

She undid the top button on her dress, pulled the material to let air into it. Her drink arrived, something dark. It was in a glass not like the earthenware beakers we got. She paid and sniffed it before taking a sip. 'I always fancied taking a trip.'

I finished my drink and pushed it across the bar then raised my hand to the barman.

Casper leant over to me. 'You having another?'

I shrugged. 'One more won't hurt.'

Maddy smiled. 'Are you two brothers?'

Casper shook his head and I ordered a whisky and drank it fast. He chatted to Maddy, asked her what she did and sat close while she told him about the shop she worked in. Even though they were side by side her eyes were on me and mine were on her. She moved around, tilting her head back and running her hands across her skin. Maybe it was partially the booze but she really was something.

As he ran out of things to say to her Casper watched the football on the TV and cradled his drink.

Maddy leant over and put her hand on my arm. 'What do you make of the town?'

Outside the scrum still rolled around the marketplace. 'Quite lively,' I said.

She raised her eyebrows and smiled. 'Oh, it's that all right.'

'We need to look out for Becky,' said Casper, eyeballing me.

'Who's Becky?' said Maddy.

'She's with him,' I said.

'I see.' She smiled at this.

'We have to get going,' said Casper.

Maddy looked at me, 'Sounds like big brother wants to move you on.'

'We're not brothers.'

I didn't move and she raised an eyebrow, finished her drink.

'You go. I'll catch you up,' I said. Having a couple of drinks and meeting Maddy had perked me up. Being stuck on the road with Casper and Becky wasn't a barrel of laughs. Now we were out of Faeston I was starting to find myself again. 'Look, Casper, you don't have to stay.'

He played with his beaker. Maddy finished her gin and gave me a smile. I was about to get us more drinks when she shifted her head and stared across the room. She moved back, away from me and dropped her head, her hand raised to her temple.

A man appeared at her side, twenty-something, in a

battered suit, shaven headed, scarred face. 'If it isn't Maddy,' he said. His voice was as thin as the rest of him.

She looked at the floor. 'Hello Noah.'

Noah rocked back and forward on his heels, touched one of the scratches on his face. 'Don't think I know you boys.'

'We're not from here,' I said. I'd met his type before. Big fish in tiny ponds.

Noah whistled a note as if he had a dog to call.

'We're on a trip.'

Casper stared at Noah. Maddy had found something interesting in her glass.

'On a trip?' said Noah. 'That's sounds good. Real fine.'

'We're just going,' said Casper, giving me a hard stare.

There was a cheer on the TV and the men watching sighed and groaned, like they'd no idea what was going to happen.

'Taking a trip is a fine thing to do.' Noah went into his pocket and took out a folded piece of paper. 'Do you boys follow?' He unfolded it and handed it to me. It was all about God and Jesus. How we had to repent for our sins. 'We meet every Sunday.' He smiled and half closed his eyes.

'Great,' I said. Noah didn't worry me. I was happy hanging around in the bar. Near Maddy.

'Not sure we'll be here.' Casper came round to me, leaned up close. 'We need to go. Get back.'

'I'm fine.'

'We need to go.'

'I'm staying.'

Casper shook his head. 'Trent, we need to get going. Meet Becky, you know?'

'You know what? I think I'm staying.'

He stepped back, lips tight. Then he turned and walked out.

Noah made the whistling sound again. 'You boys had a fall out?'

'We're fine.' I was happy for him to go. They could leave. I wasn't that bothered. I was more interested in Maddy.

She gave me a big grin. 'Where are you headed?'

'North.'

'You know,' said Noah. 'I think you should follow your friend. Carry on with that road trip of yours.'

'Maybe I will.'

He smiled at this.

As I moved away from the bar stool he walked backwards, his index finger pointed at me. He said no more and sidled out of the room.

'You're going?' said Maddy.

'At some point.'

'Fancy a few drinks? Elsewhere?'

'Why not.'

She took my hand and led me out of the bar a side way, into an alleyway that ran round the back, along cobbles that stank of piss and vomit, into a narrow lane. We passed men with women, men with men, women with women. Couples entwined as they kissed or screwed on the ground.

Maddy gave me a smile and led me to a red door with a polished plaque at the side. It had some symbol I didn't recognise and there was a knob below it. She pulled this three times and the door opened. A large woman in a tight dress let us in. She was heavily made up and equally heavily built. When she spoke I realised she was a he.

We went along a dark corridor of worn carpet into a long room set with tables. There was a bar at the far end and a small stage to our right, all lit by candles dotted around. She waved to the barman and took us to a table by the wall.

There was a performance on the stage: a woman dressed as a ballerina held a beach ball and shifted it around. There was no music or pattern to what she did. After a while she stopped and bowed forward and people clapped.

'What do you think?' Maddy said.

'I don't think I get it.'

'What do you think of the club?'

I looked around at the heavy wood furnishings and deep carpet. The dark wallpaper and coving. It had probably been a nice place at one time. Sophisticated. It was rather creepy now. But Maddy was worth being there for. With her slim body in that dress. 'It's lovely.'

She grinned. 'People like Noah don't know about this. He can't get in here.'

'Right.'

'It's our secret.'

The barman brought a bottle over and two glasses. I poured out a drink for each of us. It was some kind of wine, dark red. Maddy sipped, looked at me, into me.

I tried the wine. It was strong, sour tasting. Metallic. She laughed at my reaction then moved her chair round so she was next to me.

'I like you Trent.'

'I like you too.'

She took my hand and put it on her thigh, on the warm

material of her dress. We stayed like that for a while. She drank more and tipped some into my glass. I pretended to drink it but spat it back. It really was bad.

Another act came on, this time a man in a suit but with makeup and deer antlers. He moved around the stage with his hands in front of him like he was riding a horse. It's was odd but I didn't really care.

'I need to go to the toilet,' said Maddy.

'All right.'

While she was away the man carried on with his act. People came in and went. Some were transvestites like the fella on the door. There were a few gay couples as well. It crossed my mind that Maddy could have been more than she seemed. Maybe she wasn't quite what I'd thought.

I took a sip of the wine. Spat it back into the glass. There was a new sound in the room, a deep hum but when I looked around I couldn't work out where it came from.

Maybe I should have gone with Casper. Found Becky and left. I still could. The bike was still there. All my gear was in my bag on the floor at my side. But I needed fuel. At some point I'd ask Maddy if anywhere in town sold petrol or similar.

She slid back into her seat. 'Miss me?'

'Yeah.'

I gave her a good looking over, tried to work out if she was an attractive woman or a fella dressed up as an attractive woman. It was hard to say: she had good legs and her tits looked real but none of that proved anything. Her voice wasn't deep but again, there were ways round that. There was only one real test and that was hard to set up with someone you'd just met.

'You all right, Trent?'

'Yeah. What is this place?'

'Somewhere safe. For the misfits of the town. People who don't fit in.'

'Right.'

She took a drink and leaned towards me. 'I know what you're thinking.'

'You do?' I doubted that.

'What makes me a misfit?' She sat back and smiled.

'Yeah.' That was close enough.

The man finished his act and leapt off the stage. Ran through the room and out past the bar. People laughed.

Maddy took my hand and put it back on her thigh. 'My problem is I like company too much. Different company. Different men. Women in this town aren't meant to do that kind of thing.' She slid my hand into her dress, further up her thigh, to the top. She had no underwear on. There was just soft flesh. Warm. Nothing to worry about. She slid my hand back and let go. Then she moved over towards me, closed her eyes and kissed me.

When she pulled away her smile and changed. Eyes softened. For a second she stared at me before she took her wine glass, drank it all. Moved over to me again and kissed but this time with a mouthful of the wine. She forced it down my throat so that I nearly gagged. I swallowed it before I choked.

After that she sat on my knee. Topped up my glass and shared it with me. Bit by bit I got a taste for it.

She ordered food, a couple of small cakes and a smaller bottle of wine, this time sweeter.

'What is this stuff?' I said.

She laughed. 'You know what it is.'

'I need to ask you something.'

'Oh yeah?'

'I've forgotten what it is.' I'd lost my thread.

We drank and ate and kissed some more. More acts came on but they were much better. Similar themes but funnier; sharper. The man with the false head was the best. It was made of wood or something but I found it really funny. Maddy laughed a little but not as much as me.

Once we'd finished the second bottle she stood up and took my hand. 'You going to walk me home?'

'Yeah.'

I followed her out along the passageway. Up the lane and across town. There were several of the law-enforcement men hanging round at a crossroads. One came towards us as we lurched up the pavement but his companions pointed at Maddy and said something. They both laughed and went back to where they'd been. A thought crossed my mind about the tank and Becky and Casper. About the bike. But it was soon gone. The town lurched around us as Maddy led me on. Every now and then she'd stop and drag me into a doorway. Pull me tight against her as she clamped her mouth on mine.

At last we came to an old building, a tall place that reeled around in front of us. She unlocked the door and hauled me up all these stairs, up and up and up, bursting into a room with a bed and wardrobe and chair and little else.

Without wasting time she pulled her dress up, flicked it onto the floor and helped me strip off. We flopped into bed and then she was all over me and I was all over her. The room spun around us as we crawled over each other, round each other and into each other. As we twisted and bent into one person that breathed and sighed and groaned together.

CHAPTER NINETEEN

Night Over

I woke with Maddy lying splayed out in the bed next to me, naked. The sheet was rolled up at the far end. Sunlight shone through the curtains to light the ceiling where wallpaper hung down in curled strips.

I slid out of bed and stared down at her slim body. As her tits rose and fell. A slight twitch in her left thigh tugged at her skin. She took a deep breath and turned over. I pulled on my clothes and went to the bathroom. My head hurt and the room swayed as I went.

Only one of the sink's taps worked and it trickled out brown water. When the basin was half full I dunked my head in, opened my eyes under the water. Stared at the distorted plug. The cold water shocked the pain out of me. For a moment.

I straightened up and stared into the cracked mirror at my face split and dripping. That had been some night.

After using the toilet I went back into the room. Maddy had pulled the covers over her. I wasn't sure what to do: leave or hang around. It had been fun. Maybe I'd stay around for a while. Spend some time in Pleasure Town. They'd be work to do here. I could stay somewhere. Maybe here with Maddy. Casper and Becky'd be really pissed off with me. If they'd even waited.

I was tempted to wake Maddy. Have some fun with her. But I knew how it was with women, with anyone, when they got woken up too early. There was no point pissing her off. I went round to the side of the bed and grabbed up my clothes and slid them on. I could easily take them off again, if that was what she fancied. My jacket lay on a chair. I slid it on and went through the pockets. There was still a roll of cash. The pistol and keys for the scrambler. I looked around for my bag. There was no sign of it so I dropped down and searched under the bed. Still no sign.

The bag had to be around. That had my spare clothes in it, the bike battery. A shotgun, crowbar and roll of cash. The Gehenna stuff.

I went into the bathroom. Then back to the bed. Under the bed. Under her dress. In the wardrobe and under the chair.

When I turned round Maddy was awake. Staring at me. 'Trent?'

'I've lost my bag.'

She laughed. 'Good morning to you too.'

'It's got all my stuff in it.'

She flopped back and closed her eyes. 'It'll be around.'

'I can't afford to lose it.'

She opened her eyes again. 'Okay.' She slid out of bed, walked into the bathroom and shut the door. Even her bare backside couldn't take my mind off the lost bag.

I checked round the room several more times then sat in the chair and gazed out of the window. There was an overgrown playing field opposite where lads threw something back and forth. The shouted and ran around.

Maddy came out of the bathroom, still naked. 'Any sign of the bag?'

'No.' Part of me wanted to say fuck the bag, let's spend the morning in bed. But that was all I had. All my stuff.

She opened the wardrobe and took out a red dress. Dropped it over her head. Then she popped on her shoes from the night before. 'Ready?'

'What for?'

'Let's go look for it.'

She led me out of the building and onto the main road. I had no memory of walking along here the night before. We took it slowly and examined overgrown hedges and front gardens. Doorways and alleys.

At last we came to the club. She pulled the handle and we waited.

'Might be no one there,' she said.

'Right.'

Then the door opened. It was the man from the night before but no longer dressed as a woman. He was in an old suit with his hair parted down the left-hand side.

'Maddy?' he said.

'We lost something last night.'

He stepped aside. 'Didn't we all?'

I followed her through to the main room, empty of people and the bar shuttered. Its curtains open. The decor was more faded. Less creepy.

At the side of a table was my bag. I went to it and opened it up, raked through. Everything seemed to be there.

She smiled. 'Happy?'

'Yeah.'

'You owe me a drink.'

'Think I do.'

We walked out and back into the lane, along the passageway to the pub I'd first met her in, the one by the marketplace. There was nothing going on outside but a few men were crowded in the bar watching football again.

'Is this all that happens here?'

'Pretty much,' she said.

I ordered myself a whisky but Maddy cupped her hand around the barman's ear. Asked for something special. The drinks came, hers in a glass, mine in a tumbler, and we sat on bar stools.

'That was some evening,' I said.

'Sure was.'

'You always this lively?'

'Sometimes worse.'

We drank some more and talked. I reckoned Casper and Becky were long gone so there was no rush. No need to worry. I had my bag and time to spend with Maddy. There was just one more thing I needed to sort out. 'Is there anywhere to get fuel round here? Petrol?'

She shrugged. 'There's a place down by the old railway station. They sell all sorts…'

'Fair enough.'

'You planning on leaving?'

'Not necessarily.'

She smiled at this.

As I ordered our third drinks Casper came in.

'Where the hell have you been, Trent?'

'Here and there,' I said.

Maddy laughed. 'Are you sure he's not your brother?'

Casper flushed. 'We've been all over the place for you. Hung around all night.'

I took a drink, let it go down. 'You should have gone without me.'

'Well, I would have. But Becky, she'd have hung around here for days. In this dump.'

'Tut-tut,' said Maddy.

Casper was hopping around at this. All wound up. It was only a little fun at his expense.

But it turned sour when Noah came in. He walked over and stood by us.

'Well, well,' he said.

I smiled. 'Hello.'

'Still here. Still here. I wonder why?' He put his arm around Maddy and she recoiled. 'Maddy here, she's like a candle to a fly. Dirt to roach. Isn't that right, Maddy?'

Maddy nodded.

There was swearing from the men watching the football.

'So what you boys planning on doing?' said Noah.

'Not sure,' I said. 'I might stay around.'

Noah raised an eyebrow. 'That so? That so? I'm sure Maddy will have shown you the sights, I don't doubt.' He put his arm tighter around her. She shrunk back. 'Oh, I'm sure Maddy has obliged. Maddy is so very obliging.'

Casper leant forward. 'We're not staying, we're going. Now.'

'Are we?' I said.

'Well,' said Noah. 'Seems you boys can't agree.' He released Maddy and smiled. Then he put his hand on my shoulder. 'We have a community round here. See, people like Maddy,' he smiled and looked at her and she looked away. 'People like Maddy need watching over.'

'She seems capable of looking after herself.' I'd met plenty of tough guys like him before. Little men who liked to push women around.

'Maybe I'm not making myself clear.' He straightened up. 'You should have left yesterday. Not hung around. Now you have to pay your dues. Settle with the townsfolk.'

Casper stepped backwards. 'Come on.'

'We don't just let people wander in. Do as they wish. Just as you have, boys. If you come over to my office. Hand over a few commodities we'll see that as fair. A fair tax.' He gave Maddy a good looking over.

'I don't think so,' I said, leaning over to Maddy. I was buoyed up by the drink. Not scared of Noah and his rules and I put my hand on Maddy's knee. This seemed to be too much for him and he turned red and started opening and closing his hands. The rhythmic motion carried on for a few seconds until he flicked a punch out at Casper, catching him on the chest, a weak swing but enough to unbalance him. He reeled back, his hands outstretched as Noah pulled back his arm for another shot. In one move I stood up between them and hit Noah in the face.

It was a short right-hander that cracked him under the jaw. I'd not planned to do it but it happened automatically. Without any thought. His teeth snapped together and his head bounced back before he slumped forward. He made some noise like he couldn't breath and grabbed the bar, his head on Maddy's thigh. There was a roar from the crowd on the television but the bar was silent. Everyone watching us.

Noah straightened up. His eyes were rolled up in his

head so only the whites showed. He banged his temple and his eyes rolled back into place like they'd been jammed. He grabbed Maddy's glass and smashed it on the bar. The sound was an explosion and everyone stepped back, away from us. The base of the glass was intact with jagged edges.

He moved towards me and Casper.

'Don't,' said Maddy, 'don't Noah.' She was behind him, on her feet and she held his arm, pulled him back.

Noah shook her off, waved the broken glass around. 'Get away you, you whore!' He turned towards me. 'You could have gone. You could have walked out and left town, but you had to do this.'

'I think you started this,' I said.

He touched the blood on his lip and waved the glass. He circled until he was between us and the door.

'Put it down,' Casper said. Noah kept waving the glass and Maddy put her hands to her face. Everyone else in the bar watched.

Noah lunged at me and I stepped aside as it sliced through the air. 'You could have moved on and everyone would have been fine.' He jabbed the glass at me.

'Just put it down,' said Casper and he moved back.

I kept back but watched how Noah moved, which way he went with the glass. It was always to his right away from his body. I kept to his left.

'You had your chance and well...' Noah moved around and again lunged towards us. He thrust at Casper, to the right again. As he did so I caught his forearm, grabbed it tight. Noah cried out and I twisted, forced him down.

'You can't do this!' he said.

Then I swung down my free hand and struck him on

the side of the jaw, catching him hard. His body went limp and he collapsed onto the floor. The glass thudded onto the floorboards.

Everyone looked at me and Casper. We stared at Noah on the ground. Maddy backed away from him and us. She drifted across the room. Then one man shouted. It wasn't a word, more some kind of sound.

'Go,' said Casper.

As two men went to Noah I dashed outside, Casper close behind me. We joined the crowd in the marketplace and shoved through.

A gang of men piled after us.

'Run!' I shouted. We sprinted up the main road, away from the town centre.

CHAPTER TWENTY

Lynch Mob

The gang came after us, as we ran past a car park where old cars were dumped, rusted and door less. I thought about ducking in but we'd easily be spotted. The gang were a few metres back but the road was straight. We were exposed.

Casper was level with me. His breath came out in rasps, his hands knotted as he swung his arms out. My chest was tight and the top of my legs stung. But I couldn't slow. The gang shouted and something clattered on the road beside us.

'They'll get us,' said Casper.

I didn't answer, conserving my breath, but he was right. We were ahead of them but we'd not outrun everyone in the gang. Not in a town we didn't know.

We turned a corner, the first one we'd come to and passed an old stone church. There was a churchyard next to it. Leading into it was a track. I swung onto it picking up the pace. I hoped that Casper did the same but didn't wait or look for him. I pushed on over rocky ground between the headstones.

I ducked behind one and knelt down. As I took in great lungfuls of air I looked across at the gravestones, all with names and ages. Some were original carved stone but others were bits of concrete with names scrawled on.

Casper dropped down beside me. 'What now?'

'Wait.'

Footsteps thundered past on the road, accompanied by shouts. They'd soon realise we'd ducked out.

I raised up onto my haunches. 'Let's head off.' I led Casper off through the churchyard, past the cockeyed stones. We needed to hide out for a while or find another way back to the tank and bike. Get away from the town.

Across the road was a wooden shack with crates of malformed vegetables set in front. I pushed the rickety door open and went in. There were no windows and it was lit by a couple of tallow candles set upon a shelf. An old man stood behind the counter, his filthy face framed by a grey beard, tangled and knotted. The shelves around the room were dotted with tins and jars. Old-world wood with their labels faded.

'Is there another way out of here?' I said.

He didn't reply, his eyes on me, dark pebbles.

'We need to get across town.'

He shrugged but didn't speak.

Casper stepped forward and grabbed him by his shirt. 'Is there a back door?'

The man's faced twisted up and he jerked a thumb towards the far corner of the room. There were a couple of panels made into a rough door. A piece of rope held it shut. I opened it and stepped out into a dark lane of greasy flagstones. Sludge oozed out of the blocked drains and lank weeds grew out of the brickwork. At the far end was a steel gate that led to a road.

Casper followed out, dragging the man. The three of us walked along the lane, our feet sliding on the stones. There was no sound of the gang. The gate was locked with a heavy padlock

'Open it,' said Casper.

The man he pulled out a key and slid it into the lock, rattling it around until it turned, taking forever. Once it was off I pulled the bolt and rasped the gate open.

There was no one on the road so Casper and me walked out onto a pavement of flaked tarmac. The man slid the gate shut behind us.

'Thanks,' I said.

He didn't answer, just did up the padlock and shuffled off.

'Which way?' said Casper.

I pointed off to my left, what I reckoned was the right way, past rows of terraced housing, many with boarded windows. There was still no sign of the gang. Maybe they'd given up and gone back to the pub. Or run off in the wrong direction.

We walked fast but didn't break into a run. Casper started to skip off but I grabbed his sleeve, slowed him down. We didn't want to attract attention. The road was empty with only a couple of people on the pavement: an old man sweeping up and a girl sitting on a doorstep. He brushed away and she stared at the clouds of dust. Neither paid any attention to us.

'What was that about you staying?' said Casper.

'Just talk.'

'You spent the night with that woman?'

'What do you care?'

He grunted and we carried on.

We had to turn off to the right at some point to get back to the Eblis. With any luck Becky was waiting for us. I'd have to take a chance with fuel. At least we'd have some firepower with the tank.

We came to a junction with a larger road. Several old women stood and chatted and a couple of kids jumped around on the pavement. No sign of the gang.

'This way,' I said to Casper, pointing right. It seemed to be the right way.

Halfway down down the road there were several lads hanging around. They stood by some wasteland, the remains of a demolished building. They had an edginess, a rough look to them. Possibly they were from the gang we were on the run from. There were no side roads between us and them so I kept on walking.

Casper nudged me. 'Are they from the pub?'

'I'd think so.'

'What should we do?'

'Fake it.'

We should have split up and taken different routes. But we hadn't and here we were. If we ran they'd be right on us, and at best, we'd end up in the wrong part of town. As it was there was a slight chance they'd not recognise us.

'Make small talk; keep walking,' I said. It wasn't much of a plan but it was about all I could come up with. Casper didn't seem to have any ideas.

The lads stopped milling around and gave us an eyeball. One in particular was keen to look us over. At least Noah and Maddy weren't with them. That really would have stirred it up.

I walked straight ahead as if in a hurry to get somewhere, which I was really.

A young fella in a checked shirt stepped forward. 'Where you off to?'

'Just heading home,' I said all surprised.

'Where's home?'

I pointed ahead. There was no use making up a street name and I couldn't remember the one we'd parked on.

'Sussex Drive,' said Casper.

The lad twisted his mouth up. 'No one lives there.'

'We do.'

'The whole place is dropping apart.'

'That's where we live.'

From the across the derelict land more lads appeared and walked into the middle of the road. That was our exit blocked.

For a few seconds we stood there with the gang looking at us.

Then the lad grabbed Casper. He gripped his shirt and pulled it tight. 'You're the two from the pub.'

There were mutters from the others. Some picked up bricks and stones from the waste ground. Now we were stuck.

'Call Noah,' said a voice.

There was a cheer.

The fella tugged at Casper's shirt. 'We don't like trouble makers.'

Casper opened and closed his mouth saying nothing. There were too many of them to take on and they were winding up. They crowded round us.

'We're just on our way home,' said Casper. It was feeble but it cooled them down a little.

Then they all looked along the road. I expected to see Noah and a lynching mob but instead it was a vehicle.

With a rumble the Eblis thundered towards us. A voice boomed from the tank, electronic and amplified but clearly Becky's. 'Step away,' she said.

The lads didn't move.

'Step away. All of you.'

They still didn't shift.

Then the tank's gun fired, bullets thudding into the ground near them.

'Step back,' she said.

Apart from the man holding Casper they moved away. After a moment he too let go and stepped aside. The Eblis stopped before us. The turret popped open and Casper ran over to it. He wasted no time, jumping up, sliding in. The men glared at me as I followed but no one said a thing. My bike was strapped to the back and the tank's panels were all closed, hopefully with the engine fixed. As I slid into the turret I saw more men coming up the road to join the gang. Maybe one of them was Noah but I didn't hang around to see.

I eased myself through the narrow entrance and dropped down inside, closing the hatch behind me.

Inside it smelled of oil, stale air and some kind of chemical. There were no window just lights, cold electric light that left few shadows. Becky was at the front with monitor screens and levers, presumably the driver's position, where I'd expected Casper to sit. He was at the front of the turret and waved me into a seat at the back. He handed me some headphones, heavy things, not like the ones I'd had as a kid. He had a set for himself and Becky already wore a pair. He plugged them into a socket near him. There was one beside me so I pushed my connector in and a monitor lit beside me. Becky pulled one lever and pushed the other and there was a whirring from behind. The tank pivoted round in the road. It swung through 180 degrees and the scene on the monitor blurred for second, then settled onto an empty road. There were thumps as objects hit the hull, as the crowd regained their courage.

Casper opened a rear compartment and slid out a shell, a massive round of ammunition. He unlocked the breech on the gun and loaded it, pushed up a lever. Then the turret turned with a slow whine, so that it faced backwards. On the monitors I saw the mob behind us, waving planks of wood and holding bricks and stones. One man leant back, flicked his arm and a rock sailed through the air and bounced off the tank's flank.

Casper raised a cover on a button and pressed it. There was a roar and the Eblis rocked back on its suspension. The screens were dark with smoke. When it cleared the mob were all crouching down. A building behind them was filled with smoke and bricks rained down into its shattered interior. Beside it was a pile of rubble.

Becky hauled on the controls and we moved off and headed out of the town. Her voice crackled over the headphones again. 'Thought we'd lost you, Trent.'

'Seems not.'

'You okay about your bike being tied onto the tank? We were careful strapping it on.'

'That's fine.' It suited me for now, seeing as I was low on juice. 'Is the Eblis fixed?'

'Hope so.'

I glanced up at Casper who was watching me, his lips

tight. It was only when I kept his gaze he eventually looked away.

We drove out of the town, past the drunks and partiers. By the derelict houses. We turned off to the left at a roundabout, before the spot we'd been attacked, and joined the old by-pass, heading north.

'So where did you get to?' Becky said.

'I got lost,' I said. I wasn't going to let on that I'd planned to stay. Hang out with Maddy in Pleasure Town. It hadn't worked out and maybe it had always been a crazy idea. Now we were back on the road.

And that felt fine.

CHAPTER TWENTY-ONE

Onwards

The Eblis rumbled along the empty road. We were surrounded by open moorland with patches of trees, the Border Forest now thinned to occasional copses. Along the roadside there was the odd vehicle, picked so clean it was hard to recognise as a car.

I'd traded up here before but not much further north. Not as far as Becky and Casper were planning to go. To Arcadia or whatever the place was called. I'd be off before then. As soon as I had some juice.

It was difficult to imagine what they described existing, this ideal town. Decent people who welcomed strangers.

The only place that sounded similar was Shangri-La. Gary's community of peace and tranquillity. Set in woodland in north-east Northumberland with orchards and gardens of soft fruit. Chickens and sheep. Not that they even ate any of the animals. It was like some kind of oasis. A bubble of ideals in an idealess world.

But that was Gary.

In all the time I'd know him he'd never even lost his

temper. Not really. There had been one occasion where he'd got annoyed. The time I'd turned up to buy some home-grown.

I'd been in the Lotus then, that great car I'd once had.

I'd driven up past the prayer-flags and wind chimes. Parked in the courtyard with whitewashed buildings. He came out all friendly, dressed in the usual home-knitted thing but he started hopping around when I said I wanted to buy some grass, his big bearded face all creased up.

'I don't deal!' he said, 'It's not that kind of place!'

'All right, Gary. Sorry.'

He walked off shaking his head and I followed him, right the way through the building with its batiks and cushions, all the way to the greenhouses. They grew grapes, peppers and cucumbers alongside a few dope plants. Delicate stuff that needed the warmth. The glass was reclaimed from old shops and offices. Abandoned buildings in towns. It had taken him years to get all together but Shangri-La was his long-term project.

'Here,' he said, thrusting a bag of dried grass at me. 'Have it. I don't deal but I'm happy to give. To friends.'

So I took it and rolled up, staying around in the evening for one of his impromptu music sessions. There were tables with containers of fruit wine. Cider and pickled walnuts. Several young men and women drummed and danced. Laughed and sang. I smoked and joined in until I was too worn out to move.

Yeah, Gary had good parties.

The next day I'd driven off, through the woods with the scent of wild flowers and chimes ringing in the breeze.

I loved Shangri-La but didn't really fit it. It was a place for me to visit. No more than that.

Maybe this Arcadia was going to be the same.

Now we'd got away from Faeston, left Round Up, there was nothing holding me to anywhere, anyone. There was no need for me to go all the way into the Highlands.

Becky swung the Eblis round, dropping the speed, half of what we'd been doing. We turned off the track, heading cross-country. The tank crawled across the rough ground. It pitched and bounced.

'What's up?' I said.

'Trying to break the route up. Make us harder to track,' she said.

'You think Round Up are still after us?'

'There's a chance.'

There was a chance but it was getting fairly slim. We'd not seen a sign of them. Even if any of them had survived there was a lot of ground to cover.

If they'd survived.

We were safe enough in the Eblis. It was well armoured and had plenty of firepower.

The engines droned and I rocked from side to side. Side to side. After the adrenalin buzz of being chased I was settling down. I closed my eyes.

Then I was being shaken. Casper had hold of me.

Although the Eblis was moving it had slowed right down. Becky pressed buttons and tapped one of the dials.

'What's now?' I said.

'We need to stop,' she said. 'We're overheating,'

'I thought it was fixed?'

'Seems not,' said Casper.

'It's been creeping up again.' Becky hauled on the levers and the vehicle stopped. It settled down on its suspension. There were whirrs and clicks from behind me.

Swooshing sounds and buzzing.

Casper opened the hatch and climbed out. As Becky flicked switches and took readings I followed Casper. We were on moorland that rolled off in all directions. There were a couple of stunted pines nearby but these were the only trees to be seen. To the far south there were low hills. All other directions looked the same: gorse, heather and rough grass, laid out below creamy grey clouds. There was no one. No sound.

Becky came out and went straight to the rear of the vehicle. Casper joined her. They grabbed hold of the bike. Undid the straps and started to manhandle it off the back off the vehicle. I went and helped, making sure Casper didn't trash it in his haste to help Becky. We lowered the bike down and Casper jumped back up to the turret, leaning in. There were clicks from several servos under the rear bulkhead and Becky pulled at the handles on the hatches. She lifted up the largest panel and the smell of burning plastic came out.

While she ferreted around I checked over the Scrambler. There was a dent on its tank from where a something had hit it, probably thrown by one of the mob in town. Several stones had jammed between spokes and there was a piece of wood wedged in the cooling fins. I picked them all out and bounced the bike on its forks. Set it on its side-stand.

Becky was still poking around under the hatch. Casper stood at her side but didn't do anything.

After a while she straightened up, holding a blackened wire with a lump of melted plastic at the end. 'Guess my patch-up didn't hold.'

'Can you fix it?' I said.

'We need parts. The right parts.' She stared at Casper, like the was something they knew but didn't want to tell me.

'Go on,' I said.

Becky looked down at the busted part. 'We'll have to go to The Graveyard.'

For a moment none of us spoke.

Of course I knew of The Graveyard, everyone who worked the borders did, but I'd never been tempted to go there. It had once been a military base, full of activity in the last century and up until the twenties. But after the wars they'd used it as a dumping ground, one of many round the country. They'd left equipment there that couldn't be easily fixed. Once Collapse came the place was abandoned, the weapons were disabled or taken off for reuse, some in central Europe, others God-knows where. But they couldn't neuter everything and there were stories of a few gems still lying around.

There were also rumours about the gangs who hung out nearby, watching the place, using it as a lure to add to their booty. I'd heard enough about what they did to unwanted guests so I'd steered clear in the past. There were safer ways to make a living.

'Does it have to be The Graveyard?' I said.

'We'll find the right parts there. Proper military stuff.'

We'd have to double back to go to there, clipping the western edge of the Border Forest.

'The Graveyard's not somewhere just to drop into,' I said.

'That's the only place we'll find parts.'

'It's too dangerous and we're losing time. We can take it slowly. Not go.'

Becky stared at me. 'We need the parts.' She turned to Casper. 'What do you think?'

'Let's get the parts,' he said.

'I need to take a leak,' I said.

I went over to one of the nearby pines and pissed against it. Above me dead branches rattled against one another as the piss hissed down the trunk and onto the dry earth.

I did up my trousers and walked back over.

'Look,' said Becky. 'The Graveyard isn't a great place but we need to go there.'

'I thought you'd fixed the problem.'

'So did I.'

I was happy to hitch a ride in the Eblis but I wasn't interested in getting drawn into something else. Go somewhere like The Graveyard. The bike ready to run and I had all my kit. I'd be able to grab fuel somewhere else. This was a sensible time to leave.

'Tell you what,' I said. 'I'm off.'

'What?' she said.

'I'm leaving. Going off alone.'

'Come on, Trent…'

'I told you,' said Casper. 'I said he'd bail.'

I stared at him. 'Did you? That's good.'

Becky raised her hand. 'Trent, think about this. We're close to the Border Forest here. You don't want to be wandering around. On your own.'

'I'll be all right.'

Casper smiled. A nasty grin. 'What about fuel? Nowhere sells petrol round here.'

'And there's Round Up. They're probably still on our tail.' She took a deep breath. 'Let's fix the Eblis. Get away from here. If you still want to leave you can. Don't rush off. Not yet. At least wait until we're further north.'

'I'll see.' Actually, she had a point. I didn't want to run out of fuel near the Border Forest. But it was good to let off a little steam. Show Becky and Casper I had options.

I stared off across the moors. Dark clouds hung over the hills in the distance. Looked like there was a storm on the way.

'So, Trent?' said Becky.

I shrugged and she returned to the tank. Waited as she slid in. Dropped into the hatch before Casper. We all took our places and set off again.

Off towards The Graveyard.

CHAPTER TWENTY-TWO

The Graveyard

It was another hour before we came close to the place, old MOD signs marking its location, mist drifting in from the moors as sound dipped onto the moors in the west. Becky stopped us on the road in front of the entrance. There was no movement, nothing on the screens or the through the headphones. Maybe there was no one here. If there was, maybe they'd leave something like the Eblis alone. Maybe.

Becky turned towards me. 'We'll be straight in, pick up the parts and off.'

'It'll be easier in better light.' I said. As the mist thickened and rolled in around us.

Casper laughed. 'You scared, Trent?'

'Being stupid doesn't make you brave.'

Casper took a breath ready to say something smart.

'Look Trent,' said Becky. 'We'll be no time. And we've got enough kit here to look after ourselves.'

'Yeah Trent. Don't worry.'

I didn't even bother replying. I was stuck with the two

of them for the time being and there was no point winding Casper up. Not yet.

Becky drove off but slower than ever. 'We'll keep down to crawler speed. It's quieter.' We passed a bust up gatehouse, its barrier lying at the side. The road was chewed up and where there'd been a car-park there was now an untidy field dotted with barriers. We faced a row of low buildings, some of the windows boarded and others smashed. To the right was a small housing estate, many with doors kicked in and tiles missing. The road carried on round to the left. Wrecked equipment emerged from the fog: a burnt-out car, stripped of parts. A pile of odd shoes in a misshapen cairn.

When we came round the building there was a flat open space, probably once the parade ground. In the distance were the frames of hangers and warehouse, all without walls and roofs, open to the moors and stunted trees that surrounded the camp. Before us were rows of vehicles, armoured cars, tanks and aircraft, all mottled with corrosion, panels missing.

Becky stopped the Eblis before them, shutting down the motors and watching her own monitors. 'Any movement out there?' she said.

'You asking me?' I said.

'Flick the switches. It'll give you different views.'

I pressed buttons under the screen and the images changed colour. Got bigger and smaller. Apart from weeds moving in the breeze there was nothing. 'All clear,' I said.

'And me,' added Casper.

Becky grabbed a pistol, jumped out of her seat. I moved aside and so did Casper to let her out. The two of us watched our screens as she slid down off the tank and made towards the vehicles.

'Are you joining her?' I said.

'You kidding?' He grinned like he'd said something funny. When I didn't smile he looked more serious. 'I'm on the guns. Just in case.'

'Yeah? Think I'll head out.' I took the revolver out of my bag, pushed past him and went out after her.

The damp air muffled my footsteps as I clambered down the tank. Becky was ahead of me, scanning the wrecks. I joined her on the cracked tarmac, amongst the rows of vehicles, decaying buildings and abandoned clothing.

'Trent?'

'Thought I'd tag along.'

'Keep your eyes open.'

Apart from a sigh of wind through the undergrowth, there was no sound. With my pistol raised I walked over to the derelicts. There were dozens of them, great beetles that disappeared off into the mist. The paint was burnt off most to show white-corroded alloy and orange rust. Those with wheels wore tireless rims and the tanks had snapped or missing tracks.

'Seems deserted,' she said.

'Seems so.' Maybe I'd worried about nothing.

'Casper can stay in the Eblis. Watch the monitors.'

'Very brave.'

She ignored my dig and walked around the ruined vehicles, tapping the flank of a tracked personnel carrier. 'Looks like they've been used for weapons testing.'

The rear end was blasted clean of paint and melted round the edges, the metal warped. 'Take some weapons to do this.'

She turned and marched back to the tank, disappearing into the fog. A minute later she came back out, shaking her head. 'I'd not thought to check the readings. They're high.'

'Readings?'

'They're radioactive, Trent. They've had nuclear weapons tested on them. Part of the Final Push.'

I stepped back from the nearest tank, as if that would make any difference. I knew about some of the stuff the military had got up to. The last phase had been called the Final Push. Everything had been thrown at that. Nearly everything.

She wandered off between the vehicles and I followed.

'Is this safe?'

'For a short time,' she said.

Maybe that was what had finished off the gangs. They could have fallen sick. Died.

As we walked around she gave me a running commentary on what she thought had been done to each of the vehicles. It seemed not all of them had been nuked. Some seemed to be just worn out or damaged in practice sessions. She guessed they'd originally planned to use some for parts, but The Collapse had meant that had never happened.

Then she stopped. We were beside a huge wreck, bigger than the Eblis. Bigger than anything else. She circled it and her hand reached out as if she wanted to touch it but was afraid to.

'Is this useful?' I said.

'No. It's the FV5035. Came out before the Eblis. Different mechanicals.'

'Tell me about the Eblis.'

'You know all about it.' She moved off then stopped at another vehicle. It had a bulldozer blade and no turret but otherwise was similar to the Eblis. 'This was the 5050AVRE. Earlier model but close. Might be able to get something from it.'

'You know your stuff.'

'Hope so.'

Although the paintwork was stripped, the panels were still intact. There were a couple of wheels missing and no tracks.

She climbed onto it and tried to open the hatch. She pulled at a lever and poked around the hinges. After a minute of messing with it she swore and came back down.

'All sealed up.'

I waved the pistol. 'Can't we shoot our way in?'

She shook her head. 'No chance. But I think I can get in.'

I followed her back to the Eblis where she went inside and rummaged around. The light was fading as I shuffled on the overgrown parade ground. There was no sound from Casper inside. With the mist around us, the moors and buildings had already vanished. The tanks were just dark outlines.

Becky appeared with a multi-metre and some wires. She had a torch but no pistol. 'This should help.'

'Maybe we should head off. Come back tomorrow. Leave it for now.' Running away wasn't what I usually did but this place had too many dark corners. Maybe the gangs had gone. Or maybe they were still here. Watching us.

'Be finished in no time.' She walked back to the big

tank, her footsteps light, unaffected by the creeping darkness.

I stood at the side as she climbed up and messed with the hatch, holding the torch in her mouth as she poked wires into something. Her torch made a pool of light in the darkness. Hopefully the mist would conceal it from onlookers. If there were any.

The air was heavy with moisture and the vehicles had a damp sheen, water running down them.

She tutted and muttered.

From far off there was a crash. I turned towards it and waited for another sound. Something that would let me know if it was an animal. Or a person. There was no other sound but I walked in the direction it had come from with my gun raised.

There was an old transporter with a crane on the back, its arm raised up like gallows. It was surrounded by debris: shredded tyres and coolant hoses. Beyond the transporter there was a Land Rover with the bonnet gone, much of its mechanicals stripped. As I passed it a crow burst out, flapping wildly, cawing. The bird disappeared off into the fog and I waited to see if there were others.

There was nothing else so I walked back.

Becky had gone, the wires and meter still hanging there. I stood there in the damp air, twisting my head to pick up sounds. A low drone came from way off but there was nothing else. No voices or sounds of movement. I went over to the Eblis and the hatch opened. Becky popped out.

'It's this I need,' she said, holding some more wires. 'The set-up was wrong.'

'It's getting too dark. You won't be able to see

anything.'

'We need to do it now.'

Then there was a thud from the building, like something had been knocked over.

'Probably animals,' she said.

'Probably. But it's sensible to get out of here. Before it's properly dark.'

She shuffled around for a minute then there was another thump. 'It won't take long.' She walked down the row back to the tank. I scanned the area, watching out for movement. Listening for more sounds.

She fiddled around in her patch of light for ages. Then there was a click and the hatch open. She disappeared into it, talking to herself. Now and then the torch beam flicked up and there were rattles. No sounds came from the abandoned vehicles, just Becky as she poked around. I kept the pistol tight in my hand and stared across the heavy shadows in the mist.

There was a clunk from the rear of the tank. Becky came out with tools in her hand and torch held in her armpit. 'Triggered the servo,' she said, slipping down and round to the back. 'Technical stuff.' Raising up the engine cover she leant in and started to work on it. Her torch was balanced on the side as she felt around and muttered.

There was a rattle from way off to my right, away from the Eblis.

Becky whistled and the sound floated off across the camp. She popped the torch into her mouth and leant further in. For some minutes she shifted around as she undid something inside.

'Do you need a hand?' I said.

She grunted and carried on.

'I could hold the torch…'

Then she stood up with a bunch of wires in her hand. 'Got it.'

'Great. Let's go.'

She led us back to the Eblis, the torch flicking around the damp ground then up onto the tank. I kept the pistol raised as she clambered up and dropped into the hatch then I slid in after her. Once the hatch was closed Casper turned up the lights. They were dazzling after the being outside.

'Did you get them?' he asked.

'Hope so.' She held up the wires and connectors.

'You think they'll fit?' I asked.

'Yeah. It's a similar design.' She started up the vehicle's motors, turning us round so that we left the parade ground. We passed the pile of shoes, burnt-out car and boarded up housing estate, now only visible as shadows even when I messed with the controls on the monitors.

When we joined the road she let the vehicle pick up speed and the camp disappeared behind us.

But after a mile or so she stopped us dead, swearing to herself, before turning the Eblis round to face back.

'What's up?' I said.

'The meter. The multi-meter and wires. They're on the tank.'

'We can get them in the morning,' said Casper.

'We need them. Can't risk losing them.'

'Really?' I said.

'Really. We need to go back to The Graveyard.'

CHAPTER TWENTY-THREE

Return

She took us back onto the rough track, past the buildings now invisible in the mist, to the parade ground. We stopped at the same spot.

We sat there with the motors off, no one moving, watching the monitors. There was no sign of anything.

'I suppose I better go,' she said.

'I'll do it,' I said. Before I could change my mind I pushed past Casper and opened the hatch. I stepped out and he passed me the torch. I slid out the pistol as he sealed the vehicle behind me.

The light seemed to have faded in the few minutes we'd been away. Maybe it was because my eyes had adjusted to the inside of the tank or it was just getting dark. The nearest vehicles were shapeless shadows, the ones further off no longer visible. When I lit the torch it bounced back from the fog.

The vehicle I needed was somewhere ahead. I knew it had no turret and the tracks were bust. I couldn't remember much else.

I walked down the row with the light pointed down, the dark shadows shifting around me.

One tank looked familiar so I clambered up onto it. There was a small turret with a bent gun, not right at all. I climbed up onto the next one, slipped on the damp metal, my left foot flying backwards. As I thudded onto the steel surface I gave out a sigh. My voice echoed back off the hulks of the Graveyard. This one had a turret as well.

A crash came from some way off, a loud sound. It could have been from the Eblis, if Casper had climbed out of it and slipped like me. Or it might have been from the buildings, where I'd heard something earlier.

I moved on.

The next two vehicles didn't have turrets but were more like armoured cars. The wrong shape: I tried another row further on and shone the torch around, trying to recognise something.

This shouldn't have been so hard. Jump out and grab the gear, that had been the idea but here I was wandering around in the dark.

Then there was another sound, this time several loud cracks, possibly wood being smashed. Or small-calibre gunfire. Shots from a pistol.

With the torch low I worked down the row, methodical. I needed to find the tank, pick up the wires and go. That was all. But they all looked the same. Big slabs of metal in the dark.

Then it came back to me — the bulldozer blade and shovels built into it. That was what I needed to find. None of the vehicles nearby had blades so I moved to the next row.

There it was, the fifth one down. The torch jiggle

around as I ran over to it. With my hands tight on the grab handles I clambered up, scanning around for the wires and metre. There was no sign of them on the hatch. They'd gone.

But Becky had taken them round to the back. That's where she'd been last. I dropped down and waved the torch around. There they were: hanging off the edge of the bulk head. I put my pistol away. Grabbed the metre up and wrapped the wires around it. Shoved it all into my jacket.

Then I turned the torch off and stood at the rear of the tank, looking for the Eblis. That was when I heard the voices. No doubt about it, there were people here. They were whispering, several men, not far off. They must have seen the torch beam and were tracking over towards me. I lowered myself to the ground. There was no time to work out where Becky and Casper were so I slid under the vehicle, between the busted tracks and chassis. It had sunk into the ground so there wasn't much space and I had to lie flat, pressed against the chewed up tarmac, the torch still in my hand, gravel in my face.

For several minutes there was no sound besides my own breath. As it rasped in and out. Then they came over, footsteps and voices. They stopped near me, standing by the tank. There sounded to be four or five of them, maybe more, now invisible in the darkness. Their voices were gruff and they used words I didn't recognise. They muttered about the light they'd seen and where it was. Other stuff I couldn't follow.

If they'd just arrived it was possible they'd not seen the Eblis, mistaking it for one of the wrecks.

There was a rasp and light shone on their feet as they lit

a lamp. They talked about footprints and what they'd do if they found anyone. How they'd strung up the last visitor and slit him open. They all laughed at this.

I slid the gun out and held it up beside my head. Chances were they had their own weapons. There'd be no way I could take them all on but it felt better to have the pistol to hand. At least I'd be able to take a couple of them down with me.

As the lamplight swung around one of them raised his voice, said he'd found something. They were silent for a moment, all clustered around the tank, looking. This was it. I shuffled back, millimetre by millimetre. I came to the far side and slid out. Staying low I moved down the row, behind the other vehicles in the direction of the Eblis. Where I thought it was. The men were still standing around the tank, their lamp swinging around but not bright enough to light me. I took short steps, not wanting to trip or make a noise. If I could get far enough away I could put my torch on. Work my way back.

Then there was a shout. A rock flew through the air. Towards me. It bounced off a tank at my side.

I flicked my torch on and ran, thudded across the overgrown tarmac, ready for a bullet to thump into me, knock me off my feet. Then they could grab me and drag me off. Lynch me and slit me open.

There was one shot but it thudded into the ground off to my right. I ran on towards the end of the row, not sure where the Eblis was, where to go. The shell of an armoured car appeared out of the dark and I turned left. There were more shouts from behind me. Even if this wasn't the right way I needed to put some distance between me and the mob so I picked up the pace.

But there was no sign of the Eblis. The torchlight gave a cone of white in front of me, little else. Another shot came from behind, clanged off the body of a hulk beside me. I ducked behind a personnel-carried, going out into the next row and bending forward to keep below the vehicles' bodywork.

The men shouted. Feet clumped on the ground.

Then a bright light came on. It shone from a distance, over to my left. A powerful spotlight accompanied by the sound of motors.

It was the Eblis.

Casper and Becky must have heard the shots and powered up. I turned towards the light and ran flat out, sprinting as fast as I could. As soon as I'd gone a few metres it was clear I'd made a mistake. I was a silhouetted, easy to see in the lamp's beam. Easy to shoot.

Becky's amplified voice came from the Eblis. 'Lie down, Trent,' she said.

I dropped to the ground, fell on the stones and weeds. Knocked the air out of myself.

A second later a machine gun roared. In the stillness of The Graveyard it was deafening. A stream of shots clattered over my head, rattling and tinkling off tanks. One ricocheted into the soil near my head,

Then it stopped. Silence. Behind me I heard a couple of voices shouting, crying out. Swearing. Then the gun fired again, a short burst. Stopped. This time there were no voices.

I glanced back. The tank's headlamp caught an irregular pile. Shadowed outlines in the mist, arms, legs and heads at odd angles laid out between the rotting shells. A hand twisted out as if to catch a ball.

I walked back towards the Eblis, sticking to the side and leaving clear space just in case one of the men had survived and tried something. As I climbed the turret the Eblis' gun fired a couple of times, a figure falling back into the dim pile of bodies.

Back inside the vehicle Becky thanked me when I handed over the meter and wires. 'That got complicated,' she said.

'Yeah. 'On the monitor the bodies lay spot lit. Still. 'Thanks.'

'You okay?'

'Fine.'

Casper stared into his sight. 'Think that's it,' he said.

Becky already had her hands on the controls. 'Let's go.'

'Yeah,' I said.

We reversed out of the parade ground of rotting hulks. Dead bodies. We left The Graveyard for the second time that evening

CHAPTER TWENTY-FOUR

Strip Down

We drove on through the darkness for some time. The Eblis lumbered along as Becky kept the speed down. Watched the dials. The vehicle's lights were off yet I could see the road ahead on the monitor: overgrown hedgerows and meadows of weeds. Everything around us, in blacks and greens.

We turned off down a track taking us up to an abandoned farm. Around it were fields of weeds. There was a large yard and Becky pulled up in the middle of it.

'Listen,' she said.

There were no sounds. No movement on the screens. We were between several buildings: there was a barn with a roof that had partially collapsed. It lay angled like the bow of a ship. Opposite was a farmhouse with cracked and distorted windows from fire damage. Its interior was dark, lifeless. Beside it was a pile of timber that must have once been another barn.

'Looks dead.' I grabbed the pistol and squeezed past Casper. Popped the hatch and went out.

Mist hung over the buildings. The air smelled of damp grass and hot metal from the tank. It gave off of ticks and gurgles but otherwise there was no sound.

Becky came and stood by me. 'We had to shoot them,' she said.

'I know.'

'They wouldn't have hesitated to shoot you.'

'I'm sure.' Of all the things we'd done it was one that bothered me the least.

She came round and stood in front of me. 'Look, Trent, this trip…' She took a deep breath and kicked at the ground. 'Now we've got the parts. We can fix the tank. It's going to be fine.'

'Right.' I wasn't sure what this speech was for. What she wanted from me. All I knew was I was probably going to leave as soon as we got further into Scotland. They could head off to their dream town but once I got juice I was off.

'We never did see Nico or the Round Up crew.'

'There's still time.'

She shook her head. 'I'd guess they've gone back. Or Casper finished them off.'

'I guess.' It seemed likely but Nico was tough. A survivor. And if he was alive he'd be after us: until he got us.

Casper came out and joined us. 'Everything okay?'

'Fine,' said Becky. 'Look, it's too dark to fit the parts tonight. We'll have to do it first thing.'

I offered to collect firewood while they explored the buildings and gave them a clean sweep. Made sure there was no one hanging around.

There were plenty of old rafters scattered around so I

gathered them up and dumped them in corner of the barn. Once Becky and Casper had had a good look around she drove the tank into the barn and we set up a section of busted metal roof alongside it to make a sheltered area.

We lit a fire and warmed up tinned vegetables. Becky talked about the replacement components they'd picked up. It wasn't a particularly technical conversation but I lost interested after a while and rolled out my bedding, lying back on the packed-earth floor. The pistol was stashed at my side, just in case. As I fell asleep I thought of Scotland and the mountains. The empty Highlands away from the gangs of the border.

But I slept badly, reliving events in Faeston with Round Up and Sophie. Beating up kids and making false promises. Hanging around in my flat with the documents on Gehenna. I dreamt about the pile of bodies, the ones Casper had shot in the camp. Another where I'd found a pile of bones; nearly ended up in it. That was the one that woke me up.

I sat up in my sleeping bag and looked around. Becky and Casper were still asleep. The fire was a pile of ash and faint light came through from far side of the barn.

I slid on some clothes, taking my pistol. The Eblis was slimy with dew, cold to my touch. I walked round it and through the yard, over to a gate. The sun fought through mist that cloaked the fields. At the side of the farmhouse I undid my trousers and took a piss. It steamed onto the ground as two jackdaws rose up from a chimney stack. The birds flapped off and I did my fly.

There was movement across at the far side of the farm building, just behind the smashed gate.

A figure stood facing me, a teenage lad, skinny with a mop of hair. When he saw me he ducked behind the wall. I made my way towards him, not too fast but with the pistol raised and cocked.

When I came round the wall he faced me.

He was older than I'd first thought, in his late teens, sunken eyed and gaunt. He wore a sweatshirt and jeans. The clothes were faded and holed but clean. He stared at me but didn't speak.

'Who are you?' I said.

He half turned and looked out across the field. Then he faced me again. 'Got any food?' he said. His voice was muffled, like there was something stuck in his mouth.

I waved the gun at him. 'No.' Not for him at least. Some fella wandering around in the wilds.

'I'm really hungry.' His mouth dropped at the edges as if he was going to cry. 'Hungry.'

I kept the gun on him but he didn't seem interested. Or bothered. 'Where've you come from?'

He pointed across the field. 'I'm out of food.'

'Sorry. I've got nothing.'

He nodded but didn't say any more.

'I think you should go home.'

He nodded again then walked off. Through the gate and across the mist-heavy field. He didn't slow or stop so I left him to it. I turned and walked off back into the barn. He didn't seem like a threat but he wasn't my responsibility. The country was full of people who were hungry. I sat down on my bedding as Casper and Becky slept.

We had food but it wasn't my job to help him. He'd just have to sort himself out.

I lay back on my bedding.

It wasn't up to me to save people. He'd just have to starve.

I sat up and went over to Becky's bag, grabbed a tin of beans, proper old-world ones, and took it and a can-opener and spoon. As I walked across the farmyard I drew the gun out again. Maybe it was a trap and there'd be a bunch of lads waiting all tooled up. Maybe they sent him as bait.

When I got back to the spot I'd last seen he was still there, in the field. He must have stopped walking as soon as I gone. I slid the gun away. 'Hey!' I shouted.

He turned back towards me. When I held the can up he walked over. I offered him the can, can opener and spoon. He grinned and took them, opening up and scooping out the cold beans.

I stood there as he ploughed through them until he scrapped out every speck of sauce and leant back with his head facing up and eyes shut. The can, spoon and opener slid from his fingers.

Then he moved fast and dropped to his knees. Before I had time to grab the gun he was down on the ground, hands clasped together. With whispered words he prayed. I smiled at this. He was like Rory, my crazy god-fearing brother. He'd not been able to take a sip of water without thanking God or Jesus. Seemed this lad was the same. He finished then stood and smiled. He grabbed up the can, spoon and opener, handing them to me.

'Thank you,' he said.

He turned and walked off, back into the mist and across the field. Within seconds he vanished from sight.

If it wasn't for the empty tin and dirty spoon I'd not

believe he'd existed.

I took them and returned to the barn. Lay back on my bedding again and watched the barn brighten up.

Casper woke with a grunt. He found the can and spoon but didn't seem impressed that I'd eaten the beans. I spared him the story of the lad just in case he fancied tracking him down with the Eblis. Shooting him in the back of the head.

Once Becky was awake they set to work on the tank. As they leant into the engine compartment I took a walk around the farm. The mist had cleared and the autumn sun cut through the cool air, crisp. Golden light on the overgrown fields. There was no sign of the lad or anyone else. Just the weed-filled earth that ran off towards overgrown hedgerows and a copse of brown-leafed trees on the horizon.

For a minute I leant against the fence as Becky and Casper clattered on behind me.

There was a flash of light from the trees. A few seconds later it came again but this time there was a sound. Like something heavy being dropped. Becky and Casper were still busy and there was nothing for me to do. I checked I had the gun then walked across the field. Towards the light.

The ground was rutted and covered with thick plants: dandelions, coarse grass and thistles, still damp from the mist. I kept an eye on the copse. There was no movement. No sign that anyone was there.

As I got closer I saw that there was a structure hidden in the trees. Tall, man made. There was a fence around the patch of woods and I could make out the outline of something else through the branches: a building. I stopped in the middle of the field beside a muddy pool. This was a stupid idea. There could be anyone there. Any number of neo-reivers or crazy people. There were no sounds apart from the clanks that floated over from Casper and Becky.

So I carried on. A trampled path came in from the left so I joined it, where it led up to a section of the fence that was bust. Through the foliage I could see the building. It was brick built with an exhaust and several wires' conduits running out of it. The structure beside it was a lattice of rusted steel: an old phone transmitter. A branch had fallen from a tree and lay across the top of it. I slid through the fence and walked over towards it with the gun in my hand.

A head popped out of the building and disappeared back in. It was the lad I'd seen earlier. I put the gun away and walked towards him. He looked out again and when he saw me he grinned. In his hand was a mole grip and a tenon saw. For a moment we just faced one another. The building had several small piles set out around. One was of feathers and bones, presumably from the birds and other animals he'd eaten. Another was old food tins flattened and neatly arranged. The third was clothes all folded. There was also a bowl of water set beneath a length of guttering that ran off into the trees. To the side of it a washing line was set up with pegs on it.

'Hello,' I said.

The lad put his tools down. He came over and extended his hand. For a second I didn't respond then I took it and shook it, a ritual I'd almost forgotten. His grip was light, skin soft.

'I live here,' he said.

'Yeah?'

'My place.'

'Are you on your own?'

'Yep. Since Mum and Dad went. You want to look?'

It seemed an odd offer. But he was an odd lad. 'All right,' I said.

He stepped back and held out a hand towards the building. I ducked down and went inside. It was dark and there wasn't much in there. He had bedding set out on wooden boards. There were more clothes, again neatly folded with two pairs of holed shoes. A mug and plate with cutlery were set to the side and an old telephone lay by the wall. Its wires disappeared through a gap in the bricks.

'You like it?' he said.

'Great,' I said. 'Really smart.'

He beamed at this. I went back outside. The wire from the phone ran off towards the transmitter where it was looped around the structure in a knot. There was no sign of anyone else or that there had ever been anyone else.

The lad stared at me, eyebrows raised like he was waiting for me to do something. Now I was here and I'd seen him I wasn't really sure what I'd come over for. Curiosity or something.

'Well, nice to have met you,' I said.

'Yep.'

I started to walk backwards. 'Bye.'

He stared at me but didn't move so I backed off a little more then turned around. As I passed through the fence I glanced back. He had his hands at his side, immobile. Then he ducked into the building and started clattering around.

I crossed the field as the sun rose up over the farm

buildings, warming the air. It had been a waste of time going going over to the trees but it hadn't done any harm. Becky and Casper were busy and I'd had time to fill. The lad was on his own though he seemed to have everything he needed, so that was all fine.

I came to the farmyard and carried on towards the tank. Casper and Becky stood beside it, the engine's cover still up and tools lined up on the ground.

'Is it fixed?' I said.

'Hmm,' said Becky but her eyes weren't on me.

'Who the fuck is he?' said Casper, pointing.

I turned.

The lad was behind me, close up, holding a bundle of clothes and his plate and cutlery. He grinned. 'These your friends?'

The four of us stood without talking. The lad was tapping his foot.

Eventually Casper spoke. 'Who the fuck is he?'

'I think you've already said that,' I said.

'What did you bring him here for?'

'I didn't bring him —'

'Well, he's here. With you.'

'Let's not get worked up,' said Becky. 'I'm sure Trent has a good reason.'

Casper and Becky stared at me. The lad tapped his foot.

'Look,' I said. The lad's foot was thudding away on the ground. I turned to him. 'Can you stop that, please?' Then I faced Casper and Becky again. 'I didn't bring him over. He followed me, that's all…'

'Followed you?' said Casper. 'Where the hell from?' His voice was raised and he pointed at the lad who shuffled around, kicked up dirt.

'Calm down, Casper,' said Becky.

'Yeah, calm down,' I said.

This was too much for Casper. He went red and raised his fist at me. 'Fuck you, Trent. Fuck you.'

I didn't move. He wasn't someone who frightened me, especially when he was being so dramatic.

'Come on,' said Becky. 'Trent, just tell him, whoever he is, let him know we're going. That he can't come with us, okay? That will be all right Casper, eh?'

Casper shrugged.

I turned to the lad. He was now playing with his cutlery, tapping it against his leg. I took his shoulder and walked him across the barn, away from Becky and Casper. His body was thin under his shirt.

'Hello,' I said.

'I'm Daniel,' he said.

'Daniel.'

'Yes, Daniel. Don't call me Dan.'

'Right. Daniel. Listen Daniel. We're going soon and you need to, you know. You need to sort yourself out...'

He held up the bundle of clothes. 'Got them all. All the good ones. Ready to go.'

This wasn't going to be simple. I took a breath. He had to be told straight. 'Daniel, I know you've got all your stuff...' Across by the tank Casper grinned at me. He loved this, me telling the lad that he couldn't come in the tank. That he had to stay here on his own. Me doing as I was instructed.

I smiled at Daniel. 'Come on. Let's get you settled in.' I led him across to the tank.

Casper stepped forward.

'He comes,' I said.

'Like fuck he can —'

'He comes.' I had my pistol out at my side, away from Daniel. At that point I was ready to shoot Casper. Not kill him but certainly hurt him.

Maybe he saw this because he stepped back. 'You're crazy.'

'Possibly. But he comes.'

Becky came between us. 'Okay, Trent, okay. He comes. Four will fit. But we drop him off somewhere, you hear?'

'Yeah, I hear.'

She shook her head and walked over to the Eblis, stuck her head under the rear hatch. Casper gave me once last glance, a dirty look, then he followed her.

I was left with Daniel as he held out his bundle of clothes. 'You hang onto them,' I said. Then I waved for him to follow me.

We walked over to the tank and I helped him up the bulkhead and onto the turret. Becky closed up the rear hatch and came and joined us.

'All done?' I said.

'I think so.'

She showed Daniel how to get in. Casper picked up the tools and stood to the side of the tank, chewing at his fingernails and spitting them onto the ground. Daniel slid his feet into the turret following after Becky.

He stopped when he was halfway and faced me. 'I knew you'd come,' he said. Then he grinned and was in.

I followed and sat in the usual spot. Daniel was in the armaments seat next to Casper who'd just joined us. He was like a block of wood, responding to Becky's requests but no more than that.

The hatch was sealed and the motors started. The tank manoeuvred out of the farmyard.

We joined the main road and picked up speed, the four of us in the Eblis.

'Where now?' I had a rough idea but wanted to hear it. Wanted to know there'd been no changes.

'Galashiels then northwards,' said Becky.

There was no more conversation after that. Daniel hummed to himself and Casper fiddled with the gun controls. Becky drove and I sat back. We were headed through the Lowlands. Once we'd skirted the cities I'd be off. That was my plan now. Daniel could stay with them or I'd take him and drop him somewhere. I'd work that out later.

Midmorning we had a stop by a stream. We ate stale bread and dried meat, Casper by Becky and Daniel beside me. He gobbled his food up. Maybe he'd not found any animals to eat for a while. I tried to ask him about where he'd lived and how long he'd been there but his answers didn't make sense. Then there was all the stuff about knowing that I'd come. He said it again but I didn't quiz him. Not with Casper there.

So after a while we fell to silence. Casper stared off at the moors but Becky watched Daniel. When he'd finished his food she gave him some of her bread.

'So, through Galashiels then north,' I said.

'That's the plan,' said Becky.

I was all right with this. Galashiels was reasonable town, one of the few I liked, even if I did have some history there. If she'd suggested going through Kelso I'd have kicked up a fuss. That was where Maxwell had had his headquarters. Maxwell who I'd stolen the Gehenna details from, killing a few of his men in the process. He was dead but there'd be some of his gang hanging around and I had no wish to meet any of them. Fellas like that had long memories.

We set off again and Becky cranked the speed up. The Eblis rattled past a couple of carts filled with hay, the first vehicles we'd seen that morning.

The outskirts of Galashiels looked the same as last time I'd been there, all pre-Collapse buildings, relatively tidy, but slightly shabby like everywhere. This was one of the towns that had given up on trying to rebuild the old world. They'd gone back to simpler ways, growing wood for fuel and using animals for transport. Maybe it wasn't as lively as other places but it was safe enough.

We passed a sign advertising that it was market day. Becky slowed the Eblis and drove towards the town centre, cutting past a horse pulling a cart. People on the pavement stopped to watch us, curious but not threatening. There were shops and green spaces, many of the town's buildings in good repair.

We approached the bridge and Becky cried out. 'Shit!'

The Eblis stopped and she threw it straight into reverse so that we pitched forward. I adjusted the monitor and hung onto my seat, as I tried to work out what she'd seen. Daniel gave out a low moan as he fell forward.

'What is it?' shouted Casper.

'He's at the bridge.'

There he was, standing by the bridge's parapet. It was Nico, dressed in long coat. In his hand was a rocket launcher and behind him his Range Rover. As he set the weapon on his shoulder Becky raced the tank backwards, ignoring the carts parked at the side of the road and horses lined up.

As we negotiated the corner there was a deep thud and deafening explosion, followed by darkness.

CHAPTER TWENTY-FIVE

The Bridge

There was a flicker and the lights came back on. The monitors showed static then clouds of dust. Becky grabbed the controls and thrust the Eblis further back up the road, not worrying to wait for her screens settle down.

'Are we hit?' I said.

Daniel had his hands on his ears and rocked back and forward.

Becky shook her head, tapping buttons, adjusting settings on the controls. 'Missed us. Took out at building. Poor shot.'

On my screen the side of grain merchants' appeared out of the smoke, now without walls. Floors open to the street.

'Is there another way across the river?' said Casper.

'Not for this weight of vehicle,' she said.

'We could go back and take another route north —'

'We need to sort him out,' I said. Nico was armed with something capable of damaging the tank. If we came out in the open he'd have us. He had a vehicle with him as well so we couldn't outrun him. He'd track us down. 'He won't give up until he's got us.'

'There are loads of ways —'

'Trent is right,' said Becky. 'We've got to face him. It might as well be here.'

Daniel was still rocking in his seat, repeating something over and over.

'Don't worry,' I said. Once we got out of this, if we got out of this, I'd talk to him properly. But there wasn't time now.

Becky gazed at the screens before her as the smoke and dust settled. 'What will he do? What will Nico do?'

'Wait for a while then come for us. He might have Gregg and Will with him as well.'

She reached into a locker and pulled a walkie-talkie out. 'You ever used one of these?' She handed it to me.

'Not really. Maybe Casper should go.'

Casper grunted. He reached over Daniel and loaded ammo into the gun. Clanged the breech shut.

'You know Nico,' she said.

I did know Nico. She knew how to drive the tank. And Casper was a coward but knew how to shoot, so I probably was the best person to go.

Casper opened the hatch and I turned the walkie-talkie over in my hands. Twisted a knob so it hissed. Been a while since I'd seen one of these.

'Back soon,' I said to Daniel and I stepped out.

Debris had settled across the pavement. I picked my way back through it to the corner of the road. At the far side several horses stamped in agitation as another lay whimpering, its hind quarters crushed as blood pooled around it. There was no one on the street but people stared out from inside shops. Out at the rubble and smashed carts. A shower of masonry rattled down from the wrecked grain merchant's. There was no sign of Nico by the bridge but his Range Rover was still there.

I grabbed the walkie-talkie up, pressed the button and spoke into it. 'I'm at the corner. There's no sign of Nico or the others.' When I released the button there was a hiss.

Becky's voice came on. 'Okay. Contact me if he shows up.'

I pulled my pistol out and lined it up on the bridge. Stayed like that for some time as the horse whined and debris fell from the building opposite. Then Nico's head popped up. The rocket launcher was in his hand pointed upwards. He was too far off for me to hit him so I slid the pistol away. He shifted along the wall, moving towards the right to allow him to see the tank.

I picked up the walkie-talkie. 'Spotted him,' I said.

'Come back to the Eblis. I've got something for you.'

When I got there Becky already had the hatch to the open and held a couple of grenades. 'Know what these are?' she said.

'Yeah. You want a diversion?'

'Get as far forward as you can, then contact me.'

I set off with the pistol in one hand and a grenade in the other. The walkie-talkie and other grenade were stashed in my jacket. I made my way back down the road, my eyes fixed on the bridge, where Nico was. He hadn't moved much further, now setting up the weapon. If Gregg and Will were around they weren't beside him or in the Range Rover. Maybe they'd split up and he'd left the other two on this side of the bridge. Maybe they were dead. Maybe not. I ducked down and stayed at the side, made my way up the pavement, hiding behind the smashed carts. Nico aimed at the side road we'd gone up, the rocket-launcher on his shoulder, ready for when the tank appeared. He didn't even glance over at me.

I laid the pistol and both grenades on the ground and radioed Becky.

'Ready,' I said.

There was no reply. Nico set up the sights and was now angling further across. There was a chance that he'd clip the front of the tank from that angle and they'd not see him.

'Becky?' I said.

Again, nothing. If I couldn't contact them I'd have to do something on my own, maybe get even closer and try to hit him with the grenade, take a couple of shots.

I tried once more.

Becky's voice crackled back. 'Trent?'

'I'm here.'

'Pull the pins, count to five then throw them.'

'He's too far off.'

'Just throw them. Anywhere.'

I put down the walkie-talkie, pulled both pins, counted and threw them over the road.

I ducked down behind the remains of a cart. There was a rumble and clatter from the Eblis as it moved forward.

Then two great blasts shook the street. Glass smashed in a shop opposite and pieces of metal zinged off the stonework behind me. Into the cart.

As soon as the smoke cleared there were two other explosions. One came from behind me, a deep hollow sound. It roared over me with a blast from across the river.

It was followed by another one. This was higher pitched, sharper, accompanied by bits of stone in the air. Dust. From my position it was hard to tell who had fired which but it sounded like the first was from the Eblis. Then Nico had responded. This meant they hadn't hit him. Casper had missed.

I raised my head. The tank was behind me, intact but sprinkled with debris, the building behind it now a hollowed out ruin after Nico's second shot. Over at the bridge there was a smoking pothole in the riverbank.

The Eblis fired again. There was a great thud and smoke that sent a shockwave through the air. The buildings shook. The shell punched into the far bank of the river with a cloud of black smoke. Sprayed up earth and stone. Bits of the road and wall and god-knows what else. It cleared to show a scorched crater. Nico's Range Rover was a blackened skeleton, flames licking up one side.

Debris dropped down on me. Dust and bits of masonry. The air smelled of smoke.

I spoke into the walkie-talkie. 'I'm going to check on Nico.' I headed off, not waiting for a reply. On the way I stopped by the stricken horse. It rolled it eyes up, tongue lolling out. A great chunk of brickwork lay on its flank and blood poured out of the animal. I pulled the pistol out, aimed and fired a shot into its head. It jerked back then was still. As the gunshot echoed off the buildings I made my way to the bridge, towards Nico. My gun was raised. Ready.

All the way across the bridge I kept an eye on where he'd been, beside the Range Rover. There was no sign of him now: no movement or sound. Just the crackle of burning plastic.

There was a black circle of carbon around the wrecked Range Rover, the result of the explosion. Behind it was a great fissure in the road where the shell had finally buried itself.

Then I saw Nico. He was down by the river, on a patch of mud, face down, immobile. There was no sign of the rocket-launcher. Or Will and Gregg. It would have been handy if they'd hidden in the Range Rover but that wasn't their style. If they'd come with Nico they'd have hung around with him.

I climbed the parapet ready to go down and check on him. Make sure he was dead.

The Eblis pulled up and Casper appeared out of the top. 'Come on,' he said.

'Nico is down there.'

'Did we get him?'

'Think so.'

Casper smiled. He reached into the tank and pull out a semi-automatic, swung it round and fired twice into Nico. Into his back. There was no movement or sound from Nico. 'He's dead. We need to get going.'

I didn't move. I was annoyed with Casper, maybe because he'd shot Nico or because I'd been cheated out of it. Maybe I was just annoyed.

Back at the other side of the river people came out of the buildings, some carrying farming implements, several standing over the dead horse. I got into the hatch.

Daniel was still in his seat. He made whimpering noises.

'Your little friend is calming down,' said Casper. 'Think he's been crying.'

'Fuck you,' I said.

Casper laughed.

Daniel stared up at me. His eyes were red-rimmed, mouth turned down.

'We're going to be fine,' I said.

As I sat down Becky gunned the vehicle forward and we left town. My monitor stayed on the smoking remains of Nico's car until it was out of view.

CHAPTER TWENTY-SIX
Lonely Drivers

We carried on north. To save time we stayed on the main road, keeping a good cruising speed. I didn't say too much to Becky and Casper. I spoke to Daniel after I'd persuaded him to put the headphones on.

'It's all right, Daniel,' I said. 'That was a bad man but he's gone now. Gone.'

Daniel didn't reply but he nodded, which seemed like a good sign. This wasn't something I was used to doing, or that I was any good at, but it seemed to be what was needed. Anyway, talking stopped me thinking about Nico. About Casper shooting him in the back. I'd never liked Nico and had often wished him dead. That wasn't the way I'd wanted it done, though.

Over the next couple of hours we passed a few vehicles: an estate car turned into a cart pulled by two horses. A mutilated hatchback belching smoke. As we carried on north clouds built up into great mountains of grey. The sky darkened. Then there was a flash of lightning and a rumble that shook its way through the tank. Raindrops clattered off the bulkhead. We slowed in the deluge as the road turned into a river and pebbles rolled along in the currents. There was another flash that lit the landscape before it dropped into premature dusk. We crept on through the storm, Becky and Casper intent on their screens and Daniel rocking in his seat. The tanks hull buzzed with the electricity in the air as we made our way through the downpour.

At last the storm passed over.

The sky cleared and the sun lit the road behind and before us. The monitors showed overgrown pastures and thickets of trees. Pools of water and overfull streams and derelict buildings. And there was something behind us, a little spec of light that only showed when the sun caught it. As we drove on it stayed with us, never closer or further away. It chased us like our own shadow. I played around with the controls on my monitor and worked out how to zoom in and enlarged the image. It was a red Jaguar XF, same as Nico's second car. It had to be Will and Gregg.

'We've got company,' I said.

Casper grunted.

'Behind us.'

He messed with the sights on the turret. 'It's no big deal.'

'It's been on us for ages. Pacing us.'

'What's that?' said Becky.

'Trent's jumpy,' said Casper. 'Thinks we're being followed.'

She looked at her screen for the best part of a minute. Then she pushed the levers forward. Picked up the pace. The car matched us. Then she slowed right down and so did it. 'Think you're right, Trent.'

Casper said nothing.

'Can we hit them?'

Casper checked his sights. Took a deep breath. 'Possibly. Not clearly from this range. Not while we're moving. We could stop. Blow them away.'

'Maybe.' But they were probably armed as well. They'd see us slow and be ready. What we needed to do was catch them out. They wouldn't know about us being able to zoom in on the monitors so they'd probably assume we hadn't seen them. 'We need to pull off somewhere. Get behind them. Hit them when they're not expecting it.'

Casper raised an eyebrow. 'Sounds reasonable.'

Becky agreed and Daniel just looked worried. I told him there were more bad men but it would be all right. We'd keep him safe.

We continued on for a little while. The road was straight with nowhere to hide. The car was still on our tail. Still pacing us.

Then we descended a steep curve with patches of trees along the roadside. Becky let the Eblis pick up speed. Once we were over the brow and out of their vision she swung it down onto the verge. Off to the left. The Eblis slid, its weight resisting the turn, as we charged into the foliage. Branches slapped on the hull and we pitched and rocked as she steered it through the undergrowth, stopping us behind some straggly trees. Casper turned the turret to face the road.

We waited.

Maybe the camouflage would fool them. But how could they not spot our huge bulk behind the trees? Or the track marks on the road?

They'd be on us before we had time to aim, time to fire

back.

The seconds passed and there was no sign of the car.

Then it came past. It seemed to slow then accelerated up the road. The Jaguar disappeared out of view.

Becky reversed, twisting the Eblis round to face after them. Casper worked on the turret and sights, setting it up on the car as it raced off.

He fired. The sound filled the tank and the Jaguar disappeared in a cloud of smoke.

For a few seconds the vehicle reverberated with the blast. Casper was up close to his monitor. He stared into it and chewed his nails. Daniel rocked in his seat. This wasn't a great experience for him. All I could see on mine were clouds of dust.

'Think we've got it,' said Casper.

Becky drove off the verge and back onto the road. The tank's tracks rattled up the tarmac as we headed to where the smoke was settling. As the air cleared we could see the damage the shell had done: there was a hole punched in the road, debris scattered round it. Chunks of dry clay, gravel and tarmac. The Jaguar was half in the crater, intact but badly smashed up. Slewed to the side from its attempt to steer out of the way.

We stopped next to it and Casper clambered out first, a gun in his hand.

'Are you all right?' I said to Daniel. Sunlight and dusty air came in through the open hatch.

'Yep,' he said. His face was red and there were tears on his cheeks. I helped him out and we were followed by Becky.

The car lay on its left-hand side, the front end pushed back almost a metre and the bonnet buckled up. Will was wedged in the front windscreen, his arms splayed out and head twisted back. The glass was cracked and blood stained his face and the dashboard. His eyes were open but they were as dead as he was.

Gregg was still in his seat, flopped against the driver's door covered with blood. His eyes were shut but he moaned and moved around.

'What should we do with him?' said Becky.

Casper brandished his pistol. 'We can see him off, like his mates.'

'Like you did with Nico?'

He squared up to me. 'That's right. You got a problem with that?'

Actually, in this case I didn't. It was one thing shooting someone in the back and something else putting an injured man out of his misery. I reached my hand out towards the gun. 'No. I'll do it.'

'Really?' Casper's face slackened but he still held onto his pistol.

'Yeah.'

Daniel started to whine, a high pitched sound.

Becky put a hand on each of our shoulders. 'Not in front of Daniel. Just leave him.'

'You kidding?' said Casper.

'He'll die.'

Casper still had hold of the gun but it was aimed down.

Daniel squeezed past us and went to the wrecked car. He knelt beside Will and said a prayer. The he came round to Gregg's side and muttered something as he held his hand.

We left Will's body and Gregg in the car. Daniel walked with me, his shoulders slumped and brow furrowed. Maybe he'd wanted to bury Will. Care for Gregg. But we didn't have time for all that.

Before getting in I checked on my bike at the back of the Eblis. It had some fragments of stone on it but otherwise looked fine.

I climbed the turret and looked over at Gregg. He'd stopped moving and was slumped against the steering wheel. I'd have liked to see him finished off but Becky was right. He wasn't going to last without help. Maybe Daniel brought out the best in all of us. With a last glance at Gregg's still body, Will laid out, I got into Eblis.

None of us said anything as Casper shut the hatch and Becky manoeuvred the tank around the Jaguar.

Now that Round Up were gone things were going to be much easier.

CHAPTER TWENTY-SEVEN

Plan

We drove on further into Scotland, up through the Lowlands. Daniel hummed to himself and sometimes he put his hands over his eyes. At least he wasn't rocking in his seat.

Becky's voice crackled over my headphones. 'We need to have a chat. About where we are going and stuff.' She turned and looked at Daniel. Seemed he was the stuff.

I didn't bother to reply. Before I could jump ship I needed juice so I was fine to coast along. Another couple of miles down the road a weatherworn sign appeared with a derelict building beyond it: a disused petrol station. Perfect.

'Let's stop here,' I said. It was a long-shot that there'd be any fuel but it was worth trying.

'Already?' said Becky.

'Might as well.'

Casper had nothing to add so she slowed the Eblis and pulled in. There were rocks set up to block the entrance but the tank chewed its way over the them.

We stopped in the middle of the forecourt near two stripped down vans, their doorless bodies dented and rusty. Leaves lay rotting around them and lichen gave their roofs a green fur. The building at the far side had no windows or fittings and debris lay strewn around the entrance. Only one petrol pump remained and it lay on its side beneath a bare frame that had once been the canopy.

We all got out onto the tarmac, split and punctuated by weeds that grew through decomposing leaf-litter.

Casper and Becky started talking to each other as if me and Daniel weren't within earshot, which we were. So I walked off, over to the wrecked petrol pumps, beside one that lay on its side component-less. Daniel followed me and I lay down on the ground, peered into the pipe from the broken pump that led down into the reservoir. I sniffed. It smelled of hummus and fungi. No whiff of petrol.

I ripped the cover off another pump and turned the mechanism by hand. Tried to draw up trace of fuel. For several minutes I cranked it over, the dry bearings squeaking. When I held the nozzle to my nose there was nothing. Not a hint.

So, I was stuck with them for the time being. I walked back to Becky and Casper, Daniel behind me. They were still on about routes, the best way to skirt Glasgow and get all the way up to the loch they were aiming for. She'd pulled out a map and laid it on the ground to show the inlets and roads. I got in between her and Casper, much to his annoyance. She pointed to where they were going, Loch Fyne on the west coast. From here to there is was hard to see an easy route without going past Glasgow.

'Crossing the river is the problem,' said Casper.

'We could go east and avoid all that,' said Becky.

'That will add miles to the distance.'

'If we aim for Stirling then swing over, we'll be fine.'

'There's no guarantee that will be better.'

Becky looked at me. 'What do you think, Trent? About Glasgow. About our route north.'

Like most cities Glasgow was a crazy place, the stories of the gangs that worked the area suggesting we'd be mad to go through. But heading east would force us to skirt Loch Lomond at the top end, putting a big loop on the journey. Then again, I knew the rumours about crossing the Clyde and the tolls that were extracted, sometimes human ones. Bridges were pinch points, as we'd found in Galashiels. 'Head for Stirling,' I said.

'Still have to pass Edinburgh,' said Casper.

'Safer than Glasgow.'

'Fine,' said Becky.

Casper shrugged, indifferent.

'What do you think?' She was looking at Daniel.

We all turned to him. He was kicking at the chewed up car park with his hands in his pockets. 'Yep,' he said.

So we planned our route on the map. For now I was with them and I wanted some say in where we went. With a couple of pens we marked it out. Daniel muttered things and stood with us but didn't have much to add. As Becky cross-checked it on bigger scale maps Casper went to scavenge for food in the building and I took Daniel aside. We chatted over by the busted petrol pumps. I wanted to know what his story was. While it was quiet I wanted to sound him out. Why we'd found him where he was and whether he was still happy to come with us: complete strangers who killed people.

I started easy. 'How are you?'

'I'm okay.'

'You sure?'

'Yep.'

'Daniel…'

'Yep?'

'How did you end up where you were? On that farm?'

'We moved there. Set up.'

'Who?'

'We did.'

I watched Casper dig around in the building as Becky rechecked our route. I decided to take a different approach. 'Are you still happy to travel with us?'

'Yep?'

'You're not put off?'

'No.'

'And where do you want to go?' This would catch him out. Force him to think a little more.

'Away. Away from here.'

'Where to, though?'

He gazed around the bust-up service station, hands pushed into his pockets. Then he smiled. 'Knew you'd come. They told me.'

This was what he'd said before but with a little extra. 'They?'

'You know who.' He laughed. 'They told me. Before they went. Told me about you.'

'What exactly did they tell you?'

'That men would come. Bad and good. They'd come. And they did. Seen the bad men lots of times. You're the good one.' He grinned at this like he'd really nailed it.

I grunted. I'd never been called a good man before.

Still, there was more I needed to know. 'Who told you this? Who are they?' Maybe there'd been a group or family or friends. Maybe there were clues to where they'd gone.

He struggled with this. The grin disappeared and he started to rub his hands together. Like he was cold. He closed his eyes. Tilted his head back. 'Mum. And Jack. Told me before they went…'

'Went where?'

'Away.'

Away where?'

'Away. Away. Not back.' Then he was silent, his eyes glassy.

'Right. Thanks for answering.' So his mother and his step-dad or brother or someone had gone off. Left him for some reason. It had happened so many times. Kids abandoned by parents to fend for themselves. Sometimes they went off to die, other times it was to search for food or water or shelter. Now and then it was because they couldn't cope. For whatever reasons it had happened to Daniel.

He'd latched onto me because he thought I was a good man. Because I'd been kind to him and he'd been told that was what he needed to look out for. There were worse reasons to form partnerships but it was still going to be tricky. I'd have to work out where we were going. Or where I could leave him.

Casper came out of the building. He held two tins in his hands and swung them as he walked. They were dented and free of labels but one was big, the size of a shell from the Eblis's gun. He clanged them onto the tank's hull.

Taking out his pen knife he cut into their lids Becky

grabbed pan and plates from the tank. He tipped out tomato soup from one, more orange than could be believed. The other was sliced apricots.

We warmed the soup and shared it before having several apricots each. Daniel kept close to me the whole time. At the end of the meal the pair of us walked over to a nearby stream and washed up. Daniel took the rough off the bowls and pan and I finished off.

We worked in silence in the evening light.

Once they were all cleaned we headed back.

'Will they be there?' he said.

'What?' I said.

'When we get there. Will they?'

For a moment I walked alongside him as we held the pan and plates at our side, the sun setting on the petrol station. This could have been about the bad people or just a random thing.

When I said nothing. He tapped me. 'Will they be there?' He pulled his serious face. 'When we get there. Will my Mum and Jack be there?'

I took a deep breath. 'Maybe, Daniel, maybe.'

I carried on to the tank, Daniel moving with a lightness to him. I'd have to let him down at some point.

But not yet.

CHAPTER TWENTY-EIGHT
Ring Road

We set off on the road again, turning north at Peebles. The Eblis rumbled through the town where warehouses stood abandoned and shops derelict and empty. A car park had been turned into an encampment: tents were lined up, greens and blues. Faded shades of pink and yellow. Two old men dressed in rags stared at us as we roared by. We carried on past smart houses at the edge of the town.

Then we were back into countryside, open moorland with clumps of trees, on our way to Edinburgh. The road was quiet as the light faded. The setting sun lit the clear sky orange and gold.

Casper smiled to himself and Becky seemed relaxed at the controls. Daniel had stopped rocking and hummed. Maybe we'd all be okay. The four of us could head into the highlands and part as friends. Each go off and make some kind of a life for ourselves.

As we carried on along the road the debris started to appear out of the darkness, burnt out vehicles and busted barricades. Edinburgh had a reputation for being well organised and reasonably safe but they didn't let strangers just wander in. And we weren't going through the city, we were skirting the edge, where all the people who hadn't been allowed in hung around. At the side of the road was a message, roughly painted on the side of a lorry. *Edinburgh: Count Me Oot* it said in distorted paint.

We drove over breeze blocks with railings tied to them.

Further on there was scaffolding on a hummock.

Becky slowed the Eblis. She flicked the spotlights on and manoeuvred to light the structure. There were two decaying bodies strapped on, naked apart from underwear and sacks over their heads. A sign hung around each of their necks, saying *They Didn Pay*.

This was reivers' work. Seemed some nasty ones had set up camp on the edge of the city.

We came to a section that had steep embankments. The road had been partially blocked by massive chunks of concrete and debris, several metres high, somehow brought and dropped in. To the right was a lower section where the blocks had been blasted clear. Around us there were vans and cars. Empty and stripped. They must have got stuck here. Been picked clean. This was a bottleneck. A trap. Getting trapped here would be really bad.

'We should go back,' I said.

'I can get us through,' said Becky.

'This is a trap. Let's go.'

'Don't panic, Trent,' said Casper. 'We're safe in here.'

'This is reiver territory. We should go.'

'I can do it,' said Becky. She steered us to the lower section of the blockade. The tank rose up and tilted backwards. It juddered and crawled over the blocks, still a metre high. We moved forward then dropped down over them. There was a thump and the Eblis fell to the right, the rumble from the tracks turning to a grinding sound.

'We're caught on it,' said Becky, pushing the controls.

'Stop!' shouted Casper.

Becky still had her hand on the control, ramming it forward but the Eblis pitched and jerked. Casper dropped down and grabbed hold of her, pulling her away from the levers. The sound of the motors died down and the tank settled at an odd angle, tilted over.

'I was trying to drive us over it,' she said.

'You've busted a track.'

The tank's reactor gurgled behind us. Otherwise there was just the creak of Daniel's chair as he rocked back and forward, his hands clasped together.

'Can we fix it?' I said.

'Yeah,' Casper said. 'But we'll have to go out.' He swivelled the turret and looked through the sight as me and Becky watched our screens. The tank's headlights lit the road with long shadows from the debris. Beyond the lamps' beams it was pitch dark. I adjusted the controls on the monitors and got it onto infrared. The embankments appeared around us in ghostly shades. There was no sign of movement. Casper grabbed a box out of a locker, dimmed the light and opened the hatch. 'Coming?' he said to me.

'You all right Daniel?' I said.

'Yep,' he said but he had his eyes shut and hands on his head.

Becky handed me a torch and I climbed out to join Casper at the side of the Eblis. It was dark all around us.

I held my pistol tight. There was no sound. No

movement, the stripped vehicles behind us still in evening air.

'We'll need light to work,' said Casper.

I turned the torch on and flicked it around. The Eblis was halfway over the lower section of blocks. Either side of us was the rest of the barricade, much higher, made of piled up rubble that hemmed us in. The block that we were on had been worn down. Three thick steel rods from the reinforced concrete poked out. One had sheared-off in the track but the other two were still jammed in it where it had snapped.

Casper shook his head, put his gun on the tank and took out a selection of heavy tools, then he shouted up to Becky. 'Take the right track back a little,' he said.

A few seconds later the drive wheel started to turn and the track pulled tight before springing free of the rods.

'That's it,' he shouted up and the motor stopped. He turned to me and pointed at the rods jutting up. 'We need to hammer these flat.'

'Right.' This was going to be some work.

'There's a hammer in the tank.'

I propped up the torch on the concrete aimed at where he was working. Then I went back into the Eblis as he began removing the broken section of track.

Becky and Daniel both looked up at me when I went back in.

'Everything okay?' she said.

'I need the sledgehammer.'

She reached into a compartment and fished it out.

'I don't like it here,' said Daniel.

'Me neither.' I took the hammer and went back out.

Casper had a battery powered drill, which whirred

away on the riveted section of track. The sound bounced back off the embankment.

I put my gun next to Casper's, lined up the sledgehammer and aimed at the steel rod. It was in barely lit and when I swung I caught it at a bad angle. Second time was better and it clanged like a church bell as the rod bent slightly. I did it again, got into a rhythm and bit by bit folded it over. The sound rolled off down the road.

Casper was still busy with the drill. There was a ping and the rivet fell out of the track.

'Got it,' he said.

I hammered some more and folded over the first rod. Then I started on the second. Its position was worse and I had to take long swings. The sledgehammer bounced off. Missed.

'How's it going?' said Casper.

'It's going.'

He carried on doing something with the track and I shifted round to get a better swing. The rod started to fold over and I swung harder to flatten it down.

'That'll do,' he said. 'I need some help here.'

I put the hammer down. It was quieter than ever. I held the track where he showed me as he slid in a new pin and finger-tightened its nut. There was still no movement or sound from the embankment. Maybe we were going to get away with it.

He lined up the second pin but couldn't get it in. The track was at the wrong angle.

'Shit,' he said and he shouted up to Becky. 'Back it a little.'

'How much?' she shouted back.

'Millimetres.'

The track shifted but it now pulled too tight and the pin still wouldn't go in. He got her to move it forwards again. It went too far. This went on for some minutes. Forwards and backwards. I held the torch and watched the embankment. The faint shadows of grass. I listened for sounds: anything that suggested reivers were coming.

At last the track's hole lined up. He slid the new pin in and started to tighten it up.

As he worked there was a sound from behind us, a rustling. I turned towards the noise and flicked the torch up. The dead grass was still and there was no one there. I whispered up to Becky. 'Is there anything on the infrared?'

Before she answered there was a zing, a high pitched sound and something shot over our heads. It bounced off the tank and disappeared into the dark.

'Are you finished?' I grabbed up a pistol and aimed the torch up to where the object had come from. There was still no sign of anyone. They must have chucked it from the other side of the embankment. At least this meant they couldn't aim. It was tempting to fire off a couple of shots but I wanted to save ammo for when someone appeared. When the reivers showed themselves.

Casper grunted. 'Can I have some light?' He worked on the track as two more objects shot over our heads. One disappeared across the road and the other bounced off the hull. Landed near us. I picked it up and examined it. It was an arrow, barbed and fletched with what looked like dried skin.

'See movement up there, Becky?' I shouted.

'Nothing.'

'Nearly done.' Casper gave the track one last tap and

put the tools into the box before closing it. As he straightened up a couple of arrows flew over. One landed on the ground. The second hit him.

Stuck in his back.

He cried out and extended up, stretched out. Another caught on my sleeve, missing my skin. I jerked it out and dragged him sideways, as he moaned and tensed up. There was a sound from the bushes and several arrows bounced off the tank near me. Another caught my trousers and one hit Casper's shoe, sticking in the laces.

I dropped him onto the ground and lay beside him, behind a lump of rubble that formed part of the barrier. I raised my pistol and fired several shots in the direction the arrows had come. The shots thudded into the soil.

'Becky?' I shouted. There was no reply. 'Becky?'

Another hail of arrows came but this time there was another sound, louder. The machine gun on the tank hammered out a stream of bullets. They thudded into the embankment and pinged off rocks. There were no shouts or signs that anyone had been hit but there was silence after the gun stopped.

'Trent, Casper, are you okay?' said Becky.

'Casper's been hit,' I said.

'Shit.'

'It doesn't look critical.' Not that I could tell. But I didn't want to worry her.

'Can you both get back in?'

'I'll have to drag him. Give us covering fire.'

The turret rotated and the Eblis' gun clattered but another arrow bounced off the tank. Seemed they weren't easily scared.

'I can't see them,' said Becky.

'Just keep it up.'

There was no more gunfire for a moment. From some way off there were voices. A conversation then laughter. More talking. The reivers were planning. Working out what to do. Whether to fire more arrows or something worse. Whether to rush us.

Then the main gun of the Eblis roared out, a deafening sound as a great ball of fire appeared, vanishing into black smoke. The top of the embankment exploded in an eruption of soil and small stones, raining down on the tank and us.

This was it. I slid the pistols away and hauled Casper up onto the rear flank. I carried on to the turret, dragging his heavy body. Becky appeared and helped me. Without removing the arrow we twisted and shifted him to slide him down, putting him in the bottom of the tank on his side.

Daniel stared at him. 'Is it hurt?'

'Yes,' I said.

He leant over and took Casper's hand.

I shut the turret and scanned the screens, watching for movement. The shell might have scared them off. But there could be hundreds of them over the other side and they'd probably have other weapons besides arrows. Bigger weapons.

Casper pushed himself up as Becky slid into her seat. 'Take it back,' he said. 'Then forward. So we don't get caught again.'

I set the screens to show the road in front, checking the obstacles before us. There was still no sign of anyone out there. Maybe they'd lost interest. Becky powered up and eased us back half a metre. The repairs held as we moved.

She ran the right track on its own to twist the Eblis round, set us up for the gap. Then she eased us forward over the block and onto the road.

There were thuds on the outside of the Eblis, not loud, like rocks being thrown. If that was all they had we'd be fine.

Becky pushed us forwards, faster.

Then there was an explosion. The vehicle rocked and the lights dimmed, flickered off. They came back up but there was another blast.

Daniel cried out as the lights went off.

CHAPTER TWENTY-NINE

Off

We sat in darkness for a few seconds then red lights came on. Daniel rocked back and forward in his seat but didn't make any sound.

'Everyone all right?' said Becky.

Casper groaned and Daniel continued to rock.

'We need to get going,' I said. If they had grenades they could have other stuff. Worse.

Becky pushed the controls and we picked up speed, bouncing over rubble and burnt-out wheel hubs. There was another explosion in front of us, the screens flickering off.

'Can they do any damage?'

'I need you to drive.' Before I had time to ask why, she slid out of her seat and released the controls. The vehicle slowed. I squeezed past her and took her position as she went up into the turret. I grabbed hold of the controls and shoved them both forward. The Eblis jerked and pitched. I eased off and it steadied.

Becky loaded the gun then shifted into the gunner's

position. She checked the sights and moved the turret.

There were more blocks ahead but these were smaller. I steered to the right but the Eblis turned too hard and thudded into the embankment's side. I straightened up and increased the speed. We needed to get away. Set some distance between us and the reivers before the got a clean hit. Blew us to bits.

An explosion off to our right sprayed us with chunks of road. They bounced off the bulkhead and rattled on the turret.

Then Becky fired. The gun boomed and shook the tank. She reloaded and checked the sights, fired again. The sound filled the vehicle. I concentrated on the screens and kept the power on. For several minutes we picked our way through obstacles.

At last the debris thinned out. Becky reloaded and stayed at the gunner's position but didn't fire again. The road cleared of junk and the land around us levelled.

'Think we're okay,' said Becky. She flicked a switch and the normal lights came on.

'Hope so,' I said. My hands were tight on the controls. I eased off. Daniel was rocking with his eyes shut. Casper lay sprawled at the side.

'We need to sort him out,' I said. The arrow was now coated with blood and a pool of it had formed around him.

The road ahead and land around us was clear. But there were several things behind us. Shapes in the darkness. 'They're following,' I said.

Becky moved to my old seat and checked the screen. 'Jesus.'

The things behind us were indistinct but there were at

least two of them. I picked up the speed. The motors' pitch rose as the Eblis sat up on its suspension. There was little visible ahead so I put the lights on. There was no need to worry about attracting attention. We'd already done that and they were on our tail.

The things behind us paced the tank. Closed on us. They grew in the monitors. By the size and shape they looked to be military vehicles, squat and windowless.

'Can you hit them?' I said.

She loaded up, rotated the turret so it faced backwards and spent ages with her eyes pressed against the sights.

Then she fired.

The Eblis moved on its suspension. There was the roar of the weapon. The rear view flared then dimmed. For some time there was static and distortion. Nothing clear. Then something showed. A lump, a distorted mess. Chewed up with flames coming from it. No movement around it. She'd hit one of them. Blown it to bits.

'Good shot,' I said.

'Lucky.'

'Either way you hit it.'

'Still one out there.' But with the wreck in the road the other would struggle to get past. Even if it did it might suffer the same fate.

I kept the speed up but there was now nothing behind us. No dark shape on our tail. Casper lay on the Eblis's floor and groaned.

'How is he?' I said.

'We need to stop,' said Becky. 'Check him over.'

'Let's get well away from here first.'

Daniel shifted out of his seat and went over to Casper. He placed his hand on his forehead and held one hand.

Casper said nothing but gripped him.

We carried on for a while. The road ahead and behind was empty.

'We should stop soon,' I said.

'Yeah,' said Becky.

We came to a patch of woodland and I slowed us down. There was nothing to worry about on any of the screens, just the trees that hemmed us in.

I pulled the Eblis on the overgrown verge. It stopped with a jerk.

Becky joined Daniel and leant over Casper.

Suddenly one of the monitors lit up.

The Eblis shook as we were hit by something. It pitched to the side.

We'd been fired on.

Another vehicle was ahead of us, possibly the second one that had followed us. Maybe some other. It didn't really matter. What mattered was that it had appeared out of the trees several hundred metres up and attacked us.

Becky climbed back into the gunner's position and took the sight. She swore and moved over to the ammunition store. She'd not reloaded after the last time.

I grabbed my controls and moved us back, away from the other vehicle. It was visible now. It had heavy armour and shuttered windows. One of these was open and a long weapon poked out, no doubt an anti-tank weapon. There was a crater in the ground near us. They'd missed with the first shot.

There was another explosion and the Eblis rocked from side to side.

'Becky,' I said. 'You're going to have to fire. Now.'

'I know.'

She was at the ammunition store and messed around with the catch. She had hold of it but couldn't get it to release. She pulled and banged on it. The thing ahead was about to fire again. They'd have our range. Have us.

Daniel jumped up beside her. He moved Becky's hand aside. Opened the store, rolling out the shell and handing it to her. She took it but for a second did nothing then she opened the breech and loaded.

She was on the sights. Fired. The Eblis shook, there was a flash outside and our vehicle was filled with sound. Shifted back and forward. The screens were blank for a second then the vehicle showed again, untouched. She's missed.

'You didn't get it,' I said.

'I know.'

'You need to fire again —'

'I fucking know, Trent!' She fumbled for the ammo but Daniel was there again. Calm as anything. He handed a shell to her.

She reloaded, fired again. The Eblis rocked and the lights flickered. I watched the screen waiting to see whether she'd hit.

The vehicle was there. But it was split in two. Smoking.

A few figures staggered around.

'Take us to it,' said Becky.

I rammed the controls forward and the Eblis lurched off. She reached over to the machine gun and fired. It rattled out sending the figures backwards onto the ground. They lay still. She fired some more then stopped. There was no more movement.

I stopped a few metres away from it and we sat and watched the screens. There were flames and crackling but nothing else.

'Let's drive on,' Becky said.

'No yet.' I climbed up to the hatch, popping it open, stepping out.

'Where are you going?' she said.

'Just making sure.'

She followed after me, bringing her pistol. We left Casper and Daniel.

The air smelled of hot metal and burning plastic. Smoke came from the smashed vehicle and fires burnt around it. There were several bodies splayed on the ground. Beyond the light from the flames the road and trees were pitch black. Becky walked around with a pistol in her hand. I carried on to the other side. There were bits of metal and components all over: a wheel and suspension parts. Busted bits of panels. Amongst it was a jerry can. It stood in a burning pool of liquid so I grabbed it up. The metal was warm and something sloshed around inside. I took it to the side, away from the flames and opened it. Sniffed: it was petrol, a good few litres. I had enough fuel to leave now.

I sealed the can and walked round to Becky.

'Can we go?' she said.

'Yeah.'

There was a groan and a body slid out of the wreckage. It was a young woman, long haired and dressed in rags. Her legs were chewed up and bloody.

'Help me,' she said. She was only in her teens by the looks.

Becky held out her pistol and aimed it. But she didn't pull the trigger. She put the safety catch back on and slid it into her pocket.

Then the woman started the laugh. It was a cruel sound, harsh and loud.

I put my arm around Becky and led her away. Left the bloodied woman in the wreckage. We returned to the Eblis and I slid in, stashing the fuel at the back. 'Do you want to drive?' I said.

'Yeah,' said Becky.

We pulled off and Casper gave out a moan as he rolled against the arrow in his back. Daniel was at his side again.

'We do need to sort him out,' I said.

'I know, Trent,' said Becky.

She drove on with the lights off. The night-sights picked out the star-lit road as the trees gave way to open moorland. No one followed us and there were no other vehicles. After a few minutes she steered us across rough ground into a small valley. She flicked the lights on to show a small stream and pool with rocky outcrop. We stopped beside it.

The three of us examined Casper. He was white faced. Covered in blood. His breathing was slow and shallow. Together we took hold of him. His flesh was sweaty. We manhandled him out of the tank, Daniel at his feet and me taking the lead. Becky in the turret feeding him out. We slid him into the cool night air and laid him on a blanket on the ground.

Becky set up a torch then we stood around him like we were in an old painting or something.

'What now?' said Becky.

'We'll have to pull the arrow,' I said. The arrow's tip was stopping him losing too much blood but there was obviously some damage going on.

'Just like that?'

'We need to turn him over and have a look.' I knelt and Becky brought the light over. We slid our hands under Casper. Eased him over as he exhaled, groaned. With him turned onto his face I shone the light on the wound. The arrow was jammed in low down, just above his pelvis, close to his kidney. The tip was buried deep in his skin, well into the flesh. It was going to take one hell of a yank to get it out, if it was possible without doing more damage.

'I think we're going to have to leave this for now,' I said.

Becky shook her head. 'Not like this.' Then she walked off and came back with one of the Eblis' tools, a heavy wire cutter. She set it around the arrow and applied pressure. It resisted so I took over, really leaning on the cutter. The shaft sheared off with a crack, leaving a stub sticking of out his skin. Daniel took Casper's had as Becky dressed the wound using a first-aid kit.

'That do?' I said.

'It'll have to for now.'

We carried him back into the Eblis, slow over the uneven ground. Onto the hull that was damp with dew. Daniel slid once and Casper cried out as he bumped onto the metal. I went ahead to ease him into the hatch. Down onto the floor of the tank.

As Becky and Daniel tended to him then I took the torch and went out to check on my bike. There were marks on the side-panels and an arrow stuck between the cooling fins. There were a couple of dents in the tank and a chip off the engine casing but otherwise it seemed all right. I'd look it over properly once we stopped in daylight.

Getting round Edinburgh had been tough but that was

it now. We were on our way. I still had to decide what exactly I was doing but I had fuel. There was nothing holding me back. Rather than just go now I'd leave once we were past Stirling. Well away from the reivers. I'd find a town, somewhere small where I could set up a trading post. My own little business run by me and worked by me. I'd collect bits and pieces from the area and sell them. Daniel could hang around or make his own way.

That felt like some kind of plan.

I put the torch off and looked up at the stars. Billions of them that went on forever. I'd have to get used to not having all these gadgets, all the technology that came with the Eblis. But that would we easy enough. I climbed up onto the tank. Slid in and closed the hatch.

Daniel gave a smile and for once I smiled back.

'Ready?' said Becky.

'Ready.'

We set off again. On our way to the highlands

CHAPTER THIRTY

Highlands

The Eblis rolled across the moors, rocking us around inside it. This was just about as far north as I'd ever been. Working the borders meant just that. I hadn't headed beyond Edinburgh and Glasgow. Not as an adult, at least.

There'd been one time I'd gone up to Stirling with Lawson, before we partnered up with Jamie.

But that had been a crazy time. As bad as some of the worst stuff in the borders. Maybe that was how it was everywhere now. The whole country; whole world.

We rattled on for some time. For an hour or two. It was hard to tell. I'd got used to using clocks in Faeston. When I was kid everyone clock-watched. They had wristwatches and phones and computers all with their meetings on. But Collapse had put end to that. Apart from a few towns, the world had gone back to natural time: sunrise and sunset.

Shadows of the landscape passed by on the monitors. The road was empty of traffic. Empty of anything. A sign appeared for Stirling, busted and hanging off its posts. A little further on we past another in a similar condition. We carried on past shadows of trees.

Casper was asleep with Daniel slumped down beside him. Daniel's face was relaxed, his mouth slack. He took deep breaths and snored. Casper had tight lips, his brow furrowed.

Becky drove on without sign of tiredness. She worked the controls and checked monitors.

'How are you doing?' I said.

Her voice crackled back to me. 'Fine.'

'When do you fancy a break?'

'I'm fine for now, thanks.'

Outside light tinted the sky faint blue. Dark outlines marked the hills that hemmed us in. As we carried on the landscape appeared around us, mountains covered in mist that rolled down and filled the glens. The shadows turned to browns then to deep greens.

For the first time in since I'd gone to Faeston I felt excited. Optimistic even. I could leave anytime now. Possibly at our next stop or even a little further on. It wouldn't be as bad as the borders. Couldn't be worse.

Casper shifted around, moaning. He was waking, his clothes soaked in blood. Becky hadn't looked back at him at all, concentrating on the road ahead. Daniel woke and went over to him. Put his hand on Casper's arm. He rubbed it and whispered something.

We passed a small patch of scraggly woodland and a sign by the road, worn and hanging by one of its two chains. It said Glens Hotel. Becky slowed, turning the Eblis to the right and up a track. We pitched over the rough surface, the woods tight around us, then we came out into an open space of chewed-up tarmac and overgrown lawn. Ahead of us was a three-storey stone building, the windows smashed and the roof specked by saplings that had burst through the slates.

'So much for the Glen Hotel,' said Becky.

She parked the tank on the overgrown car park over by the trees and facing the hotel entrance. When she shut the engines down a dull whirr came from behind me but otherwise it was silent. Becky joined Daniel alongside Casper and I opened the hatch, climbing out.

The air was cool and fresh, damp from the mist but not like the heavy moisture of the coastal fog at Faeston. This was lighter, refreshing. Through the low cloud the mountains were visible disappearing up into the heavens. There was a glimpse of a peak, then it was gone.

Becky called from inside the Eblis. 'Trent. Can you help here?'

I went back in. Casper's face was flushed and covered in drops of sweat.

'He looks poorly,' said Daniel.

'Yeah,' I said. 'He does.'

I helped raise him up towards the hatch. Becky went ahead to pull him as Daniel and me lifted his legs up. After a few minutes of manhandling we had him half out. We slid him the rest of the way and lay him down on a patch of grass, covering him with a blanket.

'Shouldn't we take him in?' said Becky,

'We need to check it's safe,' I said. There'd been no sounds and there was no sign of recent activity but this looked like the kind of place for neo-reivers. Maybe it was too far north for them but it wasn't safe to assume that. I slid my pistol out and went over to the building.

The main door hung off its hinges. It led into a hallway of fungi-coated carpet and blackened walls. Wallpaper hanging off. There was a wooden desk with stairs to the left and a lift door to the right. Most of the balustrades had been kicked out of the staircase and empty hooks marked where pictures had once been on the wall. The place smelled of rot and decay.

The ground floor had a lounge off to the right with big old fire place and view of the glen through its cracked windows. There was a settee but everything else had gone. At the opposite side of the hallway was a dining room with no furniture. It led on to a kitchen with all the cupboards opened and emptied: apart from a couple of pans the place had been picked clean. Even the cooker had had its fittings taken. Rats had made a nest in the corner and there was mouse shit on the floor. Beyond that there was a storeroom and office. Whatever might have been in them had long gone as well.

Back in the entranceway I kicked at the staircase to see if it'd take my weight. The bottom one was solid but I eased my feet onto each stair just in case. They creaked but held as I worked my way up.

The first-floor landing's carpet was damp and rotted. There was a window but this had vegetation growing over it so virtually no daylight got through. What little light there was came from the rooms that lined the passageway. Most of their doors had fallen off making the exploration easy. They were empty aside from stained beds and the odd busted TV sets or smashed kettle. At the far end there was a room with an intact door which was shut and locked. I shoved it hard. It didn't give so I stepped back, pistol raised and kicked it in.

It thudded open and smacked against the wall. There were empty tins and bottles scattered across the floor. The room stank: really disgusting. I stayed in the doorway for a moment to let the stench out. Then I went back in and stepped over balled up clothes, half-finished meals on plates, old-world magazines screwed up. Shoes. Lots of men's shoes.

The bed was covered in sheets and blankets, layers of them. This was where the smell came from. I should have left the room and shut the door again. Not bothered looking in the bed. But I had to know what was there, whether it was what I expected. I pulled back the sheets. There was a body, hairy and sunken eyed, the skin tight around the face, teeth bared. I flicked the sheet back and went to the window. The lock had jammed so I smashed it off with the gun and opened it as wide as it would go. I took great lungfuls of the fresh air then held my breath and kicked around the stuff lying on the floor. There were food packets: pasta in sauce, by the looks. They were sealed and not too faded. I took several and went out, slamming the door shut.

The rooms on the second floor were all ruined, the wrecked roof having let in enough rain and seeds to turn it into an indoor garden. Firs and ferns dotted the carpets near windows while fungi fanned out in the corners.

I went back down and out to Becky, Daniel and Casper. They sat on the overgrown lawn as the sun came up through the cloud.

'Any good?' said Becky.

'Safe enough.' I pointed at Casper. 'How is he?'

'Still poorly,' said Daniel. I had to smile at that. He had a way to say it straight.

We carried Casper in and laid him out in the dining room on a section of carpet that didn't smell too bad. We turned him onto his side and Becky went back out to the Eblis.

'Is he going to get better?' said Daniel.

'I'm not sure,' I said. There was no point kidding him.

When Becky returned she brought a first aid kit, a candle and some tools. She rolled up Casper's shirt and used a needle to inject something into his back. Then she lit the candle and heated up the ends of a pair of scissors. Once they had cooled she cut the skin around the arrowhead, peeling it away. He whined as she sliced into his flesh.

'You done this before?' I said.

'Not exactly.' She held the shaft of the arrow and tugged, cutting some more before sliding it out with a tearing sound. As the blood flowed out she stemmed it with a pad, then several more, taping over the wound. Casper was now white.

I helped her bandage it all up then we left him to rest. She joined me over by the doorway while Daniel prayed beside him.

'He's lost blood,' she said. 'That was deep. And god knows what was on the tip. Reivers aren't known to be clean.'

'You did a good job on him.'

'Stuff you learn on the road.' She stared over at Daniel who now held Casper's hand. 'Should we get all out gear in?'

'Yeah, why not.' I'd not mention moving on. Not yet: not until I had a clear plan.

We brought in bags from the Eblis and dumped them in the lounge. Back in the dining room Casper still lay flat out, his breathing shallow as Daniel sat with him. Becky went off to the kitchen and returned carrying a pan.

'Might as well do our cooking in here.' She set out our food on the hearth alongside the two packets I'd found. The fire's grate was filled with ash and there were a few chunks of unburnt coal. Becky prodded at them with a poker.

'I'll get some firewood.' I was tempted just to kick out the rest of the stairs, instead I went out to the woods. Daniel came with me.

The air was cool and fresh but the sun was as high as it was going to get and had cleared some of the mist. A light breeze blew down the glen and sunlight lit the far hillside. Compared to the towns I'd worked in it was peaceful but there wasn't much to live on up here. Without becoming a goatherd, it was hard to see how anyone could survive. Maybe that was why it was so quiet.

We gathered up twigs and small branches. I had to work out what I was going to do soon. We were a long way north and there'd be fewer towns and villages to drop off at as we carried on.

It was probably best to wait and see how Casper was getting on before I made a decision. If he died, well that would shift the dynamics. Make it more attractive for me to hang around. But if he pulled through then I'd be off.

We took the wood into the hotel and I prepared a fire before helping Becky cook the food. We added a tin of soup to one packet of pasta and had quite a decent sized meal. She kept some aside uncooked ready for when, or if, Casper was better. Throughout the meal he slept on the floor taking shallow breaths. He had more colour in his face.

Afterwards Daniel helped Becky clean up the pan and

cutlery so I went out to gather more fuel.

I picked my way through the trees and after a few minutes I had a good collection of wood. I made my way across the overgrown car park past the Eblis with the Scrambler on the back: the Scrambler I'd not run for some days. It'd be sensible to check it over before leaving.

When I went back inside Daniel was at one side of Casper while Becky sat at the other. He was breathing more steadily. Maybe he'd pull through. I dropped the wood by the fire. It was warm now but it would cool down later. Especially this far north.

'I might check the Scrambler over,' I said.

'Can I come?' said Daniel.

Becky stayed with Casper and I led Daniel outside.

He was like a puppy at my side. 'What's the Scrambler?'

I laughed. 'My motorbike.' I led him over to the Eblis. 'Here, look.'

Daniel touched the bike, running his finger through the dirt. 'Needs a clean.'

'It does that.' There were a few marks on the tank and dust all over the paintwork. When I prodded the back tyre it was soft, low on pressure. 'You going to help?'

'Yep,' he said.

We undid the straps that held it in place and he helped me set it on the ground. There was part of the fuel tank clear of dust and petrol seeped out. An arrow was jammed in the cooling fins and assorted bits of gravel wedged in nooks and crannies.

'Let's wash it,' I said.

Daniel fetched a pan and a tea towel to use as a rag and we wiped the Triumph down.

Once it was clean I got him to hold the bike as I removed the back wheel. There was a piece of shrapnel jammed in the tyre and I patched the inner tube. At each step I explained what I was doing to him. I sealed the hole in the side of the fuel tank with tape as a temporary fix. We put the wheel back on then cleaned and adjusted the brakes. The sump was still full of oil so other than that it was just a case of adjusting and lubricating. Topping up the juice from the jerry can.

By late afternoon the bike was looking reasonable. We gave it a final wash and as it dried out Becky called us over to eat. She'd cooked up the second packet of pasta and added a tin of beans.

CHAPTER THIRTY-ONE
Patch Up

We sat by the fire and had our food. Casper was still rolled up on the floor. He hadn't moved since we'd removed the arrow but his skin had pinked up and he was breathing better.

'How is he?' I said.

'I think he's going to be all right,' said Becky.

'That arrow was in deep.'

'There's a lot of flesh around that part of the back.' She picked on with her food. 'It'll be cold tonight. We'll have to stack the fire.'

'There's one half-decent room upstairs.'

'We'll be better off down here. We can't move Casper.'

'Fine,' I said. It wasn't that bothered.

After we'd eaten I helped clean up then went outside with Daniel. The sun had dipped into the mist that now rolled down the glen. 'Let's start the bike,' I said.

It took a few jabs at the starter but it fired up on the third shot. He jumped back as I revved it up. For couple of minutes I let it run and warm itself. It was all fine apart from a thread of fuel that leaked from the tank. The patch I'd put there had failed. I switched off then used a piece of spare fuel line to siphon the petrol back into the jerry can. Once it was empty I cleaned the hole. It was a good centimetre wide. In my spares I had a collection of bolts, nuts and washers. I found a combination that fitted and I tightened it up to plug the hole.

Then I refitted the tank and refilled the fuel. Daniel stood close by me and sucked his teeth as the petrol sloshed around.

Once it was all done we went to gather more branches from the darkening woods.

'Are we staying here?' said Daniel.

'Just for a while.'

'Where are we going next?' Animals scurried off as we crunched on the leaf litter.

'I'm not sure.'

Daniel pursed his lips, didn't ask anymore but it was clear he wanted a plan. I'd brought him along so now he was my responsibility. I wasn't going to ride off after sunset so we were going to be here for at least one night.

We took the wood into the hotel. Becky had set out the bedding, hers next to mine and Casper's over at the far side. Daniel's was in the other corner. He went straight over to his and moved it around.

'You sure about us all being in the same room?' I said.

'Seems sensible.'

Daniel yanked his shoes off and slid into his bed. 'I'm tired,' he said.

'It's only early evening,' I said.

'I'm tired.' He lay back and stared at the ceiling. It wasn't long before he was snoring.

Becky laughed. 'He knows his own mind.'

'Seems to.'

'Should we go into the other room? We need to talk.'

'Right.' This sounded serious.

She checked on Casper. His breathing had settled down and he was lying stretched out rather than curled up on himself.

We grabbed some of the wood and she took her sleeping bag. We went through to the lounge, made a fire and sat on the settee, the only piece of furniture. Though it smelled damp it was relatively clean.

'We'll be okay here for a couple of days,' she said.

'Yeah.'

'Then we're on the home straight. Not far to the loch. To where Arcadia is.'

'I suppose.'

'You're still on for it?'

'Possibly.'

She sighed. 'What's going on Trent? What's locked in that head of yours?' She moved up so that we were close together on the settee.

'Nothing really —'

'Come on. You picked up that lad to bring along and you've not asked anything about where we are going. Are you still in?'

The fire crackled and rippled on her face. This seemed familiar to me, like situations I'd had with Sophie. Questions with no right answer. This time I was going to be straight. Tell the truth. 'Maybe I'll drop off before we get there.'

Becky stood up and went over to the fire. She leant against the mantelpiece and twisted one leg behind the other. 'We need you, Trent. We need what you can do.'

'I can't do anything.'

'Of course you can.' She stared at me as the fire popped and hissed on the damp wood. 'I didn't just invite you along for the fun of it. You're good in a crisis. When it gets tough. There are still challenges ahead.'

'Right…'

'Think about it, at least.' She moved away from the fire and stood by the settee, hands on her hips.

'All right. I'll think about it.'

She smiled, and without saying anything else, leant forward and kissed me. She lowered herself down wrapping her arms around me and holding our bodies close together.

After a minute she moved away.

'What was that for?' I said.

'Just for you.' Then she took off her shirt and trousers, down to her underwear. She slid into her sleeping bag, one edge of it held open to show her long legs and slim torso. Then she shifted around and took off her knickers and bra. Chucked them onto the settee next to me. 'Well?'

I slid my own clothes off and joined her, as the fire crackled and the building creaked around us.

CHAPTER THIRTY-TWO

Confess

Becky was up before me in the morning. I rose and dressed then went into the dining room to find her there. Daniel was awake as well, standing by her as she tended a pan of water on the fire.

'How are you?' I said, all bright and cheery.

'Fine,' said Becky. 'We need more wood.' Her face was expressionless. Flat.

Daniel poked at the fire.

'How are you?' I said to him.

'Good,' he said.

'Sleep well?'

'Yep.' He wasn't very chatty either. Maybe he was hungry. Maybe we all were. I went over to Casper. His eyes were half open and his breathing regular.

He grunted and pushed himself up. Becky appeared with a mug of warmed water. She almost pushed me out of the way to put it to his lips, letting him sip the liquid. Then she patted him on the head, holding him up, smiling at him with warm eyes. 'I'm going to heat up some of the tinned meat we've got. Fix a good breakfast.'

'I didn't know we had tinned meat,' I said.

'I've kept it safe.' She returned to the fire and opened the tin.

I went outside. The sun fought its way through the morning mist that filled the glen and hid the mountains.

The Scrambler was where I had left it, parked behind the Eblis. There was time to give it a test run before we set off. I wasn't bothered about breakfasting with Becky if she was going to be a pain in the arse.

I went back in. Daniel was at the far side of the room as Casper and Becky chatted. He seemed to have made quite a recovery. My pistol was on the mantelpiece so I grabbed it up and shoved it in my jeans. 'Fancy a ride on the bike, Daniel?' I said.

He glanced over at the other two before he spoke. 'Is it safe?'

'Yeah. It's fine.'

'Are you sure?'

'Yeah. Come on.'

'Okay.'

'Where are you going?' said Becky.

'Off on the bike.'

'You going far?'

'Not sure.'

I led him out without saying anymore. Maybe it would shake her up a little. Shake the pair of them up.

I slid onto the saddle and told Daniel to get on the back.

He hesitated then swung his leg over. For a second it seemed he was going to slid off then he grabbed me and pulled himself into place. His hands were tight around my waist.

I turned the bike's engine over and it coughed but didn't catch. It started on the second prod and I revved it, holding it at two-thousand revs for a minute, letting it warm before dropping to tick-over. It was a familiar feeling holding the handlebars, pulling the clutch in and twisting the throttle. As I slipped it into gear it gave the usual thud, hiccupping a little as I pulled off. I took it slowly along the track, as it bounced over the ruts made by the Eblis, the exhaust note roaring back off the trees.

Daniel had his whole body pulled up tight against me. At the end of the track I stopped. 'Are you all right?' I said to him.

'Yep.'

On the open road I let it rev up, right round to four-thousand rpm and the engine picked up cleanly. It slid into second then third. As I wound it up some more Daniel banged me on the back of my head. He shouted something so I slowed and pulled in at the side of the road.

'What's up?' I said.

'I don't like it.'

'You just need to get used to it.'

'No. I don't like it.'

We stayed put as the bike idled. 'Maybe we can go a little slower, let you ease into it…'

'No. Don't like it. I want to go back.'

'Let's just take a short run. Up the road —'

'No. I don't like it.'

So I swung the bike round in the road. We rode back in first and I slipped the clutch on the rutted section to keep the speed right down. Maybe I'd overdone it. Or maybe he just didn't like bikes.

As we approached the Eblis I turned the engine off and coasted in neutral to save fuel. If he didn't like riding the bike we really were stuck. I'd have to get hold of a car, or walk. Or leave him with Casper and Becky.

I stopped the bike. 'Get off,' I said. It wasn't his fault that he didn't like the bike but I was still pissed off with him.

He swung his leg over and stumbled off the saddle. I put the stand down and slid off myself.

Daniel stood there like he didn't know what to do.

'Come on,' I said. 'Let's go eat.' I guessed Becky would have prepared some food. Maybe I'd take Daniel out later. Or just sit him on it without moving. Something to get him used to the idea of it. There were options.

As we approached the hotel there was movement from the dining room, odd and rhythmic, the kind of thing that attracted attention. I pulled the pistol out and went up to the window. Becky was there with Casper. She had her back to me and it was her head I'd seen, bobbing up and down.

She was naked and astride Casper, riding him. Like she had me the night before. Now it was him she was having sex with. Her brother.

I stayed like that for a while, as she moved and he made noises, until they'd finished. It wasn't the kind of thing I normally did but this wasn't a normal situation. I'd not even noticed that Daniel was beside me. His mouth open.

I put the pistol away, grabbed his hand and led him round to the entranceway. He went to say something but I put my hand over his mouth. I could hear Becky and Casper talking. She was muttering on about how much she wanted him but he was warning her, saying I'd be back soon with Daniel. That they'd get caught. There was no talk of this being wrong or weird, just that they might be found out.

I let go of Daniel and walked into the room, standing by the doorway, waiting until Casper saw me.

'Trent?' he said.

Becky pulled her shirt back on while he lay back with his hand over his face.

'What's going on?' I said.

She slid her trousers on and went over to the pan by the fire. 'Come and eat something.'

'You kidding?'

She stirred the food. 'I'll explain.'

'I think you'd better.'

I kept my eyes on her as I walked round, sitting on the floor. Daniel sat behind me as if he was afraid to get too close to her. She spooned out food for each of us, pasta in sauce again. It had burnt onto the bottom of the pan. Casper dragged himself over and we sat spaced out around the room. Becky ate but Casper just stared at the floor.

'So?' I said. 'What's going on?'

'It's not as bad as it seems,' said Casper, his voice weak.

'Really?'

He glanced at Becky. Then over at me and Daniel. 'We haven't quite told you everything…'

Becky was now halfway through her food with no sign of saying anything.

'It was a convenience thing,' he said. 'It's not that…We needed to get you on our side. Without making it too odd, difficult for you. We were going to clear it up.'

Becky put down the rest of her food and stared at me. 'We're not brother and sister. He's my lover.'

I laughed at this, not so much as what she'd said but the use of word. Lover didn't seem to fit Casper very well. 'Right,' I said. 'So what was I?'

She shrugged and held my gaze, the look softening a little, but still hard to read. 'Sometimes stuff just happens. Stuff you haven't planned...You wouldn't have come with us if you'd known we were a couple.'

'I see.'

'And you'd have asked more. Like about where we met and such like. This made it easier.'

'And Arcadia? Is that real?'

Becky shook her head. Just a tiny movement but enough to let me know that they'd made it up. That it didn't exist.

'What else do I need to know?'

'I think we've said enough,' said Casper.

'I don't think so.' I pulled out the pistol and aimed it at him.

'You wouldn't.'

I cocked and it fired just over his head. It punched a nice hole in the wall behind him. He shrunk down, folded up on himself. The sound seemed to last for ages.

'Missed,' I said. I was in the mood to shoot both of them. Hurt them at least. They'd really messed me around.

Becky took a deep breath then straightened up. 'Okay. Okay. But Daniel doesn't need to hear all of this —'

'Yes, I do,' said Daniel.

'All right. Fine.' She took a breath, moved over to the wall. Leant back against it and closed her eyes. 'Casper was part of a gang, a big gang in the borders, once run by a guy called Maxwell – '

'Maxwell,' I said. Maxwell was who I'd stolen from. Been on the run from in the past. Maxwell had been a nasty piece of work. A real bastard and so were his men.

'Casper wasn't one of the main people. But that was where he was. I met him in Kelso and, well, you know. That was how I found out about…' She turned to Casper. He shook his head. Neither said anything else.

I'd had enough of this. I went over to him, pointed the gun at his head. Then I went round his back and leant the barrel against his injury. He cried out.

'I want some answers,' I said.

'Okay!' said Becky. 'Okay. We found out about you. About Gehenna. That you had the documents with all the details on the sub.'

'I see.' I'd been so stupid. They'd played me all along. Gehenna. That deadly sub. That's what they wanted. In a loch in Scotland, not their mysterious town. They'd made up all the Arcadia crap.

'We borrowed a bike from Maxwell's as well as the Eblis.'

'He had the tank?'

'The tank, weapons, all kinds of stuff. Once he was dead it started to unravel. So we helped ourselves…'

'Right.' I sat down again. They'd come to Faeston to find me, for what I had. There'd been no coincidences. 'It was all planned out?'

'Apart from me getting caught,' said Casper.

'Why Gehenna?'

'Why do you care?' he said.

I waved the gun at him. Then lowered it. I didn't care

anymore. 'So what now?'

She shrugged. 'That's up to you.'

The pair of them looked at me, across at Daniel.

I got up. 'I need some air.'

When I walked out Daniel followed me.

We went over to the trees. They'd played me all right, reeled me in and kept me interested. It explained a lot but there were still a few gaps. Gaps that didn't matter.

The worst part was the Maxwell link. No one decent worked for Maxwell.

'What you going to do?' said Daniel.

'I'm not sure.'

'Are you cross with them?'

'Yeah.'

'You'll feel better in the morning.'

'What?'

'That's what Mum always says.'

'Your mum's gone Daniel. Forever.'

I didn't give him time to reply but walked off into the trees, away from all of them. It wasn't his fault but he was part of all this now.

I faced back to hotel, its smashed windows catching the morning light. In front of it was Daniel just standing there. Then there was the Eblis and off along the track the Scrambler, now all tidied and ready to go.

And so was I.

CHAPTER THIRTY-THREE
Hit the Road

It didn't take long for me to pack up and even less time to say goodbye. I raised my hand and said, 'I'm off.' Becky looked like she wanted to say something but didn't. Casper just stared at the floor. I still had hold of the pistol in case he tried anything but he seemed out of it.

Then there was Daniel. He was still on the front lawn when I went out. 'I'm sorry what I said. About your mum.'

When he looked at me he blinked more than usual. 'It's okay,' he said. 'It's okay.'

'Daniel, I'm going.'

'Oh?'

'Are you coming with me?'

'You going on the motorbike?'

'Yes.'

He took a deep breath. 'I'm staying.'

'You're welcome to come.'

'Not on the motorbike.'

We stood there for a minute. Then I put my arms

around him and hugged him. It was like holding a bag full of wooden stakes. When I released him he wouldn't look at me.

'Look, Daniel…'

'Bye.' He went back into the dining room with Becky and Casper.

I walked out with my kit under my arm. It seemed further to the bike than it had before.

I turned the Scrambler around and climbed onto it. Across at the hotel Daniel was at the window. I waved to him but he didn't move.

I started the bike. It settled into a smooth tick over. Gehenna's details were in the bottom of my bag as was the shotgun, bike parts, siphon tube, money and my few clothes. There was a can of food in there as well, something I'd put there just in case. In case I had to leave like this.

I rode the Scrambler along the track, rutted and chewed up. At the end the main road was empty in both directions. Either was fine. I had everywhere open to me. Nowhere. Despite Casper and Becky messing me around, they had given me some kind of purpose and direction for the last week. Now I was drifting again.

Mist hung over the road as I headed south. There was no real reason why I'd chosen this way but we'd done the last few miles without difficulty and it was the opposite direction to Becky and Casper's intended route.

The Scrambler pulled well, cruising at a comfortable fifty despite the road's pitted surface. Frost had lifted the tarmac in places and the far side was further chewed up by the Eblis. There were clear track marks going for miles.

It was a shame about Daniel. I felt bad about leaving

him. I'd found him and brought him with me. It was because of me he was here. But it wasn't like I'd refused to take him. He'd been offered the chance to come and he'd chosen not to. Still, I felt bad.

Now I had to sort myself out.

Once I got past Stirling I'd decide where to go. There was the east coast of Scotland. Fife: Kirkcaldy or St Andrews, even. The stories about the new developments in those places all sounded interesting, even if they weren't keen on outsiders. I'd have to prove myself to settle somewhere like that.

I dodged a pothole and accelerated the bike up to sixty, swinging it round the ruts in the road. The bike really was running well.

Maybe it was time to head south, well south. There wasn't much worth seeing in the Midlands, it seemed, not from what traders passing through Faeston had said, but there were places in Cornwall that sounded good. Those that hadn't completely disappeared into the sea. There was nothing decent in the South East, of course, after what had happened to London. That wasn't worth visiting.

But there was no need to decide where to go yet.

As the miles clocked up I got back into the rhythm of travelling, that floating sensation that always came with being on the road. Moving through the scenery but not part of it, automatically driving without thinking. I passed by forest and open moors, wrecked vehicles and debris. The land fell away to the left as a small river followed the road. Eventually I'd pass Gregg and Will's wrecked car and bodies. But that was just another piece of the landscape.

A white Transit van approached from way off, the first vehicle I'd seen. There was nothing special or significant about it. It travelled at a steady speed keeping a straight track down the road. As usual I avoided eye contact or any kind of signalling just in case it was neo-reivers.

Off in the distance the sun lit a hill, a bright patch of green in the grey mist-covered land. Maybe I'd stay up here, where there was plenty of space and fewer scavengers.

The Transit swung across the road towards me, a sharp manoeuvre so it was head on. Maybe the driver had fallen asleep at the wheel. Without thinking I swung out of the way, steering to the left to avoid it. The van followed so it was still directly in front of me. I tried to go over to the right, where it should have been but it followed again, shifting to the middle.

Rather than hit it I swung further left, towards the road's edge.

The van was really close now but there was just enough space for me to skirt round it on the roadside.

Then it eased further over. I had nowhere to go.

It was going to hit me head-on. Smash into me and the bike.

I steered onto the verge, tried to ride across the rough grass.

The handlebars jerked as the front wheel clipped a stone. It skipped away to the left. Skidded. Then it was off the verge and dropping down. It fell away so that I was weightless for a second. My stomach dropped into my boots as I lost control of it. As the bike careered off the road.

As I was launched into space I saw the faces of the

driver and passenger in the van. It was Nico with Gregg beside him, his faced all smashed up but both of them grinning, smiling at me as I flew down the riverbank.

CHAPTER THIRTY-FOUR

Soft Shoulder

The bike's wheels caught the ground and it flicked onto its left side. It kicked and bounced and upended. For a second I thought I could regain control. Keep it upright, ease the brakes on and bring it to a stop.

Then it smashed into a boulder. I was flung over it and down the slope. I held my hands in front of me as I tried to slow myself, as I shot through the undergrowth. Briers and thick bracken cut at me as my momentum sent me onwards, headfirst towards the stones at the river's edge. I stuck my arm out and spun off to the right, in the direction of a pool. I'd missed the rocks but was now headed for the water. My foot caught in a crevice and I was catapulted into it, hitting it splayed out. I smacked into the pool and took a last breath before it dragged me down, into its icy turbulence. The weight of my rucksack sent me straight to the bottom. The water foamed around me as I thrashed to get out. I kicked with my feet until they hit solid ground and I burst from the surface taking in a great lungfuls of air, grasping at vegetation to pull me to the side.

The Scrambler lay against a rock nearby, just beside the small waterfall feeding the pool. The bike's headlamp was bust and tank split.

As I struggled out of the stream a thud came from the bike and it burst into flames. There was laughter. Nico and Gregg stood on the roadside. Nico had a pistol in his hand and he aimed it at me. I grabbed a breath and pushed off the side. Ducked into the river.

Shots zinged around me as I sank into the freezing pool, pulled down by the rucksack. The bullets rippled through the water, clunked into the river bed. There was no way I could surface again, not with them up there armed, but I'd not be able to hold my breath for long.

I felt in my pocket for the pistol. But it wasn't there. I'd lost it.

I pushed along the riverbed, backwards across the smooth stones. I made towards the waterfall, as another shot pinged through the water, just missing my leg. My chest felt like it was going to burst, that even lungs filled with water would be better than holding onto the stale air in them.

The waterfall growled above me and I rose up behind it, hoping there'd be and air gap that I could hide in. But my face hit rock. I moved around and found no way up. I was trapped. My lungs burned for air. Even a bullet through the head was better than this.

Then I found a patch of silver on the water, a slim bubble of air under the rock. Tilting my head to the side I slid the edge of my mouth into it and inhaled air, cold and moist but still breathable. I took in water. Coughed it out. Tried to keep the breaths shallow, to avoid taking in any more. I held myself in that spot.

But Nico and Gregg were still out there armed and after me. They wouldn't just walk off after a few minutes, they'd want to see me punched full of bullet holes. All I wanted to do was breath, avoid being in the water. I slid the rucksack off without going under. As I kept taking in the air. I fumbled with the fasteners. My hands were slow, frozen. After a couple more breaths I ducked under, as the waterfall boiled around me, the cold crushing my head like it had nails hammered into it. Stinging my eyes.

As well as Gehenna stuff, gun and food there were clothes in there and I dragged out a shirt, then spare trousers. They flapped around, distorted in the water, hit me in the face. Nico and Gregg would be on their way down to the riverbank ready to close in and make sure they'd got me. They'd come into the water.

I rose up under the waterfall and took in another couple of breaths, then ducked down again, dumping the bag and taking the shirt and trousers. I needed a decoy. A distraction for them. The jeans were similar to the ones I was wearing. The shirt was an old checked one, not the same as what I had on but near enough. They flapped around in the current as I tried to knot them together. One end of the shirt held on a belt loop but I let go before tying another one. They rushed off in the current and snagged on a rock.

My lungs begged for air. I pushed up, under the waterfall, gasping at the thin sliver of air, hoping the clothing would be enough to convince them. It wasn't great but it was all I had.

For some minutes I stayed put, my hands numb and feet immovable. There were a couple more shots into the water, possibly near to where I'd put the clothing but nothing else. Maybe that was it, they'd fired into what they thought was me and they'd go.

Then the waterfall changed, the steady rumble coming in waves, almost stopping. With the surges came other sounds, rocks being moved around above me. They were damming up the river, diverting it so they could calm the pool and see better. If they did that they'd spot me here. I felt through the bag to find anything that would help, whether a weapon or something to put into the water and colour it. There was the shotgun, filled with water, some tools, soggy money, a can of beans. And the siphon tube. The old piece of fuel line I'd used to drain the petrol. I slipped this out, pushed it into the patch of trapped air, now stilled with the water flow diverted. I held the tube in place and ducked down as far as I could go with my back flat against the rocks. The tube tasted of stale petrol, droplets of greasy water running down into my mouth. A tickle grew in my throat. I coughed and swallowed water. Tried to clear it. Breathed again.

I drew more air through the tube. Took it slow. Fought against the urge to burst out of the water and breathe deeply.

The water was now just a trickle and I could hear voices, raised but unclear. Nico and Gregg moved around on the side, distorted shapes that shifted and rippled above me. One disappeared and the other made a great movement and the water exploded as something dropped into it. For a second I thought they'd used some kind of grenade but as the disturbance settled it was clear that they'd only thrown a rock in. Two others followed then nothing.

They disappeared from the river bank. The waterfall soon returned to full flow as their dam either failed or they bust it themselves. I stayed still despite the pain in my hands, feet and head from the cold.

At last I slid up through the waterfall and surfaced beside it, ready to duck down if they'd camped out to wait. There was no one on the riverbank and no sound apart from the river rushing past. After a minute more I picked around in the water with my feet. Once I'd found my bag I slid it into the shallows and reached into the water to fetch it out. Then I dragged it and myself through the shallows. I lay out on the rocks at the side, cold, exhausted and bruised.

The river rolled past and I took in great breaths, rested. I stared at the clouds, fluffy and dark-edged. At least Nico and Gregg had gone: both of them very much alive and well. A tough couple of bastards.

I must have been there for some time, dozing as the sun fought its way through the mist and warmed me a little, not really taking away the numbness in my hands and feet. It was only when I stood up that the wound on my left arm showed, a clean shot that had nicked the bicep, bleeding a little, washed by the river.

Then I realised that Nico and Gregg would be after the Eblis. The track marks on the road would be easy to follow and they'd find them. Torture and kill them. Becky and Casper had messed me around, really pissed me off, but not enough to wish that on them. Not for Becky, at least. And there was Daniel.

I struggled up over to the Scrambler. It was a right-off. They'd finished it off with a couple of shots into the fuel tank that had set it alight. The whole thing was charred, black with melted plastic from the seat and wiring loom. The barrel was split to show a cracked piston. The front wheel was twisted and frame snapped. If I was going back to the hotel it had to be on foot. I took off my clothes, wrung them out and shook them, lying each on rocks. When I emptied my boots a load of water poured out. My socks were double their normal size. There wasn't time to let it dry properly so after a few minutes I slid everything back on, at least a little warmer, and made my way up the hillside. On the way I tipped water out of my sodden bag. Then I joined the road and headed back towards the hotel.

Despite being in sunlight I was cold, wet and the injury in my arm was making itself felt. But I picked up the pace and focussed on what was ahead. I walked faster with long strides, pushing myself on. To get there before Nico could really set to work.

CHAPTER THIRTY-FIVE

Revenge

The walk took a long time. It was a hard slog on foot. Soaking wet. Near the hotel I stepped off the road and listened. My arm hurt and water ran from my nose but I'd warmed a little. There were sounds of birds in the trees and animals moving round. A stream trickled somewhere nearby. And there was a voice. A faint voice in the distance: male, deep.

The track to the hotel had imprints from tyres, fresh wide ones that criss-crossed those from the Eblis. Further along was the white Transit, parked just out of view of the hotel. The grass was trampled down around it and the sliding side-door open. There was no sign of anyone.

A sound came from the van, low and repetitive. Things being moved or sorted. Then the voice I'd heard — a man repeating something. I ducked down and moved up to the door. It had a crew cab with six seats rather than the usual three. In the middle of the back ones was a fella shuffling a pack of cards. He was in his thirties, tall and slim with a pock-marked face. As he set the cards out he said what each was: a king or ace or three. I'd not seen him before. It looked like Nico had picked up a helper along the way. Across the seat from him was an old revolver. He was intent on his cards as he laid out the suits.

I moved away from the van into the cover of nearby trees. He continued to name the cards as he put them down. I opened my bag and slid out the shotgun. Water dribbled from the barrel. When I broke it soggy cartridges dropped out. I shook the cartridges dry, popped them back in and shut it. The mechanism felt stiff. After being in the water it had probably lost what little lubrication it had ever had. And the cartridges where likely to be duds. Still, it looked the part so that would help.

I stepped forward and stood in the doorway so that his pistol was between me and him. For a few seconds he carried on setting down the cards. Then he glanced up. At first he smiled but that soon disappeared and he reached for the gun.

'Don't.' I jabbed the shotgun towards him.

His hand stayed a few centimetres away from the pistol as he stared at me. I cocked the shotgun. Although the mechanism was stiff it worked and the hammers held.

His hand retracted and he moved back into his seat. He watched me the whole time, his eyebrows knotted down over his eyes in concentration. 'What you want?' he said.

'Just to pass through.'

'I'm not after trouble.'

'Me neither.' I reached over and took the pistol. He stiffened at this but didn't move. I swung the cylinder out. There were three rounds in place, the first lined up with the barrel. I flicked it closed, cocked it and aimed at the man. 'Get out,' I said. 'This way.'

He sighed then shuffled across the seat to join me at the side of the van. The cards fell onto the floor apart from one that stuck to his trousers, the four of hearts.

We stood by the van and I slid the shotgun into my bag.

'What now?' he said.

There was a rattling in branches some way off and leaves crunched. For a second I scanned the undergrowth but there was no sign of anyone. It was most likely a bird or squirrel.

I waved the gun at him and we went round to the back of the van. It was unlocked and I popped the door open. Inside there were bags, spare shoes and coats. Shirts and tools and tins of food. Also four grenades and a rocket launcher. The kind of things Nico liked to have around. There was a short length of rope too. 'Kneel down,' I said. He didn't move so I jabbed the pistol at him.

'Not out here,' he said. 'Not on my own.' His voice wavered as he spoke.

'I'm not going to shoot you,' I said. 'Not if you do what I say. Kneel down and put your hands behind your back.'

He knelt and I grabbed the rope, wrapping it round his wrists, knotting it tight. Then I looped it around his ankles and tied it off. Once he was secured I put the pistol and shotgun down and went into the back of the van. I ripped a sleeve off a shirt and twisted it up before pulling it through the man's mouth and knotting it behind his head. He stared up at me but didn't try to move. I took the pistol and left the shotgun in the van. It was tempting to take the grenades and rocket launcher but they were blunt weapons. If Nico and Gregg had the others trapped in there I'd need something subtler. With the gun tight in my hand I made my way towards the hotel.

There were no signs of movement at the windows. If Nico had attacked in his usual way they'd be wherever he found them, probably the lounge or dining room. He didn't move people around much, just grabbed them and made them sweat.

There was clear ground between me and the front of the building. The Eblis was out in the open with all its weapons. I went back into the woods to scout round to the back. Before moving off I stashed my bag in a tree, wedged between some of the lower branches. Then I picked my way through the undergrowth, between thin pines all on top of each other, staying in them right round to the kitchen. I stopped at the back of the house, near the kitchen so I was able to see into the back window of the dining room. A branch snapped behind me. For a second I didn't move. Then there was a hand on my arm.

'Trent?'

I turned to face Daniel. 'Shit.'

'Shouldn't swear.'

'How did you get out?' I said.

'Ran. When they came.'

'They didn't spot you?'

'Nope.'

Nico and Gregg wouldn't have expected a third person with them so they wouldn't have looked for him. Now he was here with me.

'How many are there?' I said.

'Four men.'

'You sure?'

'Yep.'

I had a revolver, the stuff in the van. And Daniel.

Inside the hotel a figure moved around in the dining room. Possibly Nico. Another one appeared, bulkier, like Gregg, moving as if he was kicking something, someone, on the floor but it was hard to tell at this distance.

There was no point charging in with four of them in there, armed up and looking for trouble. Even if they were surprised they'd fight back. I needed to draw them out. Pick them off one by one.

They'd come out if they thought there was something happening to the van. If it caught fire or something.

'Come on,' I said to Daniel. I led him towards the Transit.

The man was still tied up but he'd shuffled into to the bushes where he lay on his side. Daniel knelt down to him as if to undo the rope.

'He's with the other men,' I said.

'The bad men?'

'That's them.'

Daniel leapt back as if he'd had a pin stuck in him.

I examined the inside of the van. It had a normal fuel tank with a reserve one attached. Even though the fuel cap was locked the pipe connecting the tanks ran through the back of the vehicle. It pulled off easily enough, letting what smelled like bio-diesel leak all over the inside of the van. As it poured out I took the rocket launcher and grenades and threw them onto the ground behind me. There was a lighter underneath the coats and I flicked it into life and threw it into the pool of fuel. Yellow flames fanned out across the floor, towards the ply-boarded sides. To help it along I threw a coat on it.

I grabbed up the weapons, shoving a couple of grenades into my pockets and giving another two to Daniel. 'Come on,' I said to him as I walked into the woods. The man on the ground squirmed backwards away from the burning van.

Once we were a good few meters away I examined the launcher, reading the instructions on it. It seemed straight forward enough, even though there was only one rocket.

'What's that?' said Daniel.

'A special gun.'

The fire in the Transit crackled and sent black smoke into the woods. There was no sign anyone in the house had seen it. I set up the weapon, loading it and aiming at the doorway. It was excessive for what I needed but it was all I had.

There was a bang from the Transit as one of its window burst, orange flames curling out of it.

A man appeared in the hotel doorway, someone I'd not seen before, holding a rifle. Nico was at the window, talking to him, sending him out to explore. Maybe he suspected something or he was keen to stay with Becky and Casper. Either way he wasn't coming out.

As the man shuffled around in the doorway I took aim with the rock launcher.

Fired.

CHAPTER THIRTY-SIX

Fightback

There was a roar and the launcher moved in my hand, jerked back. With a trail of fire, the projectile exploded inside the doorway of the hotel. There was a great burst of flames and debris. The smoke settled. The doorway and much of the wall had gone and there was a hole blasted in the building. Reception was now a charred shell. There was no sign of the man.

Daniel was on the ground with his hands on his ears. The air smelled of cordite and hot metal.

I put the launcher down and raised the pistol. There was no movement from the hotel. No sign that anyone was still alive.

Daniel eased himself up and dusted twigs off his jumper with the back of his hand. He still held the grenades.

'You all right?' I said.

'Yep.'

I tapped one of the grenades. 'You know what this is?'

'No.'

'It's dangerous but it's going to help us. Help Casper

and Becky.' I talked him through how to take the pin out and throw it. We practised twice before I sent him off into the trees. I told him to count to a hundred then set them both off.

There was still no movement from the hotel.

I went round towards the back of the building, grabbing up a large branch on the way. Then I waited near the kitchen. Daniel was to set off his grenades and that would be the signal for me to go in. He was the distraction and I was the main act.

I held the gun in one hand and the branch in the other. The grenades were in my pockets. The only sound was a crackle from the van as it burned. No grenades going off.

I tried the kitchen door. It was locked and when I put pressure on the bottom of it there was no movement. Nico had probably jammed something up against it.

There was a smell of burning paint and rubber and black smoke showed over the building.

No sound of grenades. Could Daniel actually count to a hundred? I hadn't thought of that. Or had he lost count? Forgotten what I'd said?

I went over to the kitchen window and had a look in. There was an unknown fella next to the cupboards, peering out into the hallway. He hadn't seen me so I leant back against the wall.

Still nothing from Daniel.

I put the branch and gun down and took out one of my grenades. The metal was warm, smooth. I slid my finger through the pin. I'd have to break the glass then throw it in.

There was a dull thud from the front of the building. Daniel had done it. I swung the branch and smashed a pane in the window. There was another explosion at the front and I pulled my grenade's pin and threw it in.

I ducked down and turned aside. A couple of seconds later there was a blast from the kitchen. The door creaked against its frame and glass sprayed out as windows burst.

For a few seconds I waited then went to the back door, kicked it. It held so I tried again. It cracked and split and with one more kick I burst in.

The room was full of smoke and debris. A man was curled up on the floor and I went over to him and swung the stick. Hit him hard on the head with a crack. He didn't move after that. Maybe he was unconscious, or dead. There wasn't time to worry.

The door to the dining room hung off its hinges and I shoved it out the way and went through. Bricks lay scattered across the carpet and the bedding where Casper and Daniel had slept. The bags were turned upside down and contents strewn across the floor.

Where there had been a door to reception there was now an open space. The front wall had gone right the way up to the first floor where exposed joists hung down. There was a great pile of rubble where the rocket had struck. A leg stuck out of it at an odd angle. The door to the lounge was shut with debris piled in front of it.

Two shots cracked off from the front window. Gregg and Nico were probably less than a metre away, armed and angry.

There was a shout before the shooting started again. I moved up to the door, pushed it. The bricks leant against it shifted and made a noise so I stopped. Waited for a second then eased it open a few centimetres.

Gregg knelt and fired through the bust window at the

front, a semi-automatic pistol in his bruised hand. Shots sounded from the other end of the room as well. I shoved the door further open and saw Becky tied up in a sitting position against the wall with Casper stretched out on the ground before her. Nico was at the far end by the back window, firing an assault rifle into the vegetation. The back of his coat was marked with bullet holes and material showed through, presumably from a bulletproof jacket. The kind of thing he'd had lying around in Round Up central.

Gregg was fixed on the Transit. This was my one chance to get him. I raised the pistol, aimed at his head, then lowered it. This wasn't going to work: Nico would hear the shot. He'd swing round and spray me with bullets. There was no chance I'd take out the two of them.

But I still had the stick. I pocketed the pistol and took a swing at Gregg. Hit him over the head. He slumped down like a pile of laundry, face down onto the burnt carpet.

I whipped out the pistol and swung round. Aimed it at the back of Nico's head. Pulled the trigger. There was no messing around this time: he was conscious and armed and had driven me off the road. Tried to drown me. Now it was his time.

The gun clicked. I pulled the trigger again, and once more. Nothing.

He turned round, waving his gun at me. 'Trent?' He laughed. 'Drop it!'

For a second neither of us moved. Then I dropped the pistol to the ground. He'd heard me try to fire and knew it was a duff. I shouldn't have been so keen to shoot; should have held my position, tried to get him to back off. Now he had a gun and I was unarmed.

He pointed at Gregg. 'What did you do to him?'

'He's just taking a nap.'

'Thought you were lying at the bottom of a pool.'

'Thought you were lying on a riverbank.'

He came close and prodded me with the gun. His face was marked with small cuts, some healing over. There were rips and stains on his suit and his scalp bled where a patch of hair had been burnt off.

'You've caused some mischief,' he said. 'Now it's finale time. Good bye.' He raised up his rifle. Put it to my face. 'Kneel down.'

'Shoot me here,' I said. I was already dead. No need to play games. His gun smelled of warm gunpowder. Oil.

He laughed. 'It's not that easy…' He walked around me, stepping over Gregg's body like a piece of furniture, the muzzle of his weapon pushed into my head. 'Not that easy at all.' He shoved me towards Becky and Casper.

Casper's eyes were closed but she stared at me, brow furrowed.

'See, thing is,' said Nico, 'these two have locked up that vehicle of theirs. The tank. And I want to get into it. I'm guessing that you know the way in. Now, that means I don't have to be so worried about accidentally killing one of them.' He grinned, his teeth stained with something dark.

Becky shook her head, a tiny movement and Nico went over to her, grabbing her face with one hand in a tight grip, pushing in her cheeks but looking at me. 'Gregg had plans for this one. Some fun ideas.' He released her and took went over to Gregg, knelt town and touched his neck, feeling for a pulse. The only sound was the distance crackle and pop from the burning van. Nico never once let go of the gun. Even with one hand he could spray the room with bullets.

He stood up. 'Lucky for you he's alive.'

I knew what he'd do now. He'd hurt us. He could indulge his sadistic pleasures. My guess was he'd pick me or Casper to torture and make Becky watch, try to break her. He didn't know I had no idea how to get into Eblis, so that was something. And he was on his own. He had the gun, and whatever others he had hidden, but there was only him. Until Gregg came round or the fella I'd tied up got free.

The final complication was Daniel. It was hard to say what he'd do now.

'Right,' Nico said. 'Turn round, hands behind your back.'

'No,' I said.

He aimed at Casper. 'Fucking shift around or I shoot him.'

For a moment I did nothing, then I turned round and faced the wall. My hands were gripped behind me, head twisted round to watch Nico. Casper was a pain in the arse but I didn't want him shot on my account. Nico went over to his bag and dropped onto one knee beside it. With the gun still levelled at us he pulled out a length of cord. He'd struggle to tie me and hold the gun so that was an opportunity. But it was a risky one. He'd expect trouble and be trigger happy. He'd likely hit one of us.

'Right, Trent. Time to be bound up.' For some reason he found this funny and laughed as he came over. There was no sign of him putting the gun down. He wrapped the cord round both of my wrists using one hand. The gun was still in his other hand.

'Let them go,' said a voice.

I turned to see Daniel in the doorway. Over his shoulder was the rocket launcher aimed at Nico. It wasn't loaded but it was there.

Nico stared at him. 'Who the fuck are you?' The gun was limp in his hand.

Before Nico had time to respond I elbowed him hard. While he was off balance I pulled the cord off my wrists and grabbed for the gun. Nico swung it out of my range so I hit him in the face, a punch that bust his nose and knocked him back. As he wobbled I hit again, this time in the neck to make him grab for his throat. The gun was still in his grip, ready to be raised up. Fired.

I jumped at him, sending us both to the floor. Nico fought back pushing up with all his weight, unbalancing me when he got a leg raised and twisted. We were both on our sides, hands on each other as blood ran from Nico's nose, the smell of stale meat on his breath. Then he swung the gun up and caught me on the side of the head. I couldn't see him anymore and there was some loud sound. I flung my fists out but they landed on the carpet or into free space. He flipped me over so that he was on top of me then his head sunk towards my shoulder. He dug his teeth in, biting hard into my flesh, so painful it was like being burnt. I raised my knees, pushing against him but he was too heavy. Too strong.

There was a thud and his head jerked off to the side. His teeth were wrenched away and the biting stopped. I pushed up so that he fell off to the side. He flopped over and I landed on top of him. I put my full weight on him, slipping my hands around his throat. I dug my fingers in hard, deep into the arteries, the softer tissue. He croaked and gasped but I held on tight.

Only when his body was limp beneath me did I let go.

I sat up, looking down at his bloodied and slack face.

Then I straightened up and rubbed the wound on my shoulder, Nico's warm body between my knees, his hands still held in claws, the smell of sweat coming off him.

'Is he dead?' said Daniel. He held the stick I'd brought in. The one I'd hit Gregg with and that he'd just used on Nico.

'I hope so,' I said.

CHAPTER THIRTY-SEVEN

Mission

Daniel helped me release Becky. He took the gag out of her mouth and she gasped and muttered her thanks. I undid her hands and went to Casper. He seemed to have passed out so I got Daniel to help me move him onto the sofa. He lay there taking deep breaths as the building creaked around us, unstable after what the rocket had done.

'What happens now?' said Becky.

'Be sensible to get away from here.'

Not that the bike was an option anymore. Nor was the van. I stared out at the blackened Transit. I'd not even thought about that when I'd torched it. The flames had died down leaving it a burnt shell. The trees beside it were charred but it hadn't spread through the woods. I wondered about the man we'd tied up. He'd be all right. Fellas like him always were.

'Why did you come back?' Becky gave me one of those looks again. Looks I couldn't work out. But then a chunk of the ceiling collapsed sending plaster all over us.

'We need to go,' I said.

I took Casper under the arms while Becky and Daniel grabbed his feet. We carried him round Nico's body and over Gregg's.

'What about him?' she said.

'Leave him.' I wasn't going to waste energy on Gregg. We'd already left him for dead once before. One more time wouldn't matter. We carried on out, over rubble and past what was left of the other man.

We lay Casper by the Eblis. Becky slumped down beside the tank and Daniel put his hand to Casper's brow.

I went back in to grab some bits and pieces.

The building groaned around me, masonry falling from the outside and chunks of wall dropping off inside. The bags were still at the far end of the dining room, half emptied so I chucked stuff back in before grabbing them and going into the lounge. I went over to Nico and felt through his coat finding another couple of magazines for his gun. I slid them into my pocked and shouldered the rifle, picking up the bags again. A section of the chimney breast fell onto the floor so I made for the doorway. There was a great crack as I left and the far side of the lounge collapsed outwards. I ran out, over to the Eblis, dragging the bags with me. The building fell with a clatter and clonks. Thuds and crashes. A final thump that send out a great cloud of dust.

I looked back at the hotel, now a shapeless pile of wreckage. Nico and Gregg were under the mounds of bricks and wood. As were the other men. It was a better resting place than they deserved.

Becky and Daniel tended to Casper as I retrieved my bag from the tree and checked through the wet contents. I laid out damp banknotes across the warm flank of the Eblis. I still had spares from the bike but I chucked these into the undergrowth.

Becky came over. 'Thanks for your help.'

I shrugged and stretched Gehenna's documents on the tank's hull.

'What are you planning to do now?'

'I'm not sure.'

'Do you think you'll come with us?'

'How's Casper?'

'I've given him more morphine. He's resting.'

He looked ropy as hell but he was still alive. We all were. There was a noise from the building. I half expected Nico and Gregg to rise out of the debris. Start shooting at us. But it was only another section of wall falling down.

'So?' said Becky.

I had bike or other means of getting around so it seemed I was stuck with them.

I took the plans out of my bag and set them out on the ground. The waxed surface had resisted the water reasonably well. There were charts of the lochs and waterways around the coast of western Scotland. And the sub itself with all those decks and cabins. The great engines that could run for decades; weapons that could wipe out city after city.

'When you get to Gehenna, what are you going to do.'

She leant back against the Eblis, tapped it. 'Blow it. With this.'

'Serious?'

'At least, that's the plan.'

'Why?'

She laughed. 'Why?'

'Why should you care?'

'Look, are you coming or not?'

'What makes you think the sub is still there?'

'If it's anywhere, it's there.'

I laughed. 'Jesus.'

For a moment neither of us spoke. As more bricks clunked off the hotel.

'Well?' she said. 'Are you coming with us?'

'Why should I trust you?'

'You know it all now.'

'Really?'

She nodded.

'I don't know.'

'What else would you do, Trent?'

'I suppose.'

'So you're in?'

'Seems that way.'

'Good. An extra pair of hands will be useful.' Maybe she smiled at this. If she did it was soon gone.

We hefted Casper into the Eblis, loaded in our gear and set off.

As we headed along the track the hotel fell in on itself again, now a wreck of tumbled stone and bust window frames. Beside the burnt out Transit the other man stood up with an untied rope in his hand. He stared at us as we drove out onto the road.

We went further into the highlands. The roads were no more than gravel tracks, the tarmac broken in hard winters. Becky focussed on the route, checking a map now and then. Casper lay asleep in the bottom of the vehicle and Daniel sat back in his seat, relaxed.

We were going north west now, towards the coast and

the loch where Gehenna was supposed to be. I was curious about the sub, what it looked like in the metal. It seemed hard to believe it was still there after all these years.

We drove along the road through the mountains as the light faded. The engines droned and the shadows darkened around us. The cab smelled of sweat and smoke. Dried blood and pine needles.

Sections of the road had been washed away leaving loose stones. The tank pitched over the surface and slowed but didn't stop.

We took a left fork and a soon dark expanse of water appeared.

'Is this it?' I said.

'No,' said Becky. 'This is Loch Lomond. The top end. Loch Fyne is what we are after.'

Loch Lomond went on for miles and miles. Dark water with trees at side. Then we turned off to the right and soon passed another stretch of water.

'And this?' I said.

'This is the sea, Trent.'

It was at our side for a few miles. After that we drove on through featureless hills. Dark shapes that hemmed us in. There was no sign of anyone. It seemed hard to believe that the sub would still be up here. In this wasteland.

Then we came to a sign on the roadside, recent, homemade. It said BEWARE. No more than that. More signs appeared in the Eblis' lamps, some bright coloured, welcoming, others as warnings. Becky slowed the vehicle and stopped at one. It was a tall post with cockeyed writing on the board saying TURN BACK SINNERS.

'What's up?' This didn't look like reivers, just the usual

stuff from cranks and crackpots.

'I'm not sure. Just a feeling.' She clambered up and opened the hatch, stepping out. I grabbed Nico's gun and joined her.

'Where we going?' said Daniel.

'Just stay here,' I said.

The air was still, with a cool dampness that came down from the treeless hills. The road wound off into the distance, lit by the Eblis' lights. Becky went over to the sign, reading it and running her fingers over it. I joined her, keeping an eye on the hills for signs of movement, in case the people who'd written it were nearby.

'You all right?' I said.

She raised her hand. 'Listen.'

There was a low throb from the tank but little else. 'I can't hear anything —'

'Shush.' She put her finger to my lips, the first time she'd come near me in the last day.

Then I heard it, way off, faint, drumming sound and voices, cheers and shouts. Laughter.

Becky got back into the Eblis. She turned the headlamps off. I saw the light in the distance, at the end of the road and over a hill. A glow on the horizon of reds and yellows.

'What is it?' I said.

'That's where we're going. Seems Gehenna has built up its own community.'

I joined her back in the Eblis.

'Everything okay?' said Daniel.

'Yeah,' I said. But I wasn't sure.

When we moved off I set my monitor to infrared, waiting for figures to emerge from the dark and descend on us. Sometimes I spotted something, a shape that disappeared, possibly an animal, but nothing clear.

The road made its way along open ground, great mountains sitting at our side, rounded shadows on the screens. We passed a monument to someone, now defaced with animal skulls and bones.

There in the distance was the Loch. Blacker than everything around it.

We came to a sign. It said Gehenna City.

'Looks like we're at the right place,' I said.

'It does.' She eased the tank to a stop.

The road ran straight ahead, across the moors towards a bridge that led to two three-metre pillars with massive doors between them. To the side of each bonfires burned. The doors were set in a heavy fence of tree trunks that disappeared off into the distance.

'That bridge will never take our weight,' said Becky.

'And there'll be guards on the gate,' I said.

We moved off at crawler speed, a low hum from the motors.

'Where are you going?'

'See if there's another way in.' She swung us right across the soft moors, slowing as we pitched across the rough surface. We skirted round the area marked with bonfires and picked up speed. Once we were well away from the gates she turned towards back the town. Aimed for the buildings and noise.

'We might be able to stand on the tank,' she said. 'See over the fence and get some idea of the layout.'

Then the Eblis pitched forward. It fell, nose first.

She swore and pulled the levers into reverse, the Eblis' motors' roaring. I hung on tight as the engines screamed and we slid down into something. Somewhere dark and deep.

CHAPTER THIRTY-EIGHT
Camped

With the engines flat out Becky hauled back on the levers. The vehicle bounced and tracks churned at the ground outside. We were still nose down, canted at a steep angle. Daniel covered his ears and Casper rolled around as the tank jerked and lurched. One of the monitors showed faint light behind us while the other revealed the thing we were slipping into, black and featureless. The vehicle was at full power and warning lights lit in front of Becky but she ignored these, still hanging onto the controls.

Then the Eblis began to move backwards, slowly at first then picking up speed as the tracks gripped. Becky eased off the power as we moved onto solid ground. Once we were a few metres back she stopped the motors, shaking her head as she looked at the instruments.

'What happened?' said Daniel.

'Thought I was going to fry the motors.'

'What the hell was that?' I said.

Becky stared at her screen but I climbed up through the tank, opening the hatch and getting out. The sounds of raised voices, drums and music were now clear and there were buildings outlined in the distance, beyond the fence and backlit by fire. Carefully I walked ahead of the Eblis, its tracks clogged with earth and front end sprayed with mud it had kicked up. A few yards in front of it there was a pit, ten foot wide and nearly as deep. The bottom of it was lined with wooden spikes.

Becky and Daniel came and stood next to me. 'Nice,' she said.

We walked along the edge. It was the same as far as we could see, disappearing off across the moorland in a wide arc, surrounding the town with its barricade, more a trench than pit. In places it was even wider and deeper than the section nearest to us but there was no point where we'd be able to cross.

Daniel stared at the fire-lit buildings. 'I don't like it here.'

'We need to get going,' I said. There was no sign of anyone but we'd made some noise. Maybe they'd not heard it over the drumming but there was no point risking it.

We returned to Eblis and Becky drove us off across the moors. Well away from the town, behind a small hummock. She pulled out her map and shifted it around. Jabbed her finger at it. 'This is where we are.'

There was a small town marked on the edge of the loch, nothing like the size of Gehenna City. He had some other name on the map. Something tame and Scottish. The town's new name suggested that the sub was, or had been, here. And the trench implied that the locals didn't want outsiders coming in.

I pointed to a valley off to the south, hidden away by

the contours of the land and a decent distance away from town. 'We need to keep out of the way. That should do it.'

Becky agreed and drove us in a wide arc so that we were hidden from the town by some drumlins. The tank clanked and clattered like mad.

As we dipped down into the valley Casper sat up. 'Where are we?' he said.

'We're here,' said Becky.

We drove into a patch of scots pines and parked with the front of the Eblis under the branches. She manoeuvred for the best part of a minute so that the vehicle was as far in as it would go with the tree's trunks at either side of it.

When she stopped Casper lay back and took deep breaths. If his eyes hadn't been open I'd have assumed he was asleep.

I got out first. The trees were old and twisted. A breeze hissed through them and the sound of Gehenna City faded in and out: drums and voices. Shouts.

Becky and Daniel joined me and we set up bedding beneath the pines.

'We need to keep watch,' I said. 'I'll do the first shift.'

'I'll check on Casper,' she said.

'Me too,' said Daniel.

I sat at the edge of the copse with Nico's assault rifle. The sky was pitch black but the glow from the city lit up the west. Behind me Casper was fitful and made groaning noises. It was hard to tell if he was asleep or awake but he seemed to be in pain. Becky and Daniel muttered beside him.

The wind dropped but that only made the sounds louder: singing and drums.

Becky came to join me some time later. There was still noise coming from Gehenna City. 'What the hell do you think they are doing?'

'Sounds like a party.'

For a moment we sat and listened to the sounds. As cheers and drumming drifted into the valley.

'Listen, Trent…'

'Yeah.'

'What did make you come back? After you rode off?'

'I was pushed off the road by Nico and Gregg. Lost the bike.'

'But you didn't have to come back to us.'

I was going to give her a story. About me forgetting a piece of clothing and coming back for it. Something feeble like that. Instead I told her the truth. 'I'm not sure really. Maybe I had nowhere else to go.'

She didn't say anything for a while. It was impossible to read what she was thinking with it being so dark. Her breathing was steady and she hadn't moved so it was likely she hadn't taken a too much of a huff.

Then she handed me a torch. 'I'll take over now if you want to rest.'

'All right.' I gave her the rifle and went back into the trees, to where the bedding was set out. The ground was soft underneath with low bushes sprouting around us. There were animal tracks between the undergrowth and the ground was worn, strewn with loose stones. As I swung the beam around I caught Casper. He stared up at me with his eyes open. A hard stare.

I put the light out and lay down.

For minutes I lay there as the drumming continued. At last the sky started to shift from black to deep blue. Shortly afterwards I fell asleep.

I awoke to faint daylight. Shouting. Becky was by the tank. Casper faced her. He propped himself up against the vehicle and bellowed at her. He was really pissed off about something.

Daniel still lay beside me wrapped up in his bedding. His hands were tight against his ears and he twitched every time there was a shout.

'This is madness!' said Casper. 'Fucking crazy! We shouldn't have come!' He jabbed his finger at Becky as she tried to get words in. 'What are we going to do? Us, eh? What the fuck are we going to do?'

'Casper,' she said.

'We're not exactly a crack troop! Me injured, a mercenary, a moron!'

'Casper, please.'

'Fucking waste of time!'

I went over to them. 'What's going on?'

'You keep out of it!' he said.

I looked at Becky. 'Is it his medication?'

Casper turned on me, red faced. He grabbed hold of my shirt and twisted it tight. 'Don't talk about me as if I'm not here, you bastard!'

'Casper, calm down.'

He pushed a hand up against my throat. 'Fuck you!'

This was too much. I shoved him back against the tank and jammed my elbow under his chin. 'You may be ill but you're way out of line.' I had him pinned there and he squirmed but didn't have the strength to push back.

Becky put her hand on my arm. 'Trent, please.'

For a moment I did nothing. Just let him sweat. Then I let go and stepped back.

He lifted his hand to his throat and gasped. 'Are you trying to kill me?'

'If I'd been trying to kill you, you'd be dead.'

He leant forward with his hands on his knees. I felt bad about restraining him like that but he was getting out of control.

'Look, Casper,' I said.

Then he launched himself at me. It came without warning and sent me backwards so we both fell onto the ground. As the air was knocked out of me he put weight onto my chest and rained punches onto me. They were feeble and I easily blocked them. Though I could have thrown him off I let him get it all out. For the best part of a minute he carried on like that until Becky pulled him aside.

I stood up and dusted myself down as he hung onto Becky. His arms were wrapped around her and he took deep breaths. 'You, Trent, you're the one who fucked this up. With those bastards that followed us. All your fault.'

Becky patted him on the back. Then he started to cry. Great sobs that got louder and louder, the only sound between the four of us. Daniel came over. He laid a hand on Casper's back. The three of them carried on like that for ages as I stayed to the side. Once Casper had calmed down he slumped onto the ground with his head in his hands. Becky mouthed something to me but I couldn't work out what she meant. Daniel shifted his hand onto Casper's shoulder and no one spoke.

'We need to eat.' I wasn't in the mood to humour Casper. I walked off through the trees, to the far side of the thicket. A thin mist hung over the valley. There were holes dug into the ground and a young rabbit darted into one.

I picked a branch up, went over to the hole and waited. I stayed there for a while. As a breeze hissed through the branches. There was no movement up the valley or around the warren. A light mist had started to drift down off the hills.

A rabbit darted out and I thumped the stick down, catching it in the back. As it flipped over I hit out again, this time going for its head. There was a soft crack and it writhed on the ground so I hit it once more, then again, until it lay sill, eyes open. I picked up the warm body and settled myself on a fallen tree. Then I skinned it with my knife and set it aside as I collected kindling.

By the time Becky came over I had a fire going, cooking the rabbit on a spit. The smoke rolled out into the mist so there was little chance we'd be spotted. She had maps under her arm, roughly rolled up. The flesh hissed onto the hot embers, giving off the smell of warm meat.

'You've been busy,' she said.

'Thought we needed some fresh food.'

She sat near me, shifting the charts around. 'Casper's settled down.'

'He needed to.'

'He didn't mean anything. Don't get angry with him.'

'I'm not angry.'

She smiled and set the charts out holding them with stones. 'I need to look at your Gehenna material as well.'

I cut meat off the rabbit's carcass and ate a piece. It was hot, sweet. 'Will Casper want some?'

'Doubt it.'

'Daniel will.'

'Okay. I'll fetch some plates. Then we'll look at the

documents?'

'Fine.'

She went off and I picked on at the rabbit. It tasted good. All her paperwork was on the ground. There were sea charts and maps but nothing about the actual submarine. That was what they needed me for.

She came back with Daniel and several plates. They sat down and I sliced the rabbit for them.

'Can we talk about Gehenna?' she said.

Before I had time to answer there was a loud crack and bright light in the sky, cutting through the mist.

CHAPTER THIRTY-NINE

Plan of Attack

The valley lit up for a second then returned to greyness.

'Should we check that out?' said Becky.

'Yeah.' I set off up the hillside and she followed. The ground was soft underneath as we picked our way through the bushes. It was steep and we tripped and slipped on the way.

At last we came to a point where we could look out on the town. I lay down on the damp grass and Becky joined me. The town was fog-free, framed by the loch to the west with the hills beyond it. A dark gash marked the trench just below, framed by the barricade beyond it. There were numerous low buildings, haphazard looking with one taller structure in the middle. This seemed to have something big on top of it, rounded. Between the buildings figures moved in the morning light, lots of people. Voices drifted over, shouts and cheers with drumming in the background. There was no sign of what had caused the sound.

'Some place,' said Becky.

'Yeah.'

'I can't see the submarine.'

'No.' The loch was dark blue. There was nothing in it. Nothing visible.

'Do you think we'd get the Eblis up here?'

'Not sure.' Of course. That's why we came. To blow the sub. 'What's the big deal with the submarine?'

'What do you mean?'

'Why come all the way up here? Destroy it.'

'You've seen the paperwork. You know what someone could do with a weapon like that —'

'I get all that. I just don't get you and Casper doing it. You just don't seem the types.'

'What the fuck is that meant to mean?'

'I just didn't see you as —'

'As what? Someone decent?' She stood up. She was getting all wound up.

'Don't stand up Becky.'

'Fuck you.' She turned and walked down the hill.

I lay there for a while. It was probably best to let her calm down. Blow off a little steam. I still didn't see her and Casper as saving the world types. They seemed too mercenary to me. Too selfish. Maybe I'd got them wrong. Maybe not.

I looked back down the slope into the valley. The tank was invisible down there but we'd need to bring it into the open to get a clear shot. This probably wasn't close enough to be effective which would mean going through town or finding some other part of the coast to fire from.

And we'd only get one chance.

I turned back towards the town. There were shouts. Laugher and music. A whoosh and something shot up into the sky. It exploded in a pattern of greens and blues. There was a cheer. A firework. Been a while since I'd seen one. Most gunpowder seemed to go into guns these days.

For a second there was a shadow in the loch, some great black shape. Then it was gone. I stared at the water but didn't see anything else.

I went down the hill, towards the patch of trees. Away from the town. Maybe Gehenna wasn't here anymore. It might have sailed off. Sunk in a storm. If that was the case we'd have to work out what to do. I didn't want to hang around here forever. I picked my way through the bushes back to where we were camped.

Casper, Daniel and Becky sat on a log beside the fire now red embers. None of them spoke to me. Casper seemed calmed. For now. The remains of the rabbit lay on several plates. Casper chewed away at a last chunk of meat with grease dripping down his shirt.

'So what's this plan?' I said.

Becky sighed. 'Move the Eblis closer. Blow the sub out of the water. You okay with that?'

'Assuming it does exist.'

'You've seen the town's name. The trench and gates. It's here.'

'Or it was here once.'

'We have to assume it's here with everything we've seen —'

'Do we?'

Becky stood and tidied the plates. 'What is your problem, Trent?'

'I don't have a problem. But I don't want to spend the rest of my life hanging round here.'

'You didn't have to come on this trip —'

'Hang on. You were the ones who lied to me. Gave me all this shit about being brother and sister. You strung me along to get hold of the stuff I had in my bag. So pardon me if I'm not happy to trust your judgement.'

'Okay. Okay. What do you want?'

Casper and Daniel stared at me. Seemed neither had anything to add.

Actually, I wasn't quite sure what I wanted.

'Well?' said Becky.

'Well, we've not seen the sub, so it might not be here. We don't want to be hanging around her for weeks. Months…'

'If we have to, we have to.'

'And even if we do sink it, and that's a big if —'

'We will.'

'Then we'd have to work out what to do next. Where to go.'

'We leave and head off into the Highlands.'

It didn't seem like she'd thought this through at all. I was about to quiz her when she went over to the maps.

She picked one out, put it at my feet and pointed to a road tracing a route. 'Towards Glencoe.' She sat back on her haunches and stared at me. 'Do you want to talk through our plan of attack?'

'There is a plan?'

She didn't answer but instead pointed at my bag.

We all looked over at it, apart from Casper who glared at me.

She stood and went over to my stuff. 'Can I?'

I shrugged. 'Yeah.'

She raked through my belongings and took out the plans, setting them out with the plates to hold them flat.

She ran her fingers across the surface, stopping at certain details and tutting to herself. For a few minutes she did this.

'Well?' I said.

She tapped the rear section of the sub, where there was a hatch. 'This will do it. Anywhere round here. It'll blow the whole thing.'

Casper came over. 'Once we blow it and it's destroyed, we can go?'

'That's the idea.'

He sat back down and stared into the dead fire, muttering to himself. Something going through his head.

Becky kept reading the small print on the cross-section of the sub. Then she stood up. 'I'm going to go on watch.' She grabbed up the rifle and marched off holding the paperwork.

Daniel grabbed the plates. 'I'll wash up.'

Casper sat by the embers, still lost in his thoughts. I followed Becky up the hill.

She marched up ahead of me and lay down looking towards the town. The sun cleared the hills and warmed the ground, still damp. The sky was light blue above us, streaked with thin clouds. There was still drumming and cheering but it wasn't as enthusiastic as before, the pace and volume lessened.

'It's a pity we're so far off. We need to get the Eblis in closer. As close as we can get it, really. Going to be tricky to do that without being spotted —'

'You still haven't explained why you are so bothered. Why you want to blow it.'

She took a breath. 'Do you really want to know?'

'Yeah.'

'Okay.' She turned towards me. Her eyes were soft, wider than usual. 'My brother, Archie. My real brother. He was in the military. Out in the Middle East. I've no idea why he signed up, it wasn't like he was into all the fighting and so on, but he did sign up and off he went. He was there when stuff turned really nasty. When they started to panic and all the countries threw everything at each other. He had some stories, what little got back to us. Horror stories: chemical attacks and cluster bombs. I don't want anyone to face what he faced...' For a moment she didn't speak and I thought that was it. She'd said her piece. Then she started again but her voice was different. Lower. 'This isn't just some machine. A ship or boat. It's full of evil stuff and people want it. Bad people. I spent time with scum like Maxwell. Heard their crackpot plans. Ambitions. One of them will get hold of it, then we've all had it. All of us, even you Trent. We have to get rid of it. '

'I see.'

'And in case you're wondering about my brother, he didn't make it back.'

I hadn't been wondering but I wasn't surprised. 'And Casper?'

'Casper?'

'Why's he here?'

She grunted. 'Because I am.'

We both faced the town again. It all made more sense now. If I could believe her.

We stayed there for some time until the drumming slowed and there was a great sigh from the crowd, all the voices together. Then I saw the figures, a small group over by the trench, holding tools of some sort. They were near the gate, close to where the Eblis had slid in, chewing the ground up to get out again. That was where they were looking, pointing down at the earth where the vehicle had left great track marks.

I tapped Becky and pointed to them.

After several minutes they looked around and started to head towards where we were camped.

'Shit,' she said.

'Yeah.' The tank would have left marks on the heather. They'd have no trouble following them. There seemed to be about eight people, walking purposefully. If they got too close we'd have to do something. We could probably take out the group but that would also let the town know there was trouble. Even if they didn't hear us shooting they'd notice when their people didn't come back.

'Should we go back to the Eblis?' she said.

'No, they'd see us moving.'

The group were closer now, at the far end of the valley. The Eblis was hard to spot at a distance, despite its size, being all matt paint. Hidden in the trees. But it was big enough if you were looking for it.

They stopped and examined the ground. There was some discussion going on, arms waving round. Then they moved off. They turned and went back to the gateway.

'Thank god,' said Becky.

My guess was they didn't want to go looking for something big enough to make those tracks without a good sized band. 'They'll be back.' I reckoned they'd return later in the day, probably armed to the teeth.

She stood up. 'We need to go. Prepare to attack.'

'Or leave.'

Then a great cry rose up, hundreds of voices all together.

The town all hushed and the music stopped.

The loch boiled and rippled and something appeared out of it, indistinct at first, just a patch of dark that thickened and grew, joined by another section that stretched back and forwards in the water.

HMS Gehenna rose out of the loch.

CHAPTER FORTY

Blown

The submarine was black, matt that absorbed the light, sucked it in and made the surface impossible to define.

We both stared at it in the loch. It was as long as the town and taller than the tallest building. Despite the plans, and pictures of other submarines I'd seen as a kid, I'd never thought what it would be like in the metal. Seeing it for real.

The townsfolk were silent as waves rolled out from the vessel and caught the light. White crests on the dark water beside the darker submarine.

'That's it,' said Becky. 'It's here.'

'It is.'

Then she ran off down the hill. For a moment I stayed and watched Gehenna. After a short time I followed her down. Now we had to work out what to do. Becky'd be keen to find somewhere for a clean shot. Blow it out of the water.

When I got down to the Eblis she was packing up the pans and plates. At the side were some weapons: Nico's assault rifle and a couple of grenades.

'So what now?' I said.

'We need to get going —'

'Where?'

'What's going on?' said Casper.

'It's Gehenna,' she said. 'It's in the loch.'

Casper climbed up onto the turret and dropped into the open hatch. It was the fastest I'd seen him move for days.

'What's Gayanna?' said Daniel.

'It's the submarine,' I said. 'The one we came to look for.'

'Submarine?'

I told him it was a special ship, one that could go underwater. But my words were drowned out by the sound of the Eblis' motors. We had to step aside as it moved backwards through the trees.

'Where's he going?' I said.

It shot back and pirouetted on its tracks so that it faced up the hill. It raced off with a trail of earth left in its tracks.

As it charged across the rough ground Becky stood there with an open mouth.

'What the hell is going on?' I said.

She shook her head slowly.

The tank made its way up the hillside, thudding over the rocks and vegetation. It didn't slow as it ploughed its way towards the top. We needed to stop him or at least delay him. Get him to ease off before we were spotted. 'Have you got a gun?'

'A gun?' She was working in slow motion.

I grabbed up Nico's assault rifle and aimed at the Eblis. I squeezed the trigger and knocked off a couple of shots. Both zinged off the tank and it didn't slow. It surged on up the hill.

As it came to the top, it slowed. There was some clanking as it manoeuvred then it stopped facing across towards the town.

'Oh, Casper,' said Becky. She started to run after it.

For a moment I did nothing: stood with Daniel by the plates and pans and our bedding.

Then I raced up the slope towards her. Daniel came with me but she had a good head start and neither of us could get near her.

The Eblis was stationary. For a moment I thought Casper was just looking for the sub.

But then the gun fired. There was a shot that echoed around the valley and across the town.

The tank rocked on its suspension then fired again. There was no way to tell if it had hit or missed from where we were. But that was our cover blown. The townsfolk must have been aware of our presence from the sound, let alone the shells landing on or near Gehenna.

Becky was still running but before she got close the Eblis drove off. It rolled down the other side of the bank and disappeared. When I made it to the crest Becky was there with her hands on her head. The tank was several hundred metres off, racing towards the town across the rough ground.

The submarine was still in the loch and there was no sign of damage to it. But a smoking hole lay at the edge of the town down by the waterside. He'd not got the range right and had fallen short so now he was making up ground.

The Eblis approached the trench and stopped. It shifted its turret. Prepared to fire again.

There was a flash. I thought Casper had fired, but it was followed by another from the submarine. Gehenna had a weapon of its own. There was a great blast just below us, a huge thud, followed by another straight after it. The Eblis was engulfed in a ball of flame and smoke rolled out from it then there was a third flash from the submarine. The tank exploded and sent metal chunks up into the air. The hull lay cleaved in two and parts rained down on us. Becky and Daniel pulled their hands over their heads as wires and switches fell from above. A lever bounced nearby and a gun barrel jammed into the ground.

In a few seconds it was over and the Eblis lay ruptured and burning. Becky put her hands to her face and cried.

'We need to go,' I said.

'No, no!'

'We can't stay here —'

'What about Casper? What if he's —'

'He's dead, Becky.'

'No. No.'

But she didn't resist as I led her down the hill. Away from the mess that had been the Eblis. She staggered along as if she'd been hit by the debris but she was unharmed. Not physically hurt. Daniel held her hand as we walked.

Back at the copse I grabbed up what was left of our possessions. The people from the sub would be keen to check the result of their attack and I didn't want us to be around when they turned up.

I gave the bedding to Daniel and the plates and pans to Becky. She stood without moving, eyes wide. Staring off. I shouldered the rifle and led off into the valley. I didn't have much of an idea where to go but being close to the tank's track marks didn't seem sensible.

Becky refused to come but followed when Daniel drew her with him. We walked for several hours with only a stop to drink.

At last we came to another patch of trees and I sat on a log by a gnarled spruce.

'This will do,' I said.

Daniel dumped his stuff on the ground. Becky stood by the tree and stared across the valley at nothing in particular. I checked back the way we'd come. There were sounds from way off: shouts and engines but it was hard to work out if they were from the town or where we'd been.

'We need to eat,' I said.

Daniel opened his bag then started to gather up wood for a fire. I wasn't sure if it was sensible to have one yet but I let him carry on. He took out food and arranged it on three plates.

'Are you all right?' I said to Becky. She hadn't moved.

'They blew it,' she said.

'You probably need to eat something. Rest.'

'With Casper in it.'

'I know.'

She looked at me for the first time. For a moment we just stared at each other. Then she looked away. 'He wasn't always like that.'

'Right.'

'When I met him he was different. Better.'

'I'm sure.'

'It got to him.'

'What did?'

She shrugged, took a plate and chewed a hard biscuit.

We sat and ate. Daniel's fire stayed unlit as I kept my eyes on the horizon waiting for people to turn up. Track us down.

No one showed up so we set out the bedding. I still refused to let Daniel light his fire and he took a huff at this so let him play with my lighter for a while. As he clicked it on and off I watched Becky. Her face lit up in the flashes to show sunken eyes and drooped mouth. I wanted to say something comforting to her but Casper was gone and it really was over. All we had now was a chance to escape.

After a while I took the lighter off Daniel and told him it was time to sleep. He settled down and soon started to snore.

'Becky?' I said.

'Yeah?' Her voice was flat. Dead.

'I'll take first watch if you want.'

'You sleep. I'll do it. I'm not tired.'

'You need to rest.'

'No, I don't.'

I stayed awake for a while in case she dozed off but I could sense her sitting there. Not moving.

In time I fell asleep and dreamt of the Eblis being blown apart. Casper frying in the wreckage.

In the morning she was still there with her eyes fixed on where we'd come from, her bedding wrapped around her. 'They were out in the night.'

'From the town?'

'Yes, quite a few of them.' She pointed off towards the west. Where the tank had been.

'At least they didn't come here.'

'No, they'd didn't.'

Daniel fetched some water from a stream and squeezed

in a few blaeberries to flavour it. Becky stayed in her bedding as she drank.

'What now?' I said.

She drank some more, shrugged. 'Without the Eblis we can't do much.'

'If anything.'

She threw her drink down. 'Don't you think I fucking know that? We lost the Eblis and Casper and everything. Everything!' She stood up. 'Can't you say anything useful?'

I said nothing. She needed to let off steam and I wasn't going to stop her.

'What a screw up! What a waste! What a waste.' She went on like this for ages. Waved her arms and stomped around.

At last she sat down and took a breath.

'We could still blow it,' I said.

She laughed.

'I'm serious.'

'You're serious.'

I nodded and poured her another drink. For a few moments the three of us sat and drank. I wasn't even sure where that had come from. But I was serious. We were here and we had come for a purpose. It hadn't been something I'd believed in but here we were.

A breeze blew through the trees and shadows ran across the valley as the clouds were driven in from the west. Going to destroy the sub was a crazy idea. Suicide. The sensible thing was to get away. Forget about Gehenna and the town.

'We have to get into town,' said Becky. 'They must have traders coming in.'

'Yes, but they'll be suspicious after the Eblis.'

'Have you changed your mind?'

'No.'

'There's no use hanging around out here.'

'Tell you what, I'll look the place over. See if there's some way in.'

'When?'

'I'll do it now.'

'Okay.' She seemed happy with this. If we were going to do it I didn't want to end up like Casper. I'd have a look, make a plan and let her calm down.

So I shouldered the assault rifle and walked through the trees, out across the scrubland. Up the hill behind us. The sun fought through thick cloud and lit patches of the loch. Rain fell on the far shore, beyond Gehenna. The town looked the same as ever. All the low buildings and the big object in the middle. There was music and voices that drifted across the glen.

I sat on the hillside for a while. There was no sign of movement around the gates or the trench.

Then I spotted two figures walking towards the town. A woman and a young man: Becky and Daniel, heading for the entrance way.

I ran down the hill towards them.

CHAPTER FORTY-ONE

Town

When I caught them up they were approaching the bridge. 'What are you up to?'

'We're going in.' Becky marched on, not looking at me. She had her bag and mine. Daniel carried his stuff as well.

'They'll never let you in.'

'They might.'

'Stop. Let's talk about this.'

'I thought you wanted to go in?'

'I do but we need a plan —'

'We'll work it out, Trent.' She carried on so I walked with her, towards the main gate. There were remnants of burnt out bonfires on the ground at each side.

'All right. We need to work out some story.' If they came out and found us just hanging around we'd really be in trouble. After the Eblis's trick they'd be jumpy as hell.

She stopped and thrust my bag at me. 'Go on.'

'We'll say we're traders.'

'We've got nothing to trade.'

'Could sell ourselves,' said Daniel.

I think it was a joke but it made sense. 'We could pretend to be pimp and whore.'

'Fuck you,' she said.

'It's a plan.'

'For Christ's sake.'

I checked to see what was in my bag. There were some clothes, banknotes and the Gehenna stuff. The shotgun and two grenades from the tank.

Daniel raised his hand. 'What about me.'

Becky prodded me on the chest. 'This isn't some kind of joke.'

'I'm serious,' I said. 'We could get in that way.'

She snorted and shook her head but didn't argue.

'You're our star entertainer,' I said to Daniel.

He grinned and there was almost a smile from Becky. Almost.

We carried onto the bridge of heavy logs that crossed the trench. The gates were set in the barricade, held by pillars of solid stone, sculpted to look like rockets, and with steel brackets hammered through them to take the giant hinges.

Becky stood by me. 'They're the missiles. From Gehenna.'

'Are you sure we're ready to go in?'

'Look, Trent —'

'Who's there?' said a voice.

Becky stared at me. 'Entertainers,' she said. Then she whipped her jacket off and carried on removing clothes.

'Oh aye? What kind of entertainers?' A hatch opened up on the left-hand gate a couple of metres up. A face appeared, red skinned and wrinkled. 'What you got?'

Becky took off her top so she was just in a bra and

trousers then stepped back. She put her hands on her hips and thrust her head back. There was a smile on her face but her eyes were serious. Deadly serious.

I realised I had the assault rifle over my shoulder so I slid it off. Dropped it into the trench.

The face wedged itself through the hatch and two watery eyes stared out at her as she waggled her chest at him. He disappeared and there were sounds of bolts moving. Becky sighed and relaxed. The smile vanished.

A few seconds later the left-hand gate eased open and the man peered out through the gap. 'Just the three of you?' he said as he looked us over.

'Just us,' said Becky.

'Where've you come from?'

'Tarbet. We did a show at the hotel.'

'So how did you get here.'

'Walked.'

'Walked?'

'Yes, walked. Took ages.'

'When did you arrive?'

'Just now.'

'Today?'

'Yes, now.'

'You've not got a vehicle?'

'No.'

'Guns?'

'No.'

He stepped back and drew the gate with him. I let Becky go ahead then followed with Daniel.

We stood in a small quadrangle with another gate ahead of us. This one was shut.

The man had an assistant with him, a younger man. He

didn't say anything but stared at Becky in her underwear.

'What do you do?' said the older man as he bolted up the outer gate.

'Whatever the customers want,' she said.

'You performers?'

'Yeah,' I said.

'What do you do?'

'I sing.'

He pointed at Daniel. 'And him?'

'Comedian.'

Daniel grinned.

The man pointed towards his assistant. 'Joe here needs to pat you down.'

'Fine.' I raised my arms and Joe checked me over. He moved down my body with fast hand movements. He did Daniel who giggled at one point. Then he went to the bag where we'd stashed the shotgun and grenades within everything else. If they found this we'd be in trouble.

He opened the bag and poked around.

'Aren't you going to check her?' I said pointing at Becky.

Even though she was only in her knickers and bra he put the bag down and went over to her, standing close. His eyes were all over her body as he rubbed his hands together. Then he started. First he went over her backside. Across her knickers. Into them. Then he cupped her tits. Gave them a squeeze and closed his eyes. Finally, he slid a hand into the front of her knickers.

'That's enough,' said the older man.

He drew his hand out and stood back. Looked at the ground.

'Okay. You can go.'

Becky gave them a big grin. 'Thanks.'

Joe smiled and showed cock-eyed teeth in his red gums. He led us to the far side of the quadrangle and to the other gate. He hammered on it three times. 'All clear.'

There was the sound of bolts being drawn and the gate opened. Three men stood there, two with a rifle and one with a pistol.

'All fine?' said one.

'Aye, fine,' said Joe.

They waved us through. Gave us a good eyeballing. For a moment we all just stood there.

Then they stepped aside.

'Go on,' said the fella with the pistol.

'Thanks,' said Becky then she minced off.

I followed with Daniel at my side. 'Maybe see you later.'

The five men stayed at the gate as we walked on.

'Good performance,' I said to Becky.

'Yeah. I hope it's worth it.' The smile dropped and she slid on her shirt.

When I looked back the guards were still watching us.

We headed on into town, Becky pulling on the rest of her clothes and Daniel humming to himself. The road was flanked by burnt-out bonfires and pieces of bone carved with symbols. There was a long walk into town and I expected the fellas at the gate to change their mind and come after us but they never did. We'd got in but lost the assault rifle. Casper and the Eblis.

We passed allotments and pens with chickens and pigs and ducks. Open ground with sheep grazing on it.

Further on there were low buildings made of sheet metal and scraps of wood. Then repair shops for machines and others selling food and booze, drugs of some sort. Each had a sign and people milling around. There were piles of timber at the side of the road and up ahead a factory unit with a ramshackle chimney. Wires ran out of it in a chaotic knot to thread out across the town. Men carried wood in and others brought out barrows of ash they piled at the side.

We saw carpenters and tailors. More food and drugs sellers. To the right was an old school. Music played and there was laughter and shouting. It was subdued compared to what we'd heard earlier but there was still some kind of a party going on.

The houses became more solid as we continued, the originals of whatever place this had been. They were stone-build and slate roofed though some had boarded windows and patched doors.

Off to the left was a tall building. It had once been a hotel or whatever but was now covered in boards with painted symbols: yin and yang and swirling shapes. Flowers and hearts. Topping it off was a giant skull. It was made of dozens of pieces of polished metal nailed onto a wooden frame.

The road carried on down to the loch, now a lighter blue but still with that dark shape in it: Gehenna. It was hundreds of metres long, the bulbous sections front and back proud of the water with the tower topped by instruments. There was no sign of anyone on it.

'Well, here we are.' I was regretting being so keen to get in.

'Here we are,' echoed Becky.

'We need to find somewhere to stay.' I fished around in the bag and pulled out several Scottish notes from my savings. What I'd brought from Faeston. The money was damp but usable.

'Okay. Let's have a look around.'

We found a small place just off the main street. It had been a betting shop but was now run as a hotel. An old fella sat behind the counter. He was thin with a mop of grey hair and stared at us when we went in. He really gave Daniel a good eyeballing. But when he saw my money he warmed up.

'We want a room for three. One that looks out at the loch,' said Becky.

'Oh aye?'

'We need a loch view.'

'Fine.'

'Quite a town.'

'Hmm.'

'The name and the skull and the drumming. What's it about?'

He stared at her. Then he grunted and led us up the filthy staircase to the second floor. It seemed to take him ages to find the key before he shoved the door open. The room was big with a double and single beds and windows that looked out on the loch. Faded towels hung from hooks on the wall. The room was dusty but less dirty than the rest of the building.

The fella hung around for a minute then shuffled off. Once he'd gone I locked the door. Becky was straight over to the window but l lay back on the bed.

'Think I'll take a rest,' I said. After roughing it the bed felt great.

'You're some kind of fella, you know?'

'Yeah, that's me.'

She grunted and stared out at the loch. Daniel messed around with what few possessions he had: a pack of dog-eared cards and a book of birds. I just lay on the bed and watched the patterns on the ceiling. How the light shifted as the afternoon went on and the music outside got louder and louder until it drowned out any other sound.

Becky shoved me in the ribs. 'Do you want to take a walk?'

'I'm not sure.'

'Let's get a drink.'

'All right.' A drink sounded good.

'I think it's time to go and see Gehenna.'

That didn't sound quite so good.

CHAPTER FORTY-TWO

Recon

She told Daniel to stay in the room to keep an eye on things then steered me out into the street. It was early evening and men came up from the water's edge carrying small bags and wearing wellies. The music boomed off the buildings.

'Sorry about earlier,' she said.

'Earlier?'

'Forget it.'

She stopped at the quayside and sat down on a bench so I joined her. Gehenna was still in the same position, a dark lump in the evening light. There were a number of boats tied to the quay that bobbed on the light swell. The air was warm but there was a chill to it, a hint of autumn. We were well in land but the loch smelled of the sea.

Over to our right was a house with a collapsed wall and a hole in its roof. Next to it was a pile of rubble where another building had been.

'That our doing?' I said.

Becky stared at the ruins. She pursed her lips but she

didn't say anything. We sat without speaking as the music thudded through the town.

'What are you up to?' I'd been drawn into this but there'd been no talk of what she had planned. I was here but hadn't agreed to help.

'We still have a sub to blow.'

'Oh, that should be easy enough…'

'Just look.'

Gehenna wasn't as tidy as it had seemed from up the road. Parts of the hull were marked with dents and barnacles grew all along the waterline. There was a boat tied off halfway along and a hatch open on the deck at the rear.

We stayed there for ages and nothing happened. Gehenna was just part of the scenery. Then a crew member appeared at the top of the tower and walked back and forward, looking over the edge at each end.

'There's a fella in the tower thing,' I said.

'The conning tower.'

The man disappeared and a few moments later another one popped out of the hatch on the deck. He got out and walked around. He was in uniform, dark blue with a small hat. Several others joined him and chatted.

They went over to the boat. One slid in holding onto the hand of the another. One by one they clambered into it. One of the crew stood at the front with a rifle and while two men took the oars. The untied and started rowing.

We watched as they came towards shore.

'Talk to me, Trent.'

'What about?'

'Anything. Just so we don't look weird.'

'Are you hungry?'

'What?'

'You said talk.'

'Okay, yes. I'm hungry.'

'What do you fancy to eat?'

'I don't know. Ice cream, bananas. Rice and sweetcorn and other stuff that is hard to get hold of.'

The boat tied off at the far end of the quayside and the crew stepped onto dry land. The man with the gun stayed in it as the others made their way into town. Their uniforms were worn and patched in places but they still looked smart compared to the townsfolk.

'Fancy a look?' said Becky.

'At the sub?'

'Just the boat.'

'And then what?'

'Just take a look.'

She walked over towards it and I followed. She stopped and nudged me. 'Take my hand.'

'What for?'

'Just take it.'

Her skin was dry and her fingers moved around. As we got closer she gripped me tightly. The man on guard didn't even look at us as we walked past. He was in his forties, thin and clean shaven. He held his gun across his chest and stared off into the distance.

We walked on and Becky leant against a wall beside a cottage. The house had a neat garden of small plants and shrubs set in gravel. She pointed off into the distance towards the town.

'Do you think you could overpower him?' she said.

'What are you pointing at?'

'Follow my gaze and nod as if you're interested.'

I tried to act as if the low building she was pointing towards was fascinating.

'So can you? Overpower him?'

'Maybe. But he has a gun.'

'So have we.'

I looked the fella over. He wasn't big but he'd be able to whip round that gun soon enough. Even if we got a shot off we'd attract the attention of his friends. And everyone on the sub. We'd seen what that had the power to do.

'Not in daytime,' I said. 'Not when we can be spotted.'

Becky stood up and offered her hand. 'Coming?'

We walked away from the quayside to our hotel. Even when we were out of sight of the boat we held hands.

On the way back we passed a butchers so we bought three meat pies. All that talk of food had made me hungry. Pity we hadn't had the drink she'd promised.

Daniel was at the window when we went in. 'You have a nice walk?'

'Fine,' I said. I sat beside him and looked out at the submarine. The man on the quayside was obscured by the building but I knew where he was.

We ate our pies then Becky went through my bag and took out the gun and grenades.

'How are we going to do this?' I said.

'I don't know. We need to think it through.'

I was doing some thinking of my own. Maybe we'd work out a way to destroy the sub. Maybe not. Maybe we'd just hang around for a while. Then again, there were pubs and plenty of places to eat. It wouldn't be such a bad place to spend some time.

She sat at the window. Stared out at the sub. I played

cards with Daniel, an easier version of Blackjack, then he went to bed. After sunset the music carried on, loud as ever, thudding through the town. All the buildings. I played patience for a while.

Then I stood and stretched. I fancied another look around. See what else the town had to offer. 'I'm going for a wander.'

For the first time in hours Becky moved from the window. 'I'll join you.'

We left Daniel sleeping and went out.

Strings of bare bulbs lit the buildings and a couple of spotlights shone on the sculptured skull. People wandered around drinking. Laughing and dancing.

'Think it's always like this?' I said.

Becky shrugged.

I pointed towards the school, where the music was coming from. 'Fancy this?'

She didn't answer but walked with me as I went towards it.

The school's fence and signage was still there but it was now renamed *Gehenna Club*. We passed through the gate into a field filled with people dancing. They were all ages, toddlers bouncing around through to oldies leant on walking sticks. The grass had long gone and the ground was pummelled into hard-packed earth. The low building of the school block had all its doors and windows open. Power lines ran into it and there was bunting strung up hung with lightbulbs. In the school hall a DJ leant over a couple of turntables where he mixed music, just like at an old-world club.

We stood at the side and watched.

We were there for some time. As the music thudded

through us and the town.

The sky went from dark blue to black and the music picked up the pace. After a while we walked away from the school and back towards the hotel.

'This is some place,' I said.

'It is.' She stopped and looked past me and towards the loch. At the submarine lit with a couple of lights.

As we stood there I saw someone watch us. It was the man who'd let us in the gate. The older one. He frowned and stared at us. When he saw me looking back he turned and walked away.

Maybe this wasn't some place we could stay.

We carried on back to the hotel. When we went in Daniel was still sleeping. I lay on the bed and watched the patterns from the lights on the ceiling. Listened to the music. Becky returned to the window and watched the sub. I tried not to think about the fella I'd seen. What his look had meant.

Eventually the music stopped and I dozed off. Dreamt of people dancing on the deck of Gehenna.

I awoke to sunlight shining through the open curtains. Becky was on the bed beside me asleep, fully clothed. There was no sign of Daniel.

I went to his bed. It was neatly made and some clothes folded on it.

I shook Becky and she woke. Stared at me.

'Daniel's gone,' I said.

'What?'

'He's not here.'

The door opened and Daniel came in. He had a towel over his arm and his hair was wet.

'Where've you been?' I said.

'There's a shower.'

Becky slid off the bed and grabbed a towel. 'Shower sounds good.'

While we waited, me and Daniel played cards. He asked what we were planning to do for the day and I said I wasn't sure. I wasn't sure about much but it was worse for him. He'd been dragged along here without any idea what was going on. I figured he needed some kind of explanation. 'Listen, Daniel.'

'Yes.'

'Do you know why we're here?'

'To look at the submarine?'

'Yeah. That's right. To look at the submarine.' I wanted to say more but I wasn't sure how to put it. 'Anyway, this is for you.' I went into my bag and drew out some money, a bundle of notes. Thrust them at him.

'Why do I need this?'

'Pocket money.'

'Pocket money?' He put the notes in his pocket.

Becky came back with the towel tied on her head. As she dried her hair the music started up. 'Should we go take a walk?'

Daniel put his cards down. 'Yes. Please.'

The three of us went down the quayside. The boat was tied onto the sub and there were only a few fishermen around. They brought in a catch which they loaded onto a cart pulled by a donkey, taking it off along the quayside. Gulls wheeled above us and the waves lapped at the dockside. There was no movement from Gehenna or any of the crew.

Another cart came down to the seafront. It was much bigger, pulled by four horses and it carried pieces of metal and burnt fragments. It was only as men picked at it that I realised it was the Eblis. Becky stared and put a hand to her face.

We watched as they took the pieces off and drew them away to a warehouse. Bit by bit they removed sections of the tank and I wondered how long it would be before someone connected us to it. That we'd appeared shortly after it had been destroyed.

Becky stared out across the loch and said nothing. I went to take her hand but she pushed it away.

'Can we get some food?' said Daniel.

'All right,' I said.

The music bounced off the houses as I led us along the quayside to a pub. It was an old building with stained joists and ancient photos of the town on the wall. Becky sat at a table with Daniel and I went to the bar. There were a number of pumps but most of their handles were broken or missing. They only had one type of beer so I ordered three glasses of it: one pint and two halves. The barman was an old fella who jabbered on about the weather and the noise of the music.

'It's quite a town I said.'

'Aye, it is. Is that. A real party place now.'

'It hasn't always been like this?'

He laughed. 'Only since the sub came. After the accident, you know.'

'Oh?'

'Aye, you know. You want food?'

I didn't know but wasn't keen to pry. Attract more unwanted attention. The only food was soup so I asked for three bowls.

When I went back to the table Daniel was describing

everything he liked in the room. Becky didn't reply. Gehenna was clearly visible in the loch outside. So it sounded something had happened to the sub's base and it had moved here. Given the town a new lease of life. Brought its own madness.

I drank my beer and listened to Daniel talk about the pictures on the wall. He finished and grinned, pleased with himself.

'We need to get a boat,' said Becky.

'We do?' I said.

'If we can get a boat, I think I can blow it.'

'Right.'

She flicked her head towards the window. 'We need to sail out to it. Blow one of the hatches. It's its weak point. Its Achilles' heel.'

'Yeah,' I said. 'I suppose.'

She took a drink of beer. A young woman came over and dumped the soups in front of us.

I spoke once she'd gone. 'And that's the plan?'

'You got any better ideas?'

'This is good soup,' said Daniel.

I tasted mine. It was salty but had big chunks of mutton. 'Yeah, it is good soup.' I didn't have any better ideas so there was no point arguing. I'd work something out.

We ate in silence then walked back towards the hotel. On the way Becky stopped at a fishing shop. There was a rack of clothes outside. Amongst the waterproofs and patched over-trousers there were some wetsuits. She picked one and held it against herself, then me. She did this a few times until she had a couple.

'You got some cash?' she said.

I peeled off a few notes and gave them to her.

Once she'd bought them we continued back. The music was as loud as ever but most people seemed to be busy with day-to-day stuff. Shifting carts laden with wood or vegetables. Picking up provisions at one of the stores. If it hadn't been for Gehenna sitting in the loch it would have seemed like a reasonable place. Maybe it would be once the sub left.

Back in the room Becky got me to try on the wetsuit while she slid into hers. She didn't even notice me watch her as she stripped down to her underwear. Stood there half-naked. Hers was too big and had a few holes but she seemed happy enough with it. Mine fitted reasonably well but had a tear down one leg.

'Great,' she said.

We took them off and stacked them on the floor with a bag holding the gun and grenades.

'When are we going to do all this?' I said.

'All what?'

'When are we going to grab a boat? Go out and blow the hatch.'

'When it's quiet. When they aren't expecting it.'

'When's that?'

'I don't know.' She took her seat at the window to watch Gehenna. With the plans of the sub laid out before her. It wasn't surprising that she was edgy after seeing the bits of the Eblis brought in. I'd let her calm down and talk it through with her. Work out a proper plan.

Me and Daniel played cards and talked about the pictures he'd seen in the pub. How nice the soup had been. Stuff to pass the time.

Later on Becky went out on her own. She came back a

little while later. The music was cranking up ready for the evening.

She flopped back on her bed. 'There's some food there.' She pointed to her bag.

I opened it and found three meat pies. I ate one and handed another to Daniel.

After we'd eaten we played cards some more. Becky lay on her bed and dozed. Daniel went to bed once it got dark.

She didn't wake before nightfall and I lay on the bed beside her. Fell asleep myself.

Sometime later she woke me. 'It's moving,' she said. 'The submarine is on its way.'

CHAPTER FORTY-THREE
Boat

We ran out of the hotel and down to the quayside. Just me and Becky sprinting down to the loch. There was no one else around. Not even any music. She had her bag with the gun and grenades over one shoulder and the wetsuits over the other.

She stopped at the dock and pointed at a small sail boat. 'That'll do.'

Gehenna was already a hundred metres on from where it had been. The water churned up behind it as it glided off. It moved steadily but not fast. There was only the sound of the waves that lapped at the boats; a swishing sound from the sub.

Becky led off down the steps to the boat and leapt in.

'Becky,' I said. 'This is crazy. Leave it.'

'Are you kidding? This is our last chance.'

'We had our last chance when Casper blew the tank.'

'I knew you'd blame him.'

'There's no chance we'll blow it.'

'I knew you'd chicken out. You were all keen before...'

For a moment we just stood there.

'Look, Trent, I can do this alone but —'

'All right, I'll help.' I'd come so far. Risked so much already. And I didn't like the idea of chickening out. The boat rocked as I stepped into it and tilted towards the back when I sat down.

Becky untied us. There were a couple of oars lying in the bottom so she took one and shoved us away from the dockside. The boat rocked some more, worsened by her moving around as she set the sail.

'Wind's not quite right,' she said. 'You know how to sail?'

'Not really.'

The sail flapped as the breeze caught it and she pushed me out of the way as she grabbed the rudder. The boat moved off across the loch but towards the far side, not after the sub. As it picked up speed it pitched and the water slapped at the front end. She adjusted the tiller and sail so that we were aimed towards Gehenna though still at an angle.

She glanced over at me. 'You want to slip your wetsuit on?'

For a moment I didn't move, uneasy in the undulating boat, then I twisted round and pulled my boots off and slid off my trousers. I eased the wetsuit up to my waist before I took off my shirt and slid it up. Slow movements.

The boat was going quite fast and soon we cut through part of Gehenna's wake so that we jerked and lurched in the rough water. I had one arm in the wetsuit and held onto the boat's side. Once we'd cleared the rough patch she changed direction. We slowed but were now on the same course as the submarine.

I pulled on the other sleeve and grabbed a lifejacket that was lying under the seat. I slid it on. There was a chance we were going to be flipped.

'Take over,' she said.

I grabbed the rudder as she squeezed into her own wetsuit and we rocked and tossed around.

For some time we rolled around in the boat as Gehenna ploughed on through the loch. There was a great trail of steam coming from the coning tower.

Becky laughed. 'It's venting. Must be a problem with the reactor. That's why it's so slow.'

'Great.' I had my own problems. I'd never been one for boats. As a kid I'd gone out in them on holiday. Bigger boats in lakes or the sea to watch fish, or smaller ones on ponds. Never a small boat on a rough loch. I tightened my lifejacket. 'How's this going to work?'

She adjusted the rudder. 'What?'

'Us with the sub.'

'Get close, get on, blow the hatch…'

'Then?'

She shrugged. 'Get off.'

Water sprayed in our faces as the submarine plugged on and we bounced behind it.

Then I had an idea. 'How about this?'

'What?'

'You stay on the boat and I climb onto the sub.'

'Really?'

'You know how to sail. Keep the boat handy so I can get back.'

'You sure?'

'Yeah.'

'Great.' She turned away from me and concentrated on

Gehenna. She stared at it as we sailed behind it.

It sounded easy enough in my head but the sub was this big slippery thing and we were in a little boat. Maybe we'd never get that close and it wouldn't matter.

But little by little we closed on it: until we were quite near, through the wake and just behind the bow wave. We were being pulled along by it and our boat pitched and rocked with water spilling over the side.

Becky messed around in her bag, took out the two grenades, checked them over then put them back and pulled the bag's top tight. 'You take this,' she said.

I grabbed the rucksack, slid it over the lifejacket and looked over at the submarine. What the hell was I going to do now?

'We need to get ahead,' she said. As she adjusted the sail we picked up speed but the rocking became more pronounced. The boat lurched and waves slapped on its flank.

Then the bow wave caught us and we tipped over.

We flipped into the loch.

CHAPTER FORTY-FOUR

In the water

The water churned around me cold and dark. It went into my mouth, over my head. Into eyes and ears. All my warmth was drawn from me as my wetsuit filled up. The current took me, dragged me down. Down into the turbulent loch. Into the darkness.

Then I bobbed up to the surface with only my face clearing the water. The lifejacket had saved me. I took a great lungful of air and looked around. There was no sign of the boat or Becky. I tried to shout but swallowed water. Beside me was the sub, a great dark shape that churned onwards, only metres away. I flapped towards it, keen to be on anything solid. I splashed around in the water but made no progress. Then I flipped over onto my back. Above me stars shone through thin cloud. I tried to remember the swimming strokes I'd been taught in school all those years ago. I circled my legs and kicked hard. The water moved between my feet and I began to go backwards.

I was caught by a current that swirled me around. I was

tossed over in the water and flailed with my arms to try and straighten up. The turbulence worsened and I spun around, over and over, gasping for breath when my face was upwards but taking in water as well as air.

I hit a hard surface. What little air was left in me was knocked out as I thudded into the submarine's side. The rough metal scraped past and ground against me and I grabbed at it. If I slid all the way to the back I'd end up in the propeller where it would chop me into chunks.

But the sub's flank had nothing to hold, just flaws in the panels, not enough to grip. My nails clawed at its surface as it passed but there were no grips or handholds or anything. I was going to be sucked into the wake and smashed to bits. As a last effort I pawed at the hull to at least slow me down.

Then I got hold of something. There was a small recess and my left hand stuck in it. It was at the wrong angle and bent my fingers so that they felt they were going to snap but it held me. My face was now pressed against the sub, barely above the water. I took in great gulps of air but I needed to find something else. Another hold. I stretched out as far as I could with my right hand to feel for anything on the surface, further up above the waterline but there was nothing. Just metal plates. So I put both hands in the one niche. I could only get the thumb and index finger of my right hand in, but it was better than nothing. I dangled from the hull like a piece of seaweed, bashed against the metal, my head sometimes underwater. The wake of the submarine dragged at me and threatened to wash me off and to the back, into the blades.

For a second I thought about letting go. I'd drift off and in no time it would be over. I'd be sliced up and left in the sea. That would be it.

I just hung there.

Then I moved my legs around. Millimetre by millimetre I felt for a ridge on the plates. Apart from barnacles and weed it was even surfaced.

At last I found something. Only a tiny lip but it was enough. I wiggled my foot onto it and tried to put weight on it. Only a little. I braced myself between my leg and the handhold and pushed down at the same time that I pulled up. With my left fingers as tight as they would go I let go with my right hand and reached up. As far as possible. There had to be something up there. Some ridge or handhold or unevenness in the hull. There had to be. I flicked myself up and felt around up above the waterline. It was smooth, featureless. Impossible to get hold of. I tried once more.

Then I came loose.

It happened so fast I didn't realise what was going on. One second I was feeling around on the hull, the next I was off towards the rear of the sub, hands flailing and head underwater. I swirled around and tried to grab at anything, sliding towards the propeller.

Until I hit something hard. It slammed into my waist and held me with the force of the water. There was a sound like rocks rolling down a hillside. The current pulled and dragged at me. As my lungs burned for air. I was pinioned by the flow.

I was going to drown. I was underwater and couldn't reach the surface. I reached out and grabbed part of the sub that I was stuck against. It was thick and flat like a great metal table. Some kind of fin or rudder or something. Holding on I hauled myself to the left, towards the main hull. Bit by bit I moved along it, as the loch churned around me.

At last I came to the bulkhead. I touched it with my left hand and felt around. Smooth as the rest of it. But I needed air. I was desperate to take a breath. So I stretched up and tilted my head. With one leg raised on the fin I pushed up as far as I dared. My face came out of the water and I drew in a lungful of air, blew it out, then another. My body flapped around in the flow but it was worth it to have a breath. From where I was I could see the back end of the sub. The hull was lower here and I'd be able to get on it if I could just push myself up.

But I needed to get closer and that meant going under again. Taking in one more gasp I ducked down and dragged myself as tight against the main section as I could get. Then I held on with my hands and brought my feet up onto the fin. I counted to three, let go and pushed hard with my legs and leapt.

I landed in shallow water on the tail section just in front of another fin, this one upright. I clawed my hand around it and clung there, then pulled my feet up to wrap around it with my head forced up above the water. My body was still submerged but I could breathe at last. For a minute I hung there with my eyes closed and took great gulps of air.

The waves crashed around the back of the submarine and the deck beneath me throbbed with the powerful engine that drove it. I pulled myself further round and sat on a drier section of the hull with the fin behind me. Ahead was the deck and conning tower. The water around me was black. There was a hint of light in the sky. Enough to see that there was no land; no sign of the boat or Becky. We were we at sea, out of the loch and into open water.

Maybe she'd swum off and made it to dry land. Or hung onto the boat. Or been dragged through the submarine's propeller. Chopped to bits.

I pushed myself forward and made for the conning tower. When I stood up the bag dragged at my back with all the water in it. And the grenades.

That was the reason I was here. To blow the sub. Crazy as Becky's plan was, it was all I had left. I stretched up and staggered forward and waded through the water, slid on the metal as it sloped up from the tail section to the main body. It was steep so I went onto all fours and clawed my way up the wet metal. Despite being soaked it was warm to the touch. Like the Eblis, this was nuclear powered. The phrase nuclear submarine had once been common on the news. And here I was on one. About to blow it up. Or at least try.

My feet squeaked and slid on the way up the sloping hull but I made it onto the main section. The surface was different here, ridged and easier to grip and I stood straight at last. For a moment I let the water run out of the bag then I continued forward towards the hatch.

Even though the submarine was moving there was no sign of it on the deck. No rocking or pitching just a slight rumble. The hatch was in front of me and I staggered over to it. It was a massive steel construction with a circular handle. Maybe I could open it and drop in the grenades. Kill the men inside.

That didn't seem right. What I needed to do was damage it. Make sure the sub couldn't be used as a weapon. I took the bag off and set it at my side. My hands were wrinkled with the water, lit now by the faint light of dawn. At some point the crew would spot me. Send someone up to stick a bullet into my head. I drew out the grenades and shifted them in my hands: cold and wet.

Then I wedged them against the hatch's handle and made sure their levers were free to release. For a minute I shifted them this way and that. Stalled doing anything. Once I pulled them, that was it. At present I still had the option to climb up the tower. Pretend to be a lost fisherman. Ask to be let on board and share their food and put on dry clothes. Sleep in a warm bed.

Not that they'd believe that for a second.

I had to blow the hatch then go. Once I pulled the pins I had to be off. Pull, jump then swim.

I took hold of the pins, exhaled then yanked them out.

I threw them away and stepped across the hull. With a deep breath I jumped into the freezing water.

CHAPTER FORTY-FIVE

Lost

I sank down as it swirled around me. I closed my eyes and mouth and held them tightly shut until I reached the surface. I came up and took a breath as I swam on my back, arms and legs flat out. Away from the submarine as fast as I could.

There was a dull thud, a shower of sparks, then another but nothing else. The submarine carried on into the darkness. I swam more, kicked and thrashed and put further distance between me and it. God knows what could happen with the hatch blown.

But nothing happened.

It sailed off and I floated in the water now bobbed by the wake as it made its way out to sea. Maybe I'd done some damage to it. Maybe not.

I swam on as the waves flicked me up and down. My head went under then my feet.

It had gone and I was here in the water. I needed to get as far away as possible.

It was hard to work out which way was back to the

shore so I kept going the same direction. I swam backwards into the sea.

I carried on until my arms and legs ached. Waves flicked me up and down. I'd sink into a trough of dark then rise onto a crest. Up and down in the featureless sea. There was no sign of the submarine. Or land. The sun lit the desert of water a weak grey. At least I wasn't cold. The wetsuit was doing its job.

As I floated I thought of how I'd come here. Of the journey with Becky and Casper. Daniel who was now alone in the town. Abandoned, again. Faeston with Round Up and Sophie. All the stuff I'd done before.

Then I spotted something way off to my right. A black dot that rocked around on the surface. I flapped around and aimed towards it.

For ages I swam on, legs and arms pushed to move even though I was tired. Water sprayed into my face and I was chucked up and down by the waves. My head dipped under and I took in water that I spat out as I gasped for air.

The object seemed to stay as distant as when I'd first seen it. I swam on and lay back in the water. Closed my eyes and hoped it was the boat or Becky. Becky in the boat.

Stroke by stroke I closed in on it.

The object was misshapen. Dark. I thought it was some kind of animal. A great carnivore that swam around and lured in prey: a shark or octopus that would feast on my legs and eat me as I flailed to get away. This made me curl up into a ball. Think about the great dark depths below me and what might lie there.

At the next crest I stared at the thing. It was irregular

with limbs that splayed out. It rocked from side to side but there was no other movement.

I swam on towards it.

The sun shone down on it. Lit branches and a solid trunk, cockeyed and polished. It was clear that it was a tree. An uprooted tree washed out to sea. Its boughs pointed off into the water and to the sky. Leafless and striped of bark they thrust off in different directions. They rocked amongst waves of green and blue. Topped with white.

I swam alongside and held onto it, the wood smooth and solid. Then I clambered up and slumped onto the driest section where the water lapped at the edges.

I lay upon the trunk as it floated in the water. I clung to the dead tree as it swayed and dipped and rose up.

As I drifted off to sea.

Alone in the water.

Alone.

ACKNOWLEDGEMENTS

Writing can be a lonely hobby so it's good to have some people behind you.

I would like to thank George Green and Lee Horsley at Lancaster University for all the brilliant suggestions. Also Brian Baker, Andrew Pepper and Jo Baker for further guidance.

Thanks to Toby Travis and Phil Hilborne for reading through the penultimate draft.

To Tom and Janet Storrie for believing in me when no one else did.

Of course I couldn't have done it without Tara, Ethan and Lucy being so patient when I was too busy to play.

And especially to Debs Austin for all her moral and emotional support.